C000172959

THE SCOTTISH CL/
NUMBER F

BEYOND THIS LIMIT
SELECTED SHORTER FICTION
OF
NAOMI MITCHISON

THE SCOTTISH CLASSICS SERIES

1. Allan Ramsay and Robert Fergusson, *Poems*, ed. Alexander M. Kinghorn and Alexander Law.
2. John Galt, *The Member*, ed. Ian A. Gordon.
3. James Hogg, *The Brownie of Bodsbeck*, ed. Douglas S. Mack.
4. James Hogg, *Selected Stories and Sketches*, ed. Douglas S. Mack.
5. Naomi Mitchison, *Beyond This Limit: Selected Shorter Fiction*, ed. Isobel Murray.
6. John Galt, *Selected Short Stories*, ed. Ian A. Gordon.
7. John Galt, *The Last of the Lairds*, ed. Ian A. Gordon.

THE SCOTTISH CLASSICS SERIES
GENERAL EDITOR — DOUGLAS S. MACK

BEYOND THIS LIMIT
Selected Shorter Fiction
of
NAOMI MITCHISON

EDITED AND WITH AN INTRODUCTION
BY
ISOBEL MURRAY

SCOTTISH ACADEMIC PRESS
in conjunction with
THE ASSOCIATION FOR SCOTTISH LITERARY STUDIES
EDINBURGH
1986

Published by
Scottish Academic Press Ltd.
33 Montgomery Street
Edinburgh EH7 5JX

First published 1986
ISBN 0 7073 0501 2

Scottish Academic Press
acknowledges subsidy from the Scottish Arts Council
towards the publication of this volume

British Library Cataloguing in Publication Data

Mitchison, Naomi
    Beyond this limit : selected shorter
    fiction of Naomi Mitchison.——(The
    Scottish classics series; v. 5)
    I. Title II. Murray, Isobel
    823'.912[F]   PR6025.I86

ISBN 0-7073-0501-2

Printed in Great Britain by
Billing & Sons, Worcester
Typeset at Oxford University Computing Service
from a machine-readable text
prepared by Wilma S. Mack, Dollar

CONTENTS

Acknowledgments	vi
Introduction	vii
Beyond This Limit	1
The Powers of Light	83
The Wife of Aglaos	106
Five Men and a Swan	142
The Hunting of Ian Og	159
The Hill Behind	180
The Coming of the New God	192
Remember Me	205

ACKNOWLEDGMENTS

THE Wyndham Lewis illustrations are © the estate of Mrs G. A. Wyndham Lewis, reproduced by kind permission.

'The Hill Behind' and 'The Coming of the New God', both from *Images of Africa* (1980), are reproduced by kind permission of Canongate Publishing. 'Remember Me' from *What Do You Think Yourself?* (1982) is reproduced by kind permission of Paul Harris.

The editor is most grateful to Naomi Mitchison and to Bob Tait for their cooperation in the lengthy interview of September 1984 which is cited in the Introduction. The interview is one of a series sponsored and made possible by the University of Aberdeen Development Trust.

INTRODUCTION

SINCE the publication of her first novel *The Conquered* in 1923, Naomi Mitchison has been prodigously productive of books. Authorities differ on the total number of books—seventy-three seems now a low estimate, and a bibliography which included her major contributions to books, let alone her major and minor contributions to an extraordinary range of periodicals, would be a stupendous and daunting document. This unique literary career would present problems to the reader even if the books were all in print and easily available (which is sadly far from the case), because it is on an unprecedented scale: has any serious writer ever published so much, over so many years?

I think the most important—or at least the most immediate—problem is that readers are liable to be baffled, confused, even rather lost, as, gradually, a few of the most important novels are brought back into print. (*The Corn King and the Spring Queen* and *Travel Light* are available in paperback from Virago, and *The Bull Calves* from Richard Drew Publishing.) It is hard to get any notion of this literary career; we don't have even the crudest sketch map indicating the ground at various times covered. And it is hard, under these circumstances, to approach any individual work with full confidence.

It is intended that this selection of Mitchison's shorter fiction will provide in one volume a reasonably characteristic selection of the author's best shorter fiction, so that at least in this area the reader can achieve his or her own measure of the author and her work, and experience that work directly. These stories will demonstrate something of the author's range and of her preoccupations over the decades.

But in this Introduction I want to push a little further, to begin to provide that crudest of sketch maps to Mitchison's writing career as a novelist. This will inevitably be short and over-simplified: even when we disregard all the books which are not novels, the volumes of memoirs, the many books for children and young people, the biographies, poems, plays, philosophy, and documentaries, there are still too many novels to deal with in a brief Introduction. And there are at least six collections of short stories.

Some of these novels can serve very well as points on my sketch map, for they introduce—or sum up—a phase of Mitchison's fictional development, or her choice of period. Please note that this is not an attempt at evaluative literary criticism, but rather at necessary, preliminary description. My outline of these novels will necessarily ignore others for which I'd make high claims: *To the Chapel Perilous* (1955) would be a case in point. In a recorded conversation in September 1984[1] Mitchison agreed with me that this new telling of the Grail story and the legend of the Round Table through a perspective provided by two very twentieth-century newspaper reporters might even be 'as a matter of writer's art ... probably my best book.' But I hope that a brief descriptive account of some central novels will provide some kind of starting place.

The Conquered (1923) is a very sophisticated and accomplished first novel, which begins the exploration of many themes raised and examined in different epochs and areas in other novels and stories. On the face of it, *The Conquered* is about Julius Caesar's conquest of Gaul. It centres on Meromic, son of Kormiac the Wolf, a chief of the Veneti in North Gaul; and at the start young Meromic believes that all the Veneti are brothers, a perception that comes largely from their being neighbours and sharing common enemies.

The plot involves Meromic in many conflicting loyalties and involuntary or necessary treacheries. He becomes a Roman slave, and develops a disorienting affection for his master, whose life he saves, and who saves his. Already Mitchison is beginning to investigate the dehumanising effects of slavery, on slaves and owners alike: there is much more of this in her fictions set in the world of ancient Greece. Meanwhile, the rise of Vercingetorix as leader of the Gauls against the Romans widens Meromic's native loyalty from local clans with discernible common interests to a notion of all Gaul united against the enemy. All this foreshadows the way the African hero of *When We Become Men* (1965) will likewise develop wider and larger loyalties. Mitchison finds this question of loyalties 'one of the most interesting things that happens to anyone .... One's got a loyalty presumably to one's family to start with, and then it widens out to one's village, one's town, one's country. Perhaps to being a European, and finally, I suppose, to being a human being.'

So *The Conquered* is the first, clear statement of a lasting preoccupation. But it is also a book with a very topical flavour. Young Naomi Mitchison was an ardent admirer of Yeats and Lady Gregory and her first ever political demonstration was for 'Peace with Ireland'. The chapter headings of *The Conquered* are usually from Irish poetry, and her early readers were in no doubt that the novel was essentially about the contemporary Irish situation, and the nature of British Imperialist rule. Despite this subversive intention, the novel was widely used in schools and universities as an illustrative text on Caesar's Gallic Wars. The decision Mitchison had early made, that historical characters and events must be rendered in a selection from contemporary language, in a modern idiom, made the book particularly accessible to readers, whether concerned with Ireland or with Gaul.

After that first novel, Mitchison roamed happily around the ancient world for several years, producing stories of Athens and of the comparatively tyrannical Sparta, of barbarians, of the Gallic wars. The novel *Cloud Cuckoo Land* (1925) is fairly typical. The hero comes from a very small Greek island towards the end of the fifth century B.C., almost at the end of the Peloponnesian War. The rulers of the island have to choose to side either with Athens, a bullying power but a democracy of a sort, and now nearly worn out, or with Sparta, still strong, controlled by an oligarchy, and in alliance with the Persians. This conflict is recurrent in Mitchison's work: her sympathies tend toward Athens, however exhausted, a city which has represented fine ideals and may 'hold the balance of right thinking' (*Cloud Cuckoo Land*, p. 347). There is usually a radical distrust of Sparta, with the iron discipline of the Krypteia; gradually Mitchison, always in part preoccupied with present day politics, came to a view of 'Black' Sparta which bore comparison with totalitarian movements she sensed and feared in contemporary Europe. And it applied to totalitarian communism too; when she was particularly critical of the USSR on her 1932 visit, she noted in her diary, 'A lot of Sparta about this.' (*You May Well Ask*, p. 188).

The climax of Mitchison's involvement in the ancient world and Hellas came in a giant novel which took even a powerhouse of a writer six years to write, occupied as she also was with babies and young children, and the shocking death of her eldest son, and with foreign travel, and the General Strike, her own ongoing political exploration and her historical researches. (See *You May Well Ask: A Memoir 1920-1940*, especially pages 166-7). *The Corn King and the Spring Queen* is a novel on a very large scale. It begins and ends in

Marob, a mythical country on the Black Sea peopled by ancient Scythians. Marob at the start retains collective agricultural rituals in a pure and early stage, but the book charts the awakening of Tarrik and Erif Der, respectively Corn King and Spring Queen, to a more individual self-consciousness than the old community consciousness required or permitted. So the witch Essro tells Erif; 'We're ourselves. We can't only be Marob. The Corn King has to be separate too' (p. 255). And one Plowing Eve Erif finds that the complex—and guilty—individual she has become cannot reimmerse herself in her mythic role and 'cease to be herself'. She realises; 'She had lost touch with Marob and Marob's spring. She was not the Spring Queen!' (p. 313). Tarrik comes to recognise that he and Erif are 'different from any Corn King and Spring Queen that Marob has ever had', and tries to see why: 'Perhaps it was a thing that had to come one day, or perhaps Sphaeros did it to us' (p. 319).

Sphaeros is an important character, the first representative we meet here of a potentially fine Sparta, the Sparta of the revolutionary King Kleomenes, who was to embody the ideal of a king who dies for his people. Sphaeros is Kleomenes' tutor, a Stoic philosopher who introduces Tarrik, unsuspecting, to the world of ideas, including ideas of good and evil, and disturbs his peace. Later he is supplanted for Tarrik by Hyperides, not a Stoic but an Epicurean with the ideal of brotherhood, 'a community of friends who love one another' (p. 423). This idea is to be centrally important to Mitchison, whether spelt out in the Sparta of Agis and Kleomenes, or in contemporary socialism (*We Have Been Warned*), or the early Christian martyrs, or Jesus' own disciples (*The Blood of the Martyrs, Behold Your King*).

It would be ludicrous to try to summarise here the 'thought content' of the novel—it is not self-indulgence that makes it more than seven hundred pages long—but Francis Russell Hart compresses one major thread thus simply: 'Somehow, through the sacrificial death of the Spartan king in history, Tarrik and Erif Der find a personal wholeness, a healing, a sense of transcendent purpose, and can return to Marob and to the future.'[2]

The next major novel is the first in which the author turned to depict the world of the present day, *We Have Been Warned* (1935). And immediately she ran into problems of censorship—not politically, although the book is frankly but not uncritically in favour of left wing politics generally and conditions in the Soviet Union in particular—but on sexual matters. Although Mitchison had described 'far more overt sex' in historical contexts, 'apparently it's all right when people wear wolfskins and togas' (see 'A Note on the Literary Decencies' in *You May Well Ask*, pp. 171-80). Although they balked at a rape scene, potential publishers complained most of all about open acknowledgement of the existence of contraceptives. This was bound to infuriate one of the pioneers of family-planning in London, who was on the committee of the first clinic established after Marie Stopes' own. So the move from historical to contemporary fiction had built-in problems, which delayed the publication of this novel by some two years.

A new and very personal element also marks out *We Have Been Warned*. While there was no doubt an element of self-projection in Erif Der, there is something very close to identity between the author and her two main female characters in the modern novel, in spite of obvious circumstantial differences. Indeed the whole book clearly and openly reflects the author's own experience, milieux and friends: a note at the start conventionally stresses the fictitious nature of the characters, but the following group-dedication implicitly contradicts this and identifies many main characters. The situation of Dione Galton, the heroine, closely parallels that of Mitchison herself, with a young family and a husband looking for a Parliamentary career in the Labour Party. The four British backgrounds to the story, Oxford, London, Sallington and Auchanarnish, correspond to four real ones, Oxford, London, Birmingham, where Dick Mitchison fought in 1931 as Labour candidate for King's Norton, and a generalised Scottish one, probably based on a holiday at Craignish Castle, as Mitchison had very mixed feelings about the Haldane family home at Cloan, Perthshire. And the Russian interlude is based, often quite closely, on Naomi's diaries for her trip to Russia in 1932.

In fact there were more than enough impulses in this energetic writer to supply two characters she talks of informally as 'I'. There is Dione, wife, mother and political amateur, whose often naive and open-eyed attempts to abolish class consciousness lead her into sexual adventures she had not really wanted, and there is her sister, the artist Phoebe Bathurst, an unfulfilled wife and mother whose husband was irreversibly changed by the war, and whose main love interest is in an affair outside her marriage. Phoebe is essentially an artist, with a career in illustration and wood-engraving. Mitchison's various volumes of memoirs often indicate how much some aspects of her life mirrored those of both sisters.

And Dione and Phoebe of course have important things in common. They are Scottish and self-consciously so, sharing a common homemade mythology from childhood, which involves invidious figures such as the Campbell women and the kelpies, and the 'good gules lion', and the 'good witch' Green Jean, who gives Dione at last a terrifying glimpse of a violent counter-revolution and a totalitarian future. A 'magic' element somewhat corresponding to these figures is another recurrent feature of Mitchison's work, from Erif Der and other witches in *The Corn King*, through *The Bull Calves* to the good and bad magics opposed in the Scottish children's book *The Big House*. It is rarely stressed, but is pervasive, suggesting the limitations of logic and rationality in dealing with the whole range of human experience.

Dione's awareness of her Scottishness also causes some of the problems she has with other socialists, and so the book contains an early statement of a now longstanding dilemma in Scottish political life, where the Nationalists and the Labour Party tend to distrust and suspect each other's ideas or allegiances. Mitchison herself stood as Labour candidate for the Scottish Universities in 1935, and found herself for the first of many times combining socialism and nationalist sympathies in a rather lonely way. She went on to serve for many years on the Argyll County Council and such Scottish bodies as the Highland Advisory Panel and the Highlands and Islands Consultative Council.

Another element the sisters have in common with their author is their privileged birth. Mitchison was born into the enlightened aristocratic line of the Haldanes of Gleneagles, and it is no accident that she begins *Small Talk...* (1973), her reminiscences of earliest childhood, with an awareness of status. All her understanding of class, power and politics begins with the privilege of her origins, and this is arguably one hidden thread which links her admiration of kings who died for the people—Agis, Kleomenes, Jesus—to her exploration of 'the people' in community, whether in the England of the Hunger Marches or the Rome of the early martyrs. So here and later in *The Bull Calves* Mitchison directed her passionate urgency at the Haldane-equivalents, 'the intelligensia, the people who should be

xii

giving a lead'.

We Have Been Warned, with all this, remains, perhaps inevitably, a passionate and impressive novel which is full of flaws. Michael Roberts had perceptively compared this, her first contemporary novel, to any first novel, where 'you've used far more material than you can master' (*You May Well Ask*, p. 178). I find it both the most immediate and, artistically, the least successful of Mitchison's major undertakings, and yet quite unforgettable.

It is also remarkable for pinning down most clearly an idea that Mitchison still sees as vital to continuing human civilisation. Dione comes to see most ethics as 'commercial ideas'; fair deals, the scales of justice, 'the Jealous God of Scotland, the Family Grocer visiting with his wrath those who questioned the price of his sandy sugar or attempted to evade an extortionate bill' (p. 443). Her 'new idea' is in a sense as old as Aristotle, who said: 'When people are friends there is no need for justice between them'. Her idea of good will or brotherhood is 'non-commercial':

> Good will, that curious product of consciousness, of leisure and
> energy to spare and share. That thing we put out against the
> forces of interest. That extra thing. Religions and nations and
> political parties have taken it and used it as coinage, have said
> that you must only give it in exchange for value. Good will
> towards other Christians, Moslems, Jews, towards other English,
> Scots, Allies, Europeans, towards other Monarchists, Repub-
> licans, Conservatives, Labour folk, Communists; hatred and
> cheating towards heathens, non-Moslems, Gentiles, towards the
> people across the frontier or with a different-coloured skin,
> towards all the other political parties. We will give you good
> will, but you must give us in fair exchange your soul, or your
> body, or your mind. And lately, since good will has been spoken
> of more freely, since we have given lip-service to universal good
> will, distributed free as a kind of advertisement for humanity, we
> have asked instead that we should be given something to show
> for it, peace, prosperity, happiness even. If we don't get it we are
> angry about our bargain and say we have been done. But the
> whole point of good will is that it is a by-product, a thing we can
> have too much of for our own immediate surroundings and
> belongings, as a mother can have too much milk for her baby.

We have to give it away, not only in place but in time. We have to give even to the future. (pp. 482-3)

It is restatements of this basic idea, not of good will as a by-product for the wealthy but of good will in and for itself, that animate the seekers of the 'Kingdom' in *The Blood of the Martyrs* and *Behold Your King*. It is perhaps this idea and the care with which she has promulgated it that tempts one occasionally to call the anti-clerical, anti-Father-God Mitchison nonetheless 'religious'. Something made Wyndham Lewis insert a crucifix in a portrait in 1938; 'I didn't really want that crucifix but now I think he was perhaps right, he knew a bit more about me than I knew myself' (*You May Well Ask*, p. 144).

Throughout the Thirties the need for warnings such as this novel offers was growing. Between the completion of the novel and its delayed publication, even, Mitchison was personally involved in the counter-revolution of Dollfuss in what had been 'Red Vienna'. In *Vienna Diary* (1934) she details much of what she saw there, and how she departed after a hectic month, her knickers stuffed with smuggled papers. And in fiction (*The Blood of the Martyrs*, 1939) and non-fiction (*The Moral Basis of Politics*, 1938) she continued to sound the alarm.

With the beginning of the Second World War there begins the biggest hiatus in Mitchison's publishing history: there were to be no more novels until *The Bull Calves* was published in 1947. But there was no question of the writer being too busy to write in those early days at Carradale, Kintyre, the 'big house' the Mitchisons had bought as a holiday home in 1937. Naomi spent most of the war years there, coping with her own children, evacuees, Free French soldiers, visiting politicians, the local farmers and fishermen and the local Labour Party—and doing her own farming. And with isolated spells in the London blitz. Happily for us, she had been recruited by Mass Observation to keep a daily diary, and through these long months and years she piled up a million words. Dorothy Sheridan has recently edited a magnificent selection from these diaries, in *Among You Taking Notes ... : The Wartime Diary of Naomi Mitchison* (1985). All interested readers are referred there.

And with everything else that happened around her—and some times under her control—the interested reader will find there scattered references to the composition of Mitchison's Scottish masterpiece, *The Bull Calves*. The sudden loss of her last baby in the summer of 1940 underlines her need to write a book, and the publishing situation determines that, unlike many of her others, it be a 'non-immediate book.' By November 1941 it is not only to be historical, and Scottish, but actually about her own Haldane ancestors, and she is collecting materials. One purpose is service, 'to Scotland, or rather, to the dumb Scots, the ones who need to be given pride and reassurance and kindness' (*Among You Taking Notes*, p. 179).

Happily *The Bull Calves* is once again readily available, so a detailed description is hardly necessary. It is another long book—and followed by a host of leisurely, interesting and historically accurate notes. The necessarily prolonged gestation of the novel resulted in a complex structure. It is set at Gleneagles in 1746, not long after the Jacobite Rising of the Forty-Five, in which the Haldanes took no active part. The relatively slight contemporary plot involves problems when a young member of the family gives shelter to a Jacobite fugitive and there is a general attempt to hide this, first from the head of the family and then from Duncan Forbes of Culloden, who comes to stay overnight. The more colourful plot concerns the past histories of Kirstie Haldane, sister of the house, and her Highland husband, William Macintosh. These are conveyed in confidential conversations between different characters, intricately interwoven in the structure and full of fairly dramatic surprises. The thematic movement on both national and personal levels is for unity and reconciliation, and against divisiveness: past wounds, however painful, have to be healed and put into the past. So it is, again and indirectly, a political novel, in two senses. It shows its Scottish readers a possibility of reconciliation over the past: as Mitchison says: 'it very much doesn't take sides ... and there's no nonsense about the Prince.' In a wider sense, it draws parallels between the Scottish political situation of 1746 and the world situation two hundred years later, with the culmination of a disastrous war, and people being called on to clear up the mess.

It does have, also, a personal angle. Mitchison here examines her family history with relentless honesty: 'what was great fun was doing the characters who were actually my ancestors, and one's sort of interested in the genes.' More, she uses the novel to treat indirectly one of the most crucial relationships of her own life, the close and often painful relationship with her brother Jack, the geneticist, which is mirrored in the complex love of Kirstie and her enigmatic brother Patrick; 'Patrick in a sense is partly based on my brother, so that it was all very close to the heart.' But this novel is not in the confessional mode of *We Have Been Warned*, and such information from the author is fascinating but non-essential.

Although Mitchison has written many more books since *The Bull Calves* than she had written before it, a very large proportion of these are for children or young people, and so not part of my crude map of the adult fiction. There are two new areas of concern that have become characteristic of her later fiction, and which I must point to to complete that sketch. About 1960 began Naomi's friendship with an African student called Linchwe, the future paramount chief of the Bakgatla of Botswana, and her annual visits to Mochudi have since been an important part of her life, as she has become mother to both chief and tribe.

Her fullest account of all this is in *Return to the Fairy Hill* (1966), but see also *Mucking Around: Five Continents over Fifty Years* (1981). The kind of impact it had on her fiction can be gathered from *When We Become Men* (1965). But, as I have already suggested, while the setting and characters of that fine novel are quite new, part of the way the main character's horizons are changed is implicit in *The Conquered*, when Meromic gradually discovers his larger loyalty to the whole of Gaul. The freedom fighter Isaac has to learn a more complex lesson here, for he learns the smaller loyalty Meromic knew from the start, to the local tribe, at the same time as the larger one, to black Africa. And that larger loyalty is again akin to Dione Galton's idea of good will in *We Have Been Warned*.

As it was characteristic of Mitchison to remain open to new experience, in her African relationships and in the fiction that came out of them, so the other 'new' feature of the later Mitchison is also characteristic. This most flexible and prolific of historical novelists has for more than twenty years now been calling her readers' attention to problems of the present, problems on a world scale, problems even of the future. So an element of science fiction enters her work. In *Memoirs of a Spacewoman* (1962) her interest might be described as pushing her notion of good will beyond earthly or humanoid forms, in her heroine's attempts to understand—and, importantly, to communicate with—alien and often unattractive life forms from other worlds. But in both *Solution Three* (1975) and *Not By Bread Alone* (1983) the central problem is an extension of the very real and present problem of feeding the world's people. The author's abiding interests in botany and genetics very much influence both of these. In *Not By Bread Alone*, which she refuses to call science fiction, a scientific breakthrough which revolutionises food production does not produce happiness with the elimination of starvation. And the new root crops begin to poison whole populations: only a return to the ancient eco-system of Aboriginal Australia suggests a way forward.

Solution Three is a thorough and successful piece of science fiction in which population problems are solved by conditioning people to homosexuality and all new human births are clones from the best two sets of genes available, and the wonderful new food plants, again from the best genes, suddenly become appallingly susceptible to diseases. The novel carefully underlines its message about the need for preservation of gene banks: Mitchison said in September 1984: 'What I was saying was something which *at that time* had not happened, but which is happening, I'm afraid, now.'

The only problem I had in selecting the following stories was having too big a choice of fine pieces. This was exacerbated by the fact that so many of the best pieces are on the long side, by conventional measure. Under these circumstances it was easy to yield gracefully to the author's doubts about stories written before 1930: I didn't entirely share these doubts, but willingly acquiesced.

With the exception of the first one, the stories are presented chronologically, and can easily be related to my 'sketch map' of the longer fiction. The reader can see at a glance what marks out *Beyond This Limit*: it was the result of a very special collaboration between Mitchison and Wyndham Lewis, who was the illustrator, and text and pictures are inextricably linked. It has only previously been published as an elegant slim volume in 1935. The heroine, Phoebe Bathurst, had already appeared in *We Have Been Warned*, as Dione Galton's artist sister, saddened by the marriage of a former lover. This story was composed in the autumn of 1934, some eighteen months after the completion of the novel, and the mood is different. The mode of composition is surely unique. 'What we did was that one or other of us would get ahead. He would do a picture and I would say, what's that of?—perhaps what was going to happen, and then *I* rushed ahead ... and so on.' The major characters were so clearly in some sense Lewis and Mitchison themselves that she did not bother to say that: 'He was acting as the guide of souls and with this great black hat he always wore, and I was wearing this headscarf that I always wore .... It was a bouncy book, and I think the way we both enjoyed doing it is reflected.' There is a fuller account of Lewis and Mitchison and *Beyond This Limit* in her memoir *You May Well Ask* (1979 pp. 143-152).

The Powers of Light was another illustrated slim volume (1932): it was inspired by the cave paintings at Lascaux, which made a 'tremendously strong' impact on Mitchison. Even for her, this is reaching a very long way back into intuited history. 'The Wife of Aglaos' perhaps needs a note of editorial defence: it comes from a volume of stories and poems called *The Delicate Fire* (1933) and is originally part of a five-story group, the story of 'Lovely Mantinea'. Mantinea was a Greek city which was destroyed by Antigonos of Macedonia in his war against Kleomenes, and its citizens were all sold into slavery as a reprisal for a previous atrocity, women and children on the spot, the men in gangs taken to Macedonia. The five-part story details the subsequent experience of several of these former citizens as slaves. It has a tight unity, and could have been published as a novel, but I have extracted the second part, which stands well on its own, and which in this selection has to 'stand for' all Mitchison's Greek stories.

'Five Men and a Swan' and 'The Hunting of Ian Og' were published in a collection called *Five Men and a Swan* in 1958, but the war diary shows they were written in 1940, in the long gestation period for the Scottish novel *The Bull Calves*. Both the Carradale fishermen and Neil Gunn particularly admired 'Five Men and a Swan', but *New Writing* refused it in 1941. Gunn's praise was gratifyingly, but not I think unreasonably, high. The African influence and subject matter presented in my 'map' by *When We Become Men* are indicated here by two fine stories from *Images of Africa* (Canongate, 1980), and the relatively recent open preoccupation with present and future is marked by a grim little story, 'Remember Me', from the most recent collection, *What Do You Think Yourself?* (Paul Harris, 1982). That the preoccupation with present and future is ongoing is nicely illustrated by a letter from the author

of July 1985, where she writes: 'As you will realise, "Remember Me"
is rather out of date. Bombs were a lot smaller when I wrote that.'
These stories will speak for themselves. I think they are some of the
best of the short fiction.

Notes

1 This unpublished interview is my source whenever I quote Mitchison
   without further acknowledgrment.
2 In *The Scottish Novel: A Critical Survey* (1978), pp. 187-88.

BEYOND THIS LIMIT

TWO women had arranged to have tea together, in the flat of one of them which was in a rather distant and not so fashionable quarter of the Left Bank. At this hour of the afternoon half Paris still lay between them, to be crossed between now and a vaguish teatime by the visitor. They did not know one another at all well; neither could speak the language of the other with any measure of subtlety equal to the ideas which they might wish to convey. Neither was expert with tongue nor brain; both lived by the hand and eye. The owner of the flat was a Frenchwoman, painting correctly a few years behind Picasso. The visitor was an Argyllshire Scot, and her medium was in general wood-engraving, although sometimes she took to colour, especially when in love. She was wearing a linen dress with a wide striped skirt and plain bodice; there were silver buttons all down the front of the bodice, and most other women would have noticed that in one place it was held together by a safety pin. That is, she had no chic, although the dress was becoming enough to the kind of woman who was, as it happened, Phoebe Bathurst.

For a time, in the traffic, her mind had not been working at all; it had gone blank and outward like a cod's eye. At the moment, she was vaguely glad at not thinking, but aware that at any interruption the thing would start again. She came to a crossing and had to wait for the signal shrilling of the bell. Impossible, even for the sporting Britisher, to cross without. In this pause her mind woke up and began working again. This jolted her so that she did not take her chance of crossing immediately the bell started. When she did take it she was almost too late and had to give a final rabbit jump on to the opposite pavement.

Clever Phoebe, she said to herself, as she reached the pavement and the snarling taxi-pack tore off after other prey. It would most certainly have been more traditional to go to the Rockies and shoot bears, which are always supposed to cure a broken heart, but it was cheaper to come to Paris and fully as dangerous. Also, those who go

3

to the Rockies have to spend almost a week in a liner with nothing to occupy them but the broken heart. Whereas Phoebe was ingeniously contriving to evade or fail to recognize her heart-break for hours at a time — with luck. And now, she said to herself busily, can I possibly find the right bus? No, I don't think I can, I shall take the metro. As well to recognize one's limitations.

The peculiar noise of Paris, assailing sharper nerve centres than those which cope with London, now faded. Phoebe Bathurst stepped down into the wide tunnels of the metro, where at least there is still the deliberate forest trotting of biped footsteps, long lost to streets of traffic. Phoebe's ears jogged her mind into the slightly discomforting perception that her heels were lower than those of the average Parisienne, making less angular clickings; she clutched her crocodile-skin bag, raking up small change. She was pleased with it for giving her just the right amount of centimes for her third class ticket. Nice bag, good bag.

It had been with her now for nearly five years, going everywhere with her. It had stayed decorously in Argyllshire with her mother and the children, never for weeks opening at the compartment which held lipstick or other even less respectably Scottish objects. It had been dropped about her sister's garden in the intervals of weeding or argument. It had been with her much to art dealers, private presses, and highbrow affairs of one kind and another which might be purchasers of her very delicate and specialized wood-engravings; she was famous for her flowers and animals, which, on the whole, she found preferable to people, though she was not above doing a spot of high-class pornography if the private presses really insisted on it. The crocodile-skin bag, then, knew the feeling of cheques nestling into it, all deliciously ready to turn themselves into frocks for herself and the children, into lunches, into books and theatre tickets and subscriptions to suitable causes, usually indicated by her sister. Those cheques which the gravers and scorpers and box-wood blocks made for Phoebe seemed always to turn into other things very quickly. She was hard put to it sometimes to keep up with this puzzling business of living, when things were so continually turning

4

into other things. Francs to centimes, pounds to railway tickets and the crossing of space, which itself was sometimes map inches readily held in the brain box under the little felt hat and sometimes uncounted flashing waves and trees and fields, or babies into real people, things seen explosively by instants into small, grave, graved lines, eggs into omelettes, one's own lover into another woman's husband.

That was the most surprising change of all, the only one that couldn't be altered, couldn't be foreseen, couldn't, apparently, be turned into something else again. Possibly because it was so very difficult to realize, to see at all clearly. It was always behind one. But if it got in front so that it could be seen? So that she could contemplate, without dodging, Phil and May married for ever and ever and herself not in that picture at all. Well then, she might be able to turn it into something, do something with it, take action. Because, for instance, one got into the train having taken one's ticket, one loved and educated the people into whom one's babies grew, one ate the omelette, at the other end of this journey one would get out of the metro and go to tea with that not very interesting painter-friend who had been one's excuse for coming to Paris. But there was nothing to be done about Phil. Not now. The time for that was past. Odd that apparently one can't interfere with past time, only remember it in very great detail, the exact texture of the skin between the eye and the temple, the exact shape of the leaf on the tree . . .

Dangerous to start thinking about these things. Watch between the slightly swaying shoulders of other passengers the bright or drowning reflections in the inky glass, or watch those reflections leap aside from the lighted swirling station, full of grand advertisements and ticket collectors settled there like solid flowers among the bird-darting passengers, and dark peculiar passages leading perhaps to machinery or other railway lines. When you can't bear to go on watching all this, speculate on the work and tastes of the other passengers. But not their loves. No, better be inhuman, think of the design of the perfect metro carriage. Look in your crocodile-skin bag and see that everything is there which should be there. Especially of course your new little metro ticket. And your return ticket to London and your home and your job and your children. How dreadful to be without a ticket in Paris, here alone under the streets and the wild taxi-packs. Or if you discovered that it was the wrong ticket. Or the kind of ticket that's no good. *Un billet pas valable.* If by some dreadful mistake, the kind of accident that happens to stupid people, to women who paint or write or moon about through life instead of stepping briskly from place to place or person to person, if, as you had been thinking at the last station, you had disappeared by error or oversight of the ticket-collectors, down one of those peculiar passages above which are written *Au delà de cette limite les billets ne sont plus valables*, well then — But of course the ticket is there. So far.

In any given woman's given bag, are tickets of various sorts, tickets of admission only rarely to heaven or hell, more ordinarily to those parts of middle earth which are within our familiar limits. Here, for instance, was Phoèbe's metro ticket, in the outside pocket of the crocodile-skin bag, and inside it was her return ticket to England. There also was her Club membership card, her Gorilla Arts Theatre card, and her British Museum Reader's card, not to speak of the Royal Horticultural Society's card which she had borrowed from her sister and forgotten to return, the day she went with Phil to draw irises: that excessively lovely Iris Susiana, the mourning iris, which appears already as the invention of some master draftsman. And here, tucked behind the mirror was the platform card for that Defence-of-our-Liberties meeting which she had so completely forgotten, because Phil had turned up from Oxford that afternoon and they had gone to a concert instead. Five shilling pink concert tickets. Tickets that let one into respectable places, music and books and flowers, persons with sufficiently, but oh, not dreadfully, advanced ideas. Nice square pink ideas like tickets. So, then, it is all right to come away to Paris so long as one's tickets come after one, little pink lambs in the belly of one's crocodile bag. Nothing to chase one in Paris so long as one's crocodile is with one, nothing to chase one from Concorde to Etoile by Marbœuf. And at Etoile no doubt

one changes for Grenelle, though it would have been quicker probably to take a bus, but one will change there on to the other line, simply and decorously, with the knowledge that one's ticket is there, is *valable*. At Etoile, the star, the star which has been brought down within one's limits and ticketed. So there is no need to be chased by the image of Phil who will in ten days have married May Furnivall among seasonable flowers in the College Chapel, nor need one be chased by the idea of our Liberties which are certainly in need of defence, but not by Phoebe, not to-day thank you. Nor need one be chased by the books which have not been read and the drawings which have not been made, nor even by any one particular

phrase of music which clearly cannot be heard above the noise of the metro. Although in there, behind that notice, in the tunnel where our tickets are no more use to us, such a phrase of music remembered from the pink ticket concert might well become so powerful as to chase one on cloudy wings with a neck stretched straight at one and at the end of the neck a fierce beak as piercing as wood-wind and carefully directed towards one's heart. There is nothing for it but to run.

Phoebe ran and ran and the station must have been a long way back, with the lighted trains coming noisily in under their wide arches. She had certainly been pierced to the heart, but that was some time ago. Since then the wood-wind Creature, the piercing oboe, the cloudiness that was no doubt the beginning of the cello's answer, had gone right through her, come out ahead of her and flapped away into a dazzle. Phoebe Bathurst was chasing it; she had to try and get it behind her again, for unless she did that why was she in Paris at all, why not at home? Unless she did that it was still ahead, as also the pink-ticket concert, and Phil breathing beside her, the very slight movement of Phil's listening body under the rather old flannel coat, closing against her's as the phrase took them. And if that was ahead instead of behind, where and why were the last two months? And if once two months get dislocated out of the calendar there is no telling what may happen to anything, books or drawings or flowers or art theatres or persons with the right ideas about liberty of thought and all that. Nothing is safe, nothing dependable, no ticket.

But of course that was so.

Round the next corner she met the ticket-collector. He seemed rather a pleasant man; his horse was grazing beside him; it was a white horse with a golden bridle and the grass was very green. The ticket-collector was wearing a single unwilted blossom of Iris Susiana in his button-hole. He said: 'Tickets, please', and Phoebe turned and whistled to her crocodile, which, not being able to run as fast as she could, was still several yards behind. It came up with her and unclosed. She pulled out all the tickets, flustered as usual, before remembering that she had put the metro ticket for convenience into its nostril. She handed the whole bunch to the ticket-collector.

'*Ces billets ne sont plus valables*', he said, and handed them to the horse, which ate them. He added, in English this time, but without a trace of the B.B.C. accent which she had somehow feared: 'No good, I'm afraid. Not beyond the limit. You'll have to pay.'

'But one of them was my sister's,' said Phoebe, visualizing the Royal Horticultural Society's membership card, 'and she was thinking of trying gloxinias.'

'Other peoples' tickets are no good either,' said the ticket-collector kindly, 'and the gloxinias are trying enough themselves, without her trying them any more. You'll notice them if you go on.'

Foiled on that, Phoebe asked: 'Well, how much will another ticket be?'

'You'll pay at the other end,' said the ticket-collector, 'and as to

12

how much, that'll just depend. I take it you're going to help.'

'Oh yes,' said Phoebe, 'Oh yes, I want to help!' And then noticed she didn't know what about. 'If only you'll *tell* me!' she said, 'People never tell one anything, they expect one to ‧understand. They expect one to have opinions about things, art and politics and morality and all that . . .'

'Oh opinions,' said the ticket-collector, 'You'll need them when it rains. Because if you get rheumatism you won't be much good, will you? But I shouldn't bother about them in ordinary weather; they're no use except when it's wet. Not here.'

'Capital,' said Phoebe, 'then I can just get on with chasing the Creature. That *is* it, isn't it?'

'Of course,' said the ticket-collector kindly, 'now, my horse thinks it has gone into the middle of Etoile. Naturally, the pressure is more intense there. You can manage densities?'

'I think so,' said Phoebe, 'but are we all closing in?'

'Closing or expanding, according to whether you're going back or forward. What do you expect? My horse says you look like an ‧expander: try. Of course, you'll probably get there first. If so, hold on.'

'How do I start?'

'Well, just remember what's going to happen and follow it up very closely. It's merely a matter of concentration. Keep an eye on my horse.'

Then it occurred to Phoebe that in a moment the horse was going to lift its head from the green grass and look at her. She remembered a grass blade that was going to lie on the horse's white muzzle and the expression of its eyes and ears watching her expand, as, by the way, she was now doing. There, it was looking up now, just as she had remembered it was going to. She was pressing out through the radiations of Etoile and now had expanded milkily above Paris. Looking down through herself she was aware of spikes and roughnesses and the crawling, tickling traffic, the mite-like burrowing of the

metros. The centre of Etoile had, however, ebbed away, expanding on its own, and the question was whether she could catch up with it; she was so occupied in remembering the immediate next moment and following it up that she could not be certain what was going to happen as between her and Etoile. The great curve of the world, spinning under her, shouldered away the afternoon; important to keep inside the pull of gravity. The smudge of London dirtied green England, trailing off arterial legs, blotched with the red and brown of suburbs. The Thames valley was deeper green, wound through by the blue Thames, brooded over by cloudy Phoebe. As she overlapped Oxford she caught sight of the Creature, folded gargoyle-like into a Gothic crevice, its neck coiled down on to its wings. Rapidly aware of its settling there, after flight over Reading,

Brighton, the wide Channel, the district of Caux, Rouen, Paris, herself, she palpitated down into contractions, and as she did so, Etoile also contracted into heavier and brighter densities all round her, so that a few steps would take her to the middle. The Creature, as she closed on it, had swooped down, landing just beside the Martyrs' Memorial. She had very nearly been taken unawares by the densities and had contracted down to about three foot six when

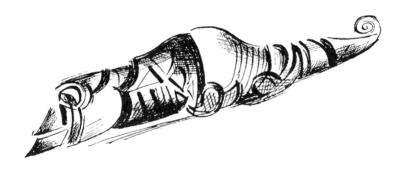

the feeling of pressure, especially about the chest, recalled her and she came back to her ordinary size.

All the time she had hold of the Creature, by its two wings. It seemed quite impassive and unaware of her, but, at the moment when she was at her smallest, it shook itself and looked at her with a pair of jolly brown eyes above a soft, freckled, snub-nose under a green cotton hat, and, as she came to her full height again, it said 'Dance me!' So, being the kind of person who usually did what children asked them to, Phoebe danced the pinky-brown arms and light body in the green flowered frock, so suitable for summer in Oxford, and, turning to May, said: 'What a lamb!'

She then went on with her interrupted conversation with Professor and Mrs. Philip Bickerden about the new work on thermodynamics

19

which had so startlingly followed the establishment of the new laboratories at Oxford by the Planning Commission of World-Soviet-States, but which had failed to shake the Martyrs' Memorial. She was rather bored with the Bickerdens, especially Phil; it was very odd to think that once she'd broken her heart over that nice old word-spinner, the Professor of Theoretical Aerostatics with his grey rather yesterdayish beard — but of course, he didn't have a beard then — did he? No, of course he didn't. And in those days there was no sub-tropical garden outside Balliol — 'You mustn't pick those

flowers or the proctors will come!' said May with age-old maternal silliness to her youngest. As if there weren't enough heads on the gloxinias for a hundred little girls from North Oxford! Still, perhaps it was better not to pick them while they were in the middle of a concert. She and the Bickerdens stopped for a moment to listen. 'What dreadful stuff they relay nowadays!' said May.

The mauve gloxinias were as always dreadfully sentimental; they lifted up their heavy, waxy trumpets, the stamens thrilled, shedding the most uncalled-for pollen, as the waltzes burbled out of them. The pink were sugary and vocal, their heavy, velvet leaves imitating a corsage which might be suitable for diamond butterflies. The Bickerdens and Phoebe passed on to another bed, where the

humming of a symphony concert rose more pleasantly from deep crimson trumpets, although even here one was aware of something not quite right either about the sentiment or about the transmission. The purple were closed, since they kept themselves to themselves and Brahms. 'You know,' said Phoebe, 'I really do find gloxinias very trying.'

'Trying yourself!' said a red gloxinia, putting out its tongue at her, and immediately the whole bed put on softly crashing brakes of finale, and began instead to talk back at her. 'You didn't try, anyway!' 'You were told to hold on, but did you?' 'Not she! Never even tried to!' 'Now it's off again just when we thought we'd got it!' 'Said she wanted to help, but much use she's been! Now, if they'd tried us gloxinias!' 'Hi, you, Phoebe, why didn't you hold on?'

'Oh dear, oh dear,' said Phoebe, becoming more and more bothered, 'I meant to, I really did! But it wasn't the Creature.'

'Yes it was,' said the gloxinias, flicking snake-tongues at her, 'it only changed itself, and you hadn't the sense to hold on!'

'But how could I have, with the others there?'

'They were only part of the projection, silly!'

'But then,' asked Phoebe, faltering, looking round for a sight of the Bickerdens, or Balliol, or the Martyrs' Memorial, or one glimpse towards what had been or was going to be North Oxford, and finding at present nothing but banks of gloxinias, 'Then perhaps Phil isn't real? I mean, he wasn't, or at least he isn't going to be . . .' From somewhere behind her, at shoulder level, a gloxinia clicked and whirred into a soprano trill. 'Perhaps none of them are really going to be like that?' Phoebe said, now almost to herself, 'Perhaps — perhaps after all I'm not going to be able to get bored with Phil?'

A whole bunch of pink freshly-watered gloxinias winked at her, closing completely but for a slip of tongue. When they opened again they were starting on Mendelssohn.

'You're just a set of nasty little gramophones!' said Phoebe, 'and I shall advise my sister not to try you!'

'Probably she finds it a little difficult to keep them in the right heat,' said the old gentleman with whom Phoebe was now talking, 'gentle and constant', and he sighed as though thinking of the silver-haired old lady who would now, but for the unkindness of fate, have graced his equally silvered tea-table. 'But of course not so touchy as orchids,' he went on; 'You see?' and he pointed to the distinguished group of orchidaceae: 'My own!'

At this some of the orchids preened themselves up, with a delicate tortion of already fantastic petals, while others tossed their heads. The deep stems of cymbidium stood meekly, but with a soft inward pride, upholding blossom and tender buds. It was one of the commoner sort, a cattleya, true haberdasher's orchid-colour, which stared at Phoebe and said 'Are you a member?'

Phoebe at once remembered the Royal Horticultural Society's card, and retrieved it without difficulty from her crocodile which was fraternizing with the orchids in a pleasant atmosphere of tropical tales. For a moment she wondered how the ticket-collector's horse had disgorged it, but quickly supposed it to be a duplicate. The cattleya, however, after one glance, turned from orchid colour to a richly indignant purple: 'That ticket, my good woman, is no use to us!' And indeed, as she now saw, it was an obvious forgery.

Dreadfully ashamed, she realized that there was only one thing to be done. Having arrived on false pretences, she must justify herself at the flower show. She sprang, as though on the ticket-collector's winged shoes, up on to one of the stands, coming down neatly on to an empty flower-pot, which, she realized with considerable satisfaction, had been filled with a nice, sweet, well-rotted

24

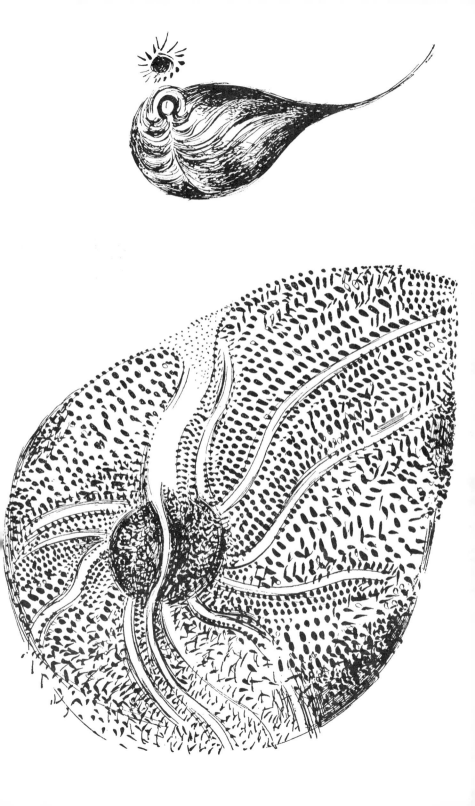

loam, just the thing for Phoebe Bathurst. In a few minutes her exhibitor came round with a watering-can: a delicious drink permeated up through her stem, strengthening and stiffening her tissues which had become somewhat limp during her encounter with the orchid. Her leaves tilted a little upward; she lifted her many-rayed flower towards the source of light. If only the delicious drink could now be followed up by a chorophyl-gratifying hour of sunshine!

And this was exactly what happened. A window was opened, a cloud passed, direct light poured in on Bathurstia Phoebe. Happily she drowsed in it, tingling with floral well-being, breathing out sweetness. With semi-maternal, semi-aesthetic complacency, she observed that one of her buds was opening. Its outer rays, after a delicate and becoming hesitation, parted, stiffening a little to the impact of the sunlight. All was well.

From time to time vague shapes moved past her. Once one of them, passing abruptly within her ken, trickled a finger along the edge of her shapeliest leaf, yet she scarcely shrunk away, accepting this shadow or double of her exhibitor, so much less intimate than any visiting bee or butterfly, whose proboscisced curiosity might well have formed a nodal point in her flowery afternoon. But the Show seemed empty of any buzz-winged Nosey Parkers.

For another space of sun-drugged existence she stayed secure among her sister flowers, vaguely aware of them, but not wondering whether they were in any way like herself. And then, immediately in front of her, occurred an area of rough white, which might have been the snow-covered tundras or a sky full of white cloud, or, for now it seemed to be patterned with lines, the side of an Essex house white-washed over a plaster decoration; it was, however, the nose of the white horse, and behind the white horse was the ticket-collector. Bathurstia Phoebe was not interested in the ticket-collector, had no memory of him, gazed sunwards. But the ticket-collector seized her by the stem and pulled.

Hideous and terrible, the wrenching out of rootlets, the crushing of sappy leaves! Her root was dragged from the earth as once children had been dragged from out of woman Phoebe, with parting of hidden

27

fibres, which had sheltered and nourished them. In this opposite of child-birth, the floral Phoebe writhed in remembrance, in a recapitulation of life from seed-bed to Flower Show, all now in vain.

'Really!' said Phoebe to the ticket-collector, 'You aren't a very polite man!'

'Sorry,' said the ticket-collector, 'but after all, you cut me dead yourself. And we've got to discuss the next move.'

'I'm afraid I wasn't awfully good,' Phoebe said, now recollecting her failure, frowning as she brushed a speck of earth from her skirt.

'That's all right,' said the ticket-collector, 'people who manage it the first time never are. We'll do it all together next time.' Come along.'

Some of the plants were prepared to help, but not others; the more delicate ones were fussy about leaving their exhibitors, though when the ticket-collector whispered: 'Coming, Susie?' the lovely Iris came at once. Most of them wanted to be carried, but the horse was willing. Phoebe hoped the gloxinias wouldn't recognize her, but as she passed they shot out mocking relayed oboe notes at her, not really painful but a little bruising. She was so occupied with the flowers that she had not particularly noticed the other visitors to the Flower Show. Now she became aware of them, not so much by looking at them, as through their looks at her. The old gentleman of the orchids patted her head and she scowled at him, annoyed with her hair for bobbing so on her neck, wishing she was grown up and could twist it into a lovely bun at the back and have long enclosing dresses that would stop people touching her – horrid old gentlemen that said they were Daddy's friends! — and then she'd be sure of herself and not make awful mistakes like when she'd said at tea — in front of the visitors — oh dear! Everything would be so easy then, nothing to be afraid of, no one making remarks she only just couldn't understand, no one interrupting when she was thinking about flowers, mooning about them, no one saying she ought to sit up and draw perspectives properly instead of scribbling shapes —

'Phoebe,' said the ticket-collector, 'you didn't come back to the

right size after being planted. You've got to expand a bit more if you want to be now.'

'What rot,' said Phoebe, 'it's Now now!'

The horse whinnied a long giggle, the white horse among the gloxinias. And Phoebe became incredulously aware that in two years she would indeed put up her hair, but it would be no fun; there would after all be no security and no uninterruption, for the carriage horses would be requisitioned and never come back and her own pony would be sold and she would cry for nights and nights, only secretly because of being patriotic and the WAR a black interruption over everything, and one had to accept it, one *did* accept it, one didn't think of the fun one wasn't getting out of being grown-up — and years and years after, what was more awful still, one would forget all about one's pony, it was other things to cry about secretly at night — oh, oh, I can't be going to turn into that sort of woman even if I'm going to be an artist, even if I'm going to be a genius and I mean to be, I'm not going to turn into a woman who likes being touched by a *man*, oh please — Gasping and expanding Phoebe clutched on to the mane of the horse.

'You see,' said the ticket-collector, 'you wouldn't have been allowed into the Reading Room at that age. And we've reason to believe IT may go there.'

Ah, thought grown-up Phoebe, looking solidly at the solid British Museum, here's something I can understand. They walked up the steps with their hands in their pockets, laying plans. The crocodile varied this, not having pockets, by laying an egg. The pigeons, delighted, promptly claimed. 'Who else shall we get?' said the ticket-collector, 'there are several possible ways of escape and we have to guard them.'

'I know some of the people in the print-room,' said Phoebe, doubtfully, 'but I don't suppose they've ever gone beyond any limits.'

'No,' the ticket-collector answered, 'I doubt if we shall get any help from the officials. And the Lo Han won't; he always kept to the limits. In fact I suspect him of being one of the Guardians. But there are the Emperors.'

31

'Caesar and Augustus shoved the limits back, but I don't think they ever went past them,' Phoebe said thoughtfully, 'and we don't *really* want the others, do we? They might side with IT. Besides, they're only busts.'

'There are the winged Assyrian bulls, if one could get it into their heads in time.'

'No!' said the horse, 'I bar those Bulls. They've got six legs. It would make me feel ordinary. Same with the giant scarab.'

'What about the mummies?'

'Yes,' said the ticket-collector — they were standing now by the post card stall — 'I'll try for them. Will you get the people from the vases, Phoebe? You'll find that some of *them* went beyond the limits.'

'Those ones will be at the back of the cases — or put away! This isn't Munich. The ones we show here believed in limits, μηδὲν ἄγαν and all that.'

The horse snorted derisively: 'They only said that because they couldn't do it! I've got some friends on the frieze. The Panathenaia wasn't a Sunday school treat. They'll be a bit of all right, my friends! Mind you don't get kicked nor yet bitten! I'll have a chat with the harpies while I'm about it.' And off he went at an echoing trot through the cast room, while Phoebe and the ticket-collector posted the flowers round the main entrance, disguised as picture post cards of the Persian Miniatures.

After that they went up the main staircase together.

'Where do you think IT is?' whispered Phoebe.

'Most likely turned into something,' said the ticket-collector, looking carefully round the bronze age, 'now, there's a sword I don't remember, look, the enamel's rather odd, if it *is* British first century. Watch . . .' As they watched the sword quivered self-consciously under the glass; it felt it had overdone the red enamel, rather in the worst Gallic taste of the period than in the respectable British mode of Verulamium. 'That's your Creature,' said the ticket-collector with a satisfied buzz of his heel and cap wings, 'but it's awkward about the glass case. Perhaps I can unlock it.' He

32

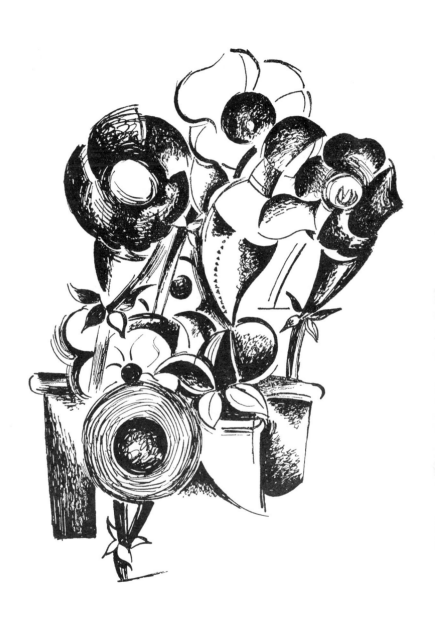

took a bunch of keys out of his pocket and started on the lock. Phoebe felt a curious remnant of normal shock and horror. What would happen when they noticed? But the visitors seemed as remote and unreal and un-noticing as other visitors to the British Museum always do. There were three school girls and a mistress, improbable already, but becoming rapidly more so with every draught of the ancient world which they sucked in, not to digest but to swell themselves out with a wind of paleish imaginings. There was a thin student, remote too in a prickly jungle of academic issues, from which he could only peer out like a very small tiger afraid of the white men with guns. There was a provincial couple, no doubt on the mummy-track, who supposed that the ticket-collector had authority — as perhaps, thought Phoebe, he has, for after all I know nothing about him, perhaps he is the director or one of the trustees, the Archbishop of Canterbury on his afternoon off, because after all, the Arch-bishops *must* have afternoons off or they'd burst through their gaiters, wouldn't they. With her mind's pencil she began to clothe the ticket-collector in gaiters, apron, purple vest and collar, authority, checking up one's ticket of admission to heaven. And when that definitely isn't one's kind of place, when one hasn't got certificates of baptism, confirmation, and love-honour-and-obeyishness, well then, he drops it all and becomes the collector of whatever other tickets one has. Tickets of admission to hell, or wherever it is that Phoebes go. He must be all that, Phoebe said to herself, watching him try one key after another, because he takes things for granted, things, I mean, like the Creature, that *are* so, but *oughtn't* to be. And he's certain, or at least his horse is, which comes to the same thing, when you compare it with my utterly idiotic crocodile. Well, not utterly, she thought, as the poor crocodile licked her hand, weeping an almost genuine tear, because it does carry my pencil and note-book and I can draw. And then she thought, how fortunate that I'm exhibiting at Redfern's, I can just walk in, because if I'd had to have a ticket it wouldn't have been any use now! And as she thought that the key turned in the lock and she became again intent on the sword.

Slowly the ticket-collector began to lift the lid, and Phoebe's hands tensed to grab on the bronze blade still perhaps cutting. But the sword, winking for a second those red enamel eyes, made, I fear only too clearly, not in Britain but in Bibracte of the Haeduans, gave a wriggle all along itself, budded a quantity of prickly and evil-looking little legs, twisted its hilt into a flat invertebrate head, and rushed millipede fashion through the crack of space under the lifted lid. Phoebe flinched, tried to catch it a moment too late, and, equally too late, the ticket-collector slammed the lid, but failed to catch even its last segment. It slithered with extreme rapidity across the floor and round the corner towards the Etruscans. 'Hell,' said Phoebe.

'Anyhow,' said the ticket-collector, 'the Creature has changed itself twice since it's been here, the third time it's got to be itself.'

'Of course,' said Phoebe comforted, 'well, we'd better see who can be got.'

They were in with the Etruscans now. The man on the sarcophagus lid with the long slanting eyes and the curious nose, beckoned them over. 'I heard IT say to itself,' he said in a rather breathy voice, lisping the *s* a little, 'that IT was going down to the inscriptions to have forty winks. IT said you'd never spot it there.' 'Coming?' asked Phoebe. The sarcophagus man stretched his legs and long toes, then smiled and shook his head. 'I have settled my account with the Limits,' he said, and lapsed back into ancient clay.

They went on through Greek and Roman life, into the Vase room, where the ticket-collector left Phoebe and himself went through to the Egyptian section to wake up the mummies. Phoebe passed the first lot of lateish vases; they were no use. But the red-figured Attic vases were promising. These people had contracted down into the hard density of the past, difficult to see into, the centre of Etoile, the star. Which of them were in her world, had passed beyond the limits? Not, clearly, the young men exercising or making love, at banquets or preparing for decently sporting and amateur battles. Not, clearly, the young women at their toilet or assisting the young men, not even the lovely white-figured girl reaching up for the apple, the topmost apple of Lesbos. She went on slowly scrutinizing towards the black figure vases. There were of course the Gods. But had they,

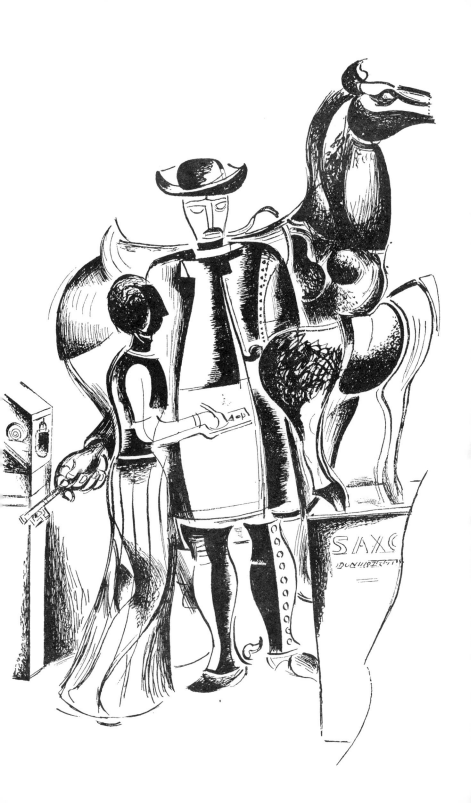

did they? Swan-riding Aphrodite, have you passed beyond the limits? Or were you born between the deep sea and the golden shore, so that there was no need to journey, as we journey driven by your relentless son, from London and music and our own work, our own homes and children and ordered things, to a week in Paris and the hope of forgetting, and our hearts pierced by the memory of the oboe, and so beyond the barrier, to the place where concepts do not hold? Father Zeus, with your nice little bundle of fireworks, have you even so much as looked over the edge since the day you decided to forget Grandfather Kronos and become a respectable Führer, standing there between Right and Left, between Atropos and Clotho, between Diké and Themis, pretending they don't exist? You'd pretend IT didn't exist, wouldn't you? And you, Apollo, you wouldn't go beyond the limits, would you, my dear? You should be my God, you're supposed to look after the artists, but you don't, do you, the Muses keep you from straying away from Helicon heights, jolly to sit among the girls in those Alpine meadows of yours, bright heady green when we're all parched below, kind-starred with gentian and autumn crocus, aren't they, my Phoibos, sweet to loose-sandalled feet, happy with cow-bells, foreshadowing Nestlés, Apollo of Neuchatel, Apollo of Berne, of Zurich, Apollo of Safety First in

lovely Lucerne! Artemis, Artemis, goddess of Roedean, you always kept within the limits: from within, chastely, you mourned Hippolytos or smote your erring maidens. Athene? . . . I wonder. She stared at the great Panathenaic amphorae, the prizes in the games, each with its strange, striding Athene. If you were goddess of Athens, didn't you have to cross limits? Doesn't that happen if you are the Maiden of a democracy?

Athene said, striding on; 'I've no time to help you, I have my hands full, still. Too many worshippers, mostly fools. Get Koré. She will know.' Then her mouth snapped silent.

Phoebe remembered that Koré was Persephone, the girl who went to Hell and came back. She looked for a vase and found one with the meeting of Mother and Daughter at Enna. The Daughter turned her head and stepped forward in the white, flowered-bordered chiton, expanding through two and a half millenia into kind woman-flesh, and said: 'I will help you, Despoina Horōn.'

It was gladdening for Phoebe to be Lady of Limits; she knew now that earlier she had been uncertain whether she was anyone. She said to Persephone: 'Koré, I see that you know everything. Do you come with us?'

'No,' said Persephone, 'for it might be I should be called back. But I shall lend you my one who was born beyond all limits. Take care of her.' And with that Persephone shrank back towards the vase, but left in her stead a shadow that solidified into a girl about eleven years old, dreadfully thin, and dark-eyed with two long plaits of storm-black hair, so alone that Phoebe suddenly thought with violent tenderness of her two, surely now safe, staying with their grandmother in Scotland, well on the known side of the limits. But at this she heard the juicily tripping first notes of the 'Bonny Banks of Loch Lomond', as performed by an English tenor, and only then noticed what flowers the child Skiageneia wore in her hair. 'My dear,' she said, 'have you got to have gloxinias?'

'Father gave them to me,' said the daughter of Persephone and Hades, 'but I don't mind losing them, Despoina.' She threw them on the floor where the tune cracked and scraped and broke off.

40

'Thank you,' said Phoebe, 'do you know who we ought to get?'

'Yes,' said Skiageneia, 'this is where I play, mostly, so I know them all. Once I found a toy mouse that someone had left. Someone littler than me, I expect. But of course I had to let it go again in the morning,' she ended gloomily.

'Oh my poor duck,' said Phoebe, 'won't your father let you out properly?'

43

'No,' said Skiageneia, 'and by the way, you know, don't you, you'll have to go and talk him round about taking me off now? But he's not so bad. You'll be able to do it, won't you, Despoina?' She took Phoebe's hand.

Phoebe thought with very considerable apprehension that she would not at all like to interview Hades, but, being a mother, said to the child: 'Of course, my lamb. How long can you stay?'

'Well,' said Skiageneia, 'if you can square father — oh, I could stay *quite* a long time. A thousand years or so. You wouldn't mind, would you, Despoina?'

'I'd love it,' said Phoebe firmly, 'now, who shall we get?'

'Let's get Iris and Niké,' said Skiageneia and went over to a vase and whispered. Out came two early fifth-century ladies in fluttering blue-spotted pleated tunics with stiff and apparently inadequate red-spotted wings. They had very womanly figures, on which Skiageneia beamed approvingly, before saying to Iris: 'You go and get Theseus and Thetis,' and to Niké: 'You get Ariadne and anyone else who'll play.'

Phoebe interrupted nervously, not sure how much to say in front of someone else's child: 'But do Thetis and Ariadne . . . ?'

'Oh yes. They squash Theseus: he needs it. And oh' — she shouted after Iris — 'You get Orpheus!' Iris and Niké went off in long noisy hops, a flutter of spotted wings like jays bouncing through a forest. They did not seem to interrupt the two or three rather shadowy visitors who were admiring the vases or wandering through them for want of anything better to do. Skiageneia pulled at Phoebe who bent down to be whispered to: 'Shall we get Lord Dionysos? He's always coming into our country, and his people are half of them beyond the Limits too. But . . .'

'But what?'

'Well, one never knows quite what he'll do. Oh, here are the others back. Let's ask them.'

Iris and Niké had no opinions, neither of them being paid to think: they were merely prepared to obey orders from Hades' only-begotten daughter. Orpheus was dazed and vague, picking at his

44

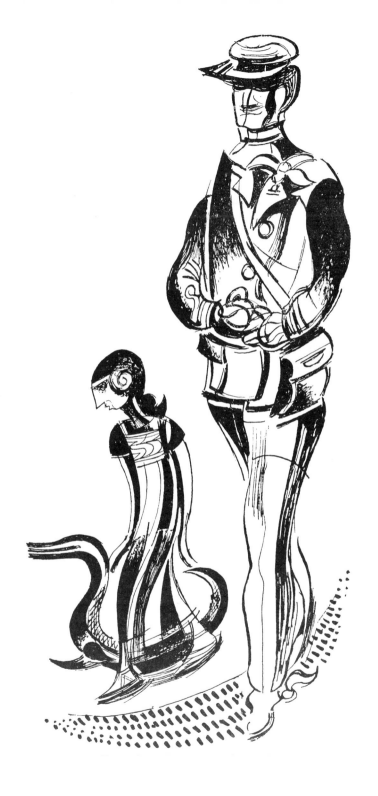

lute, watery-flowing Thetis faintly against, but young Theseus, the
thin short tunic fluttering round his unembarrassed loins, said the
more the merrier. Cretan Ariadne, curled and painted, observed
negligently that he would perhaps be convenient. Phoebe was
doubtful, but the child suddenly clapped her hands: 'Oh come on!
Iris, go fetch him, and see that he's properly grown-up this time!
I can't bear him when he's just being a big school-boy,' she added
firmly. Ariadne was smiling slightly; she had made friends with the
crocodile and was now inspecting her curiously un-English make-up
in the little mirror she had extracted from its ear.

They were now in the second room. Skiageneia suddenly pointed
to the fat Corinthian jars: 'Oh Despoina, shall we have the Zoo?' But
Phoebe, rather nervous of what the horse might think of winged
panthers, spotted eagle-dogs, antelope-snakes and such-like, decided
against. At the head of the stairs they met the ticket-collector; he
seemed cross. Phoebe hastily asked the child if she knew him.

'But of course, Despoina. He often comes with — oh, things for

Father: you wouldn't understand perhaps.' She nodded to him: 'Well, how are the markets?'

The ticket-collector nodded back at her and then began explaining, with what was, for him, an extreme lack of calm, that none of the mummies would come. They were all first-class Cook's tourists with quantities of tickets guaranteeing them complete freedom from interruptions and inconveniences; their luggage was labelled for the divine weighing-machine, and each one of them had handed out to the ticket-collector so many signed and certified Names, Symbols, insurance coupons, cheques and counterfoils, bills of lading, contracts, invoices, F.O.B., C.I.F., F.P.A., etc., that he had given it up and come away without so much as the Kha, Khu or spiritual body of one single princess. On the other hand, he had enticed a Chinese tiger from the Edward VII gallery; heavily cat-like, it swathed itself round his legs, with lamping looks and a loud, throaty purr.

It was now that Orpheus, coming clear of that daze, due perhaps to the tumult of wave-lengths through which he and his lute had passed during an expansion of three millenia, perceived the ticket-collector and shuddered. And the ticket-collector said to him in the most unexpected way: 'So you thought this was a second chance, Orpheus? But you used up your Return, you know. And it would be too late now.'

Phoebe, now audience, echoed the shudder; she had trusted the ticket-collector, supposed him kind: why this? 'It's not a second-chance universe, Despoina,' said the child at her side, looking pitifully but without help, from her great eyes at the tall quivering Orpheus.

'But it *is*!' said Phoebe — for had she not missed the Creature once?

'Mechanically, yes,' said Ariadne, fellow-countrywoman to strange adventurers, 'in the shape. But not in the internal structure. There is only re-discovery and mutation.' But Phoebe, not Cretan nor mechanically minded, a shudderer at minotaurs, could not admit this to her mind, westernly certain that every individual must be his or her own redeemer.

And then, as they stood at the head of the stairs, out flew Iris and

alighting made a craft sign which the ticket-collector returned. Behind her came bearded and flashing Dionysos, and with him his shadows and magics, the nymphs and satyrs and fauns and ramping vines. A long grape tendril cast itself down among Skiageneia's heavy hair; she brushed it away, and Ariadne with a flick of her hand removed a couple of satyrs. Nymphs held a shadow wine-jar to Orpheus who drained it eagerly amid noiseless laughter from the Bacchic creatures. No use, thought Phoebe, even real wine is no use. When I heard about Phil and May I drank half a tumbler of cooking brandy in the kitchen and it had no effect at all; the children noticed nothing, even.

They went down the steps, the great vine of Dionysos unrolling and rippling ahead of them over the balustrade, hooking a goat foot here and there or squeezing a shadow oread till imagined curve of breast or thigh burst into soaking showers of dark wine. And at the bottom of the stairs, up came the white horse and crowding behind him, hog-manes and proud little heads, horse-lips curled to whinny, round legs and barrels, clean muscles of croup and shoulder, the Parthenon ponies. Beyond them, making trial flights along corridors and under door arches, the gross bodies and strong, ill proportioned wings of the harpies. 'Well,' said the horse, prancing, 'What about it now!'

The ticket-collector smacked the nose of a horse which was trying to bite him: 'We shall need your toughs. All exits must be guarded. IT is in the main hall among the inscriptions. The flowers are watching, but are not mobile enough to stop IT! You, horses, IT's a proleterian, a charcoal burner from Acharnae, go for IT! IT may bolt into the Reading Room: Phoebe, you and the child guard there. Or up the stairs: your spear, Theseus — the tiger will help. Thetis, block all water ways. Ariadne at the Roman gallery. IT will probably take its own shape; if so, Iris and Niké can outfly IT, and the harpies bring IT down. Lord Dionysos will fill all corners with his magics. You, Orpheus, had best obey orders this time.'

Here came a scream from Thetis whose ear had been tweaked by a nibbling harpy. Theseus jabbed it with his spear: it rose squawking. Most of the horses were now gripped and bestridden by smooth or hairy legs of nymphs or satyrs, and were keeping reasonably quiet. Phoebe missed her crocodile, but supposed it would turn up as usual. She was quite resigned to the lack of interest among the normal Museum denizens; some of these were visited by the creatures of Dionysos, in what Phoebe considered a most informal way, but it appeared not to incommode them in the least. It was only at the Entrance Hall that the faithful crocodile turned up from the new rooms with the men of Ur and Um. They were distinguished-looking in their Sumerian way, but not very brilliant conversationalists. It was, thought Phoebe, natural that they should be rather Woolley after all that time. They wandered about, murmuring umm and ur, and were pushed into corners or down the umbrella racks. The flowers had kept watch and were eager to report, but Olympian Iris refused to notice the lovely alien Susiana.

All took up positions. Orpheus stepped into the central space, and stepping silently after him, the ticket-collector, one tight hand on the nape of the bowed musician's neck. Then it began: those single sweet notes and the following voice, that vibration through heart and brain, through the galleries, the Elgin marbles, the Aztec crystal, the hived Reading Room. Listening, the Museum pigeons softly crowded the cornices, sparrows and starlings edging between them, for a

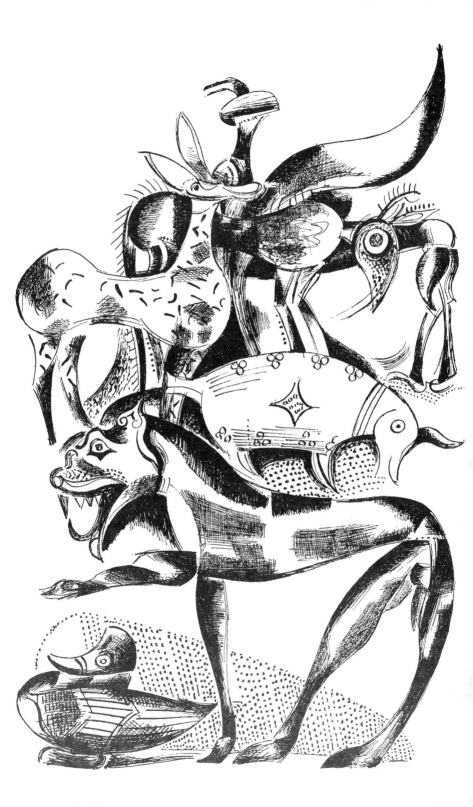

moment storm-silenced. In the Museum, cats, mice, beetles, flies, curators and sub-curators, stayed very still. And the Creature, its millipede segments glistening like new boots in Bond Street, crept half out from behind the Potidaea inscription, flattening itself to receive the sound waves. All round the hall summer-deep silence held the mares and stallions of Athens; the Dionysian ghost riders drooped forward; Gods, demi-Gods and mortals listened timelessly, standing or hovering; alone the Chinese tiger purred a delicate bass. And slowly, foot by foot, the ticket-collector moved towards the Creature and away from the musician.

Then Phoebe, watching, through the music crystal, the intent pale face of Orpheus, saw it crinkle and sharpen with pain and rebellion, and a moment later there came a terrible sound from the lute and voice, a noise of breaking and discord in the foundations of life. The Creature swelled and changed hideously into itself, and all else rushed upon it. IT towered like a pheasant out of reach of the snapping horses, the springing tiger, evaded the spear of Theseus and the flung clue of Ariadne, zigzagged like a woodcock from its winged pursuers, and ducked, below their level but above Phoebe's, crashing through the swing doors into the Reading Room.

Phoebe had just time to see the ticker-collector, with one arm at rigid, relentless right angle, hounding the tiger on to Orpheus, just time to see the squealing riot of the horses begin. And then she had snatched Skiageneia out of it all and was pulling her along into the Reading Room, after IT.

And, a few minutes later, in a hideous mist of shame, Phoebe Bathurst was turned out of the Reading Room, not only having made a noise and disturbed the sacred peace of the rightful, the householder-guaranteed, readers, but also NOT HAVING HER READERS TICKET. Unforgettable humiliation for a highbrow, for a respectable, Museum-fearing, law-conditioned bourgeoise! Because of Phoebe, hard things would justifiably be said of women, above all of women artists, newspapers would publish cruelties, Phil would see them — or worse, May. She crept towards the stony exit, scarcely noticing the emptiness of the hall, the fact that the pavement was not,

55

apparently, strewn with blood and torn poet's flesh. If the Romans, keepers of Limits, headed no doubt by the Pontifex Maximus in person, mocked at her from the mouth of their gallery, she did not notice them. It was only out on the terrace that she realized that Skiageneia was still with her, dressed now in grey flannel shorts and a blue aertex shirt, and snivelling in a way most unbefitting the child of Hades and eleven years old at that.

'I'm so hungry!' she wailed suddenly, and clutched on to Phoebe.

Now having something immediate to do, Phoebe's crushed womanhood asserted itself against her highbrow shame. 'We'll go and have tea at once,' she said, 'I'd like a cup of coffee myself, and as for you, I'm going to give you all the cream buns and pink cakes you can possibly hold.'

'Where?' said Skiagenia, brightening up.

'At my club. Oh hell, that horse has gone and eaten my Membership card or if the crocodile's got it, it'll be a wrong 'un and there's sure to be a row. Or I shall do something awful myself. No, I can't go to my club any longer. How peculiar! It was a very ordinary club. I suppose that's why . . . No, we'll go to a tea-shop. Only I haven't any English money on me, only francs.' Skiageneia looked like crying again. 'No, I'm just not going to let that interfere. Come along: when the ticket-collector turns up again, we'll make him pay.' She took the child's hand and firmly walked her off to the nearest Bloomsbury tea-shop.

It struck her at once that the cakes, obviously made with affection and fresh butter, looked like cakes used in the days when one was young and shy and, taken out to tea by aunts, never got quite the required feeling of careless and lordly fullness. Here was cream and crisp stickiness, blonde tints of sugar, heat-brunetted nuts. Perhaps the demi-god child, hungry, was cramming them all into her own vision? Phoebe lingered a moment at the window, but Skiageneia pulled her along: 'Come *on*, Despoina!' Oh well, either the ticket-collector would turn up — and have to pay — or else she'd square them somehow, suddenly discover she'd lost her purse, produce a visiting-card (or would that be rash — yes, probably it would), leave

56

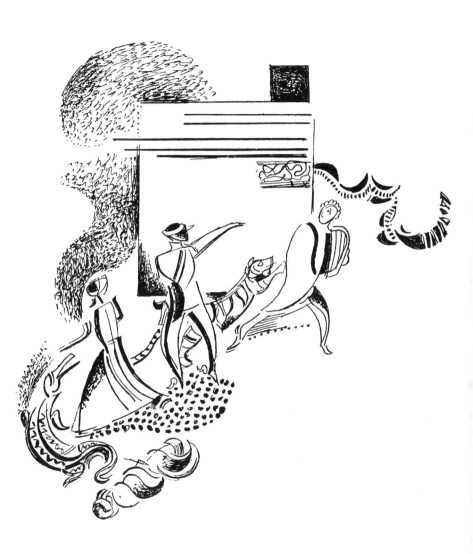

her wrist-watch as pledge, all rather un-ladylike, but *the child was hungry*. Not greedy, or only incidentally, but really hungry, as low-brow children are in Poplar and North Kensington and Bow. Odd, that.

Phoebe chose a table, mostly because its central vase held a friendly iris, while the child dashed to the counter and piled a plate with cakes. As she came back she made two mouthfuls of a cherry tart. A waitress approached: Phoebe ordered black coffee for herself, then at an urgent whisper from Skiageneia a strawberry ice-cream soda. The waitress held out a negligent official hand: 'Needs, please.'

'Needs?' said Phoebe doubtfully, wondering if the crocodile would be the least use. Skiageneia with a funny sideways look bolted a cream bun.

'Needs,' repeated the waitress, bored. 'Certificate of necessity. Oh, go on, you know! Those *ticket* things saying you need the food!'

'You don't mean,' said Phoebe with a small horrid heart-thump on the key-word, 'that you're attached to a hospital or something?'

'Hospital?' said the waitress. 'Why, whatever do you mean?'

'Well, I mean . . . this is an ordinary shop, isn't it, where one . . . pays . . . ordinarily?'

The waitress turned her head: 'Here, Rosie, here's a customer who hasn't got a ticket and doesn't know what Needs is!'

'You get the Manageress, that's what I say,' said Rosie, regarding them curiously and patting her grand chestnut head. In the meantime Skiageneia laid into the cakes and Phoebe became very nervous indeed.

The two waitresses went out through the door behind the counter, and Phoebe said half to herself, trying to rationalize it: 'Well, I suppose this is a good idea . . . if it's what it sounds like. But oh, why on earth in a Bloomsbury tea-shop?'

'On earth,' giggled Skiageneia, 'but we're beyond the Limits!'

'Oh . . . yes . . . but then she said tickets.'

'These aren't your sort of tickets. *Are they?*'

'But if we're *there*, where was the British Museum?'

59

'Oh, it's the border-land. Like Enna. It always was. But you wouldn't expect things to be quite the same after what happened, especially with me here, would you, Despoina? . . . Oh, I'm lots fuller now. But I haven't nearly finished.' She jumped up for a minute to pull a broken tendril of shadow-vine out of Phoebe's back-hair: 'Stupid stuff! We never got it all combed out of Naxos.'

The Manageress came in, a woman with the same kindly but confusing competence that Phoebe had associated with the ticket-collector. 'I'm afraid . . .' Phoebe began. 'No tickets again!' interrupted the Manageress, 'Well, well, well!' She bent down and ran a hand over Skiageneia's thin legs and knobbly knees and elbows, tipped up her chin, looking at face and neck: 'You finish that plateful, Miss!' she said sternly. 'Ice-cream soda? Hmm, yes, if you take half a glass of milk as well.' She turned to Phoebe, looked at her professionally, picked up her wrist and felt the pulse: 'Black coffee indeed! What you'll get is a nice pot of china tea and some protein with it. Go along and choose your sandwiches and don't forget the tickets next time.'

In gentle assuagement Phoebe did as she was told. Tiger and Reading Room receded. 'But don't they know you?' she asked the child.

'Not like this,' grinned Skiageneia, and shamelessly loosened the belt of her shorts. Phoebe found herself becoming all bothered with tenderness for this child of Hades, uninnocent, warily polite, leader into snares, laughter at misfortunes — Ah, no more use calling names at her than at Phil . . . 'What shall we do now, Despoina?' she said, ducking to lick a blob of cream off her shirt.

'We ought to wait for the ticket-collector. Where do you think he is?'

'I expect he's clearing up. Don't you? It was his own fault about Orpheus, of course. But did you see the way that lovely, lovely tiger jumped on to Orpheus, just two seconds' sailing with his claws out, and then scrunch! Oh I do wish Father would give me a tiger! Do the tigers at the Zoo kill people just like that when they get loose, Despoina? Oh do let's go to the Zoo now!'

'I hoped you hadn't seen,' said Phoebe in a little, choked voice, 'I tried to get you away.'

'But why? I liked it.'

'Then you can't have seen. My dear . . . the Zoo tigers *never* get loose.'

'But perhaps if *I* went . . .'

'NO!' said Phoebe, and was silenced for a moment. Then she went on, hesitating, a mortal in the divine presence, a parent uncertain about pijawing another parent's child: 'Look, my lamb, you wouldn't be thinking or saying any of this, if you knew what it really is.'

'But do *you* know what it really is, Despoina?' asked the child politely, the child who had perhaps been politely observant of souls newly arriving in Hades. No, no, what nonsense — stick to common sense, kindness, decency, the Froebel and Dalton systems . . . so long as one can.

'I know more than you do, Skiageneia,' Phoebe answered firmly, and then: 'You see, you look about as old as my Clemency, and . . .' Her voice maddeningly quivered; there were corridors and barriers and expanding star densities between her and Clemency, more than a normally ticketed railway journey between this London and that Scotland. And it seemed as though the shadow-born child knew it all, and smiled. Pomegranates. Oh, oh, had she now eaten pomegranate seed sandwiches in the domain of Hades' daughter?

But in that moment of thick panic, the ticket-collector walked in, the tail-end of a sarcastic remark to the horse flung over his shoulder. The nice, white, upper-world horse, only just wingless, only just planting hoofs on turf, or, as now, on ringing pavement! Phoebe longing to rush out and clasp her arms round his neck, knotting her fingers through his mane, instead restrained herself, flicking a tea-leaf with the point of her spoon. The ticket-collector said: 'There's news now that IT is going to be principal speaker at the meeting to-night. We'd better be going along.'

'What happened to Orpheus?' said Phoebe, not rising.

61

'The Vase Rooms are all in apple-pie order,' reassured the ticket-collector.

Yes, apple-pie. Sliced apples. Slicing claws. You put the lid on afterwards. 'What did you do to Orpheus?' she said.

'You saw,' said the ticket-collector, and then: 'I killed him. But he had already been dead for about three thousand years: or will have been: if he ever lived. Anyhow, why worry, Phoebe?'

'She can't help it,' said Skiageneia, 'she hasn't been about the markets like you have. Besides, bits of her are in different places, aren't they, Despoina? And going different ways, and some faster than others. But you could draw a lovely picture of Orpheus and the tiger, and him. Couldn't you, Despoina?'

'I think you are devils,' said Phoebe, thinly. And yet she knew she *could* draw all that — if she chose. But she wouldn't choose! They looked at her so kindly and patiently, both of them, rather puzzled, waiting for her to become ordinary. No, they weren't devils. Devils are on the human side of the limits: not here. 'Well,' she said, sitting up, 'have you a plan?' It seemed somehow probable that when IT was caught, everything might fall into line and become so simple that she would be left laughing and astonished at all her misunderstandings.

Yes, the ticket-collector certainly had a plan. IT would be on the platform at the meeting, and there, naturally, Phoebe would also be, just behind IT. And yes, thought Phoebe, with a platform ticket one's usually within reach of the speaker, and she remembered backs of necks which she had watched and noted whilst the faces whose muscles were attached to them were talking. Then Skiageneia kicked her under the table. Indignantly she said to the ticket-collector: 'You know perfectly well that your horse ate my platform ticket, and if my crocodile has a duplicate it will only get me into trouble!'

Caught out, the ticket-collector smiled and ducked; even the wings on his cap, normally at official steady and erect, gave a slight quiver. 'Can't help being the Company's servant,' he said, 'and it's in the Union regulations as well.'

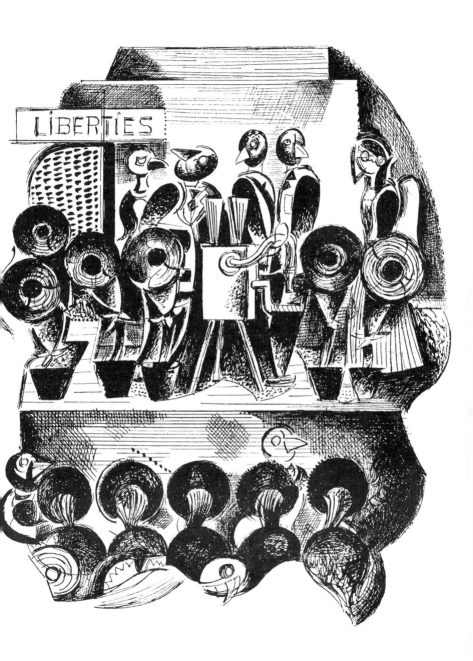

'But you're supposed to be a guide,' Phoebe scolded at him, 'a nice lot of guiding you've done for me!'

The ticket-collector drew the mourning iris out of his button-hole and smoothed it with one finger. 'I only guide the dead,' he answered, 'and you aren't anywhere near dead, are you? Makes it very awkward for me, I can tell you. Worse than gloxinias. You see, I can't guide you: it wouldn't do. But we're on the same line. Of course, if you'd rather be dead . . .'

'No, I shouldn't!' said Phoebe, 'and I wish you'd stop!'

'All right,' said the ticket-collector, 'I'm sure I don't want to talk shop. It was you that started it. Well, come along. We can very likely catch the Creature from the body of the hall.'

The meeting had not yet begun when they got there, but the platform was banked with gloxinias — ('More like a prize-giving,' said Phoebe. 'You wouldn't get people to come if there weren't prizes,' the ticket-collector whispered back). They were all shades of mauve, wine and light purple, usually with spots; with rigid and earnest trumpets some sang the Red Flag, others God Save the King. Two stewards brought on to the platform a machine with three legs, a handle, two funnels at the top and a long, flexible nozzle. Phoebe supposed, and rightly, that this was the dialectic.

The speakers came in with their ideas neatly done up in half dozens; they poured them into the funnels; the chairman supplied the sausage skins and turned the handle. Out came the syntheses, all ready to be taken home and cooked. So far it was difficult to distinguish the Creature, but it seemed probable that at some point this would as usual become clear.

The meeting, like all good meetings, decided on Liberty. Phoebe had been to other meetings which had done that, and had then gone home to Kensington, Hampstead, and the evening trains for Oxford or Cambridge, apparently unchanged. She was, therefore, surprised and delighted when the chairman picked up the liberty sausage with its long string of concomitants, and began his prize-giving speech, at the end of which all the audience, including Phoebe and the other two, turned into swallows and, tipping beautifully off their chair

65

backs into space, circled and darted in glory through the hall.

Exquisite freedom now for swallow-Phoebe, steel-blue, stream-lined, ever falling with careless velocity forward on to air-currents which cushioned her light body and stiffened wings into a guided bounce! Rules of the air, worked by the simplest quivering of feathers, averted, not once or often but always, any collision of swallows. Lucent moths floated and fluttered ceaselessly up from the platform, to become their play and food. And now, observing their audience, Chairman and speakers hastened too to put on the wings of liberty. One took the heavy rat-body and small eyes of a herring gull, another became a wagtail, the Chairman shook himself into a downy owl. But the Creature was forced into reluctant sprouting of its own scaly dragon wings.

Then with one great swerve and tumble the forked swallows swept down on IT, seizing on IT with sharp tiny claws. At that the Creature, humping itself, bolted down one of the funnels of the dialectic. The owl-chairman busily pounced on the handle and ground it, flapping, but unfortunately omitted to notice that there was nothing at all in the opposite funnel. The consequence naturally was that a great blast of hot air poured out of the nozzle, bouncing the birds upwards in astonished backward flappings, jumbling them out of the upper windows of the hall, falling and recovering over roofs and streets, swept leaf-high over respectable squares, dodging wireless masts and chimney-pots, ruffled and scattered. Some were swept into bed-rooms, some into factories or railway stations, some into the Houses of Parliament and the Albert Hall. Phoebe was tossed into a stall in Row D of the Gorilla Arts Theatre, thus avoiding all difficulties with the box-office.

Expanding and softening again after her bullet-headed swallow flight, she perceived for a moment the future of liberty, the great sausage, of mankind no longer impacted and painfully colliding, but close and yet mobile as the swallow-pack, aware of proximity yet unhampered by touches; the ready inter-gliding of ideas, cutting across one another as beautifully as the swallow *now* darts through

66

the body space of the swallow *then* and is himself darted through by the swallow of the immediately succeeding moment. Next, noticing by the look of the critics' backs that she must have arrived in the middle of the third act, she ingeniously allowed herself to expand very slightly over-size and then contracted sufficiently to remember the first two acts. Getting it all in a breath, like that, she nearly fainted with sharp boredom. She wriggled round in her stall, looking for someone to whisper with. There were all her highbrow friends, the women with bell-smooth or carefully tempestuous hair, chrome or dark, the men who wrote or painted or in some other way put themselves across as geniuses to the softer-headed of the women. They had all paid their subscriptions with more or less eagerness, or had induced someone else to pay for them; their membership tickets had followed duly, one for each, little square boats of model modern drama to float them, a-tiptoe for the light, over the rumbling seas of Europe. And she herself had her crocodile curled up and sleeping on her lap, and her neighbours did not know that his belly was now empty of safety-boats.

The couple on the stage were having the denouement worked out upon them. Phoebe looked round her again and this time she saw the ticket-collector and Skiageneia sitting three rows behind her. He looked rather tough and proletarian, as though he had been picked up at a coffee stall or off a lorry by one of the more particularly elegant young men, and she looked as though she were enjoying the play; it was, after all, possible that in Hades even the Gorilla Art Theatre would be an excitement.

The people on this stage went on talking. Phoebe said to herself: Oh God, this is all damn stupid. And then to her horror heard the whole audience round and behind her sighingly repeat the same words in the same tone. And a moment afterwards, as though that had been the lifting off of a lid, all over the theatre people began to say exactly what they were thinking about. Single voices rose, reminiscent or irritated or matter-of-fact. Their amateur solidity blotted right out the voices on the stage. They spoke mostly of their personal and intimate lives, details of love strategy, bed-tactics; and Phoebe was deeply shocked and distressed to find that she was not the only one to whom things appeared in that light. She had always somehow hoped, having been brought up as a lady, that other people at least led nice, pure, idealistic lives, that not everyone had found out either themselves or their loves. It seemed now that this was not so. Terrible nakedness! But there were some people who spoke of money, the men mostly in terms of pounds, the women of shillings or even pence, such pence as differentiate stockings or pop into gas-meters for scrambled eggs. Or again a voice would speak of some discomfort of the body which it inhabited, of a tickling throat or an aching belly; one wondered whether it was the beginning of cancer; a pregnant woman murmured a sweet torrent of love-words towards the child whom she was beginning to feel. Some again talked of politics, a very few of beauty; but several writers assumed loudly that the play would have been better written by themselves. One or two simple wants were clearly stated; there were those who longed only for a drink. Someone in a box, who might have been the author, said with extreme conviction: 'Oh hell, oh hell, oh hell.' The ticket-collector said: 'All change here for the down line.' But Skiageneia said: 'IT's just in front of you now — oh catch him, Phoebe, squeeze

him!' And Phoebe became aware that the neck in front of her, the rather wrinkled reddish neck folding down into a soft collar, which she had thought belonged to Mr. X of the *Morning Muckrake*, was really more like a dragon's neck, had wavers of green blood running under the skin, would be hard to grasp.

As she grasped it the neck slid round in her hands, revealing undoubtedly the face of Mr. X, who would know her for Phoebe Bathurst, would see that the art critic boycotted her. But was it, after all, quite Mr. X, wasn't there something wrong somewhere, the eyes, was it? Yes, the eyes not human, not soft coloured or possibly kind, but red and hollow and bottomless like a beast's, or like flames leaping towards you, leaping out of brain caverns, volcanoes, sulphur-smelling, invading outward past singed lashes darting at your own, only obstinate terror now cramping your hands to hold on. Phoebe wrestled next with a pillar of flame, always about to burn her to charred horror. IT changed under her hands to thundering water, falling through an abyss on which she could barely poise. Choking, grabbing the slipping water, IT changed again to a naked body she knew, to Phil. 'No!' she screamed, 'No!', not even for this flesh would she now relax her two hands, though they shuddered and longed, aching to be gentle. For a space now the Creature changed kaleidoscopically, giving her no moment for adjustment; from live flesh it became dead, snake, thorn-bush, flapping conger, ice-block, death-smelling test-tube. She held. And at the last IT changed into a very small and loathsome bird, with greenish feathers and points of mite-eaten baldness on head and rump; it looked at her with fading rat-coloured eyes; it might once have been a basement parrot watching unmoved horrible cruelties practised by huge stertorous cooks on country kitchen maids. The ticket-collector had a large wire cage, and Skiageneia was holding open the door. 'Put it in there,' the ticket-collector said, 'and it can never escape.'

She did so; Skiageneia fastened and locked the wire door. The nasty little bird did not even flutter, but sat on the perch as though that had always been its appointed place. There was a brass ring

71

on the top of the cage. Phoebe picked it up, Skiageneia took the suitcase; they got out of the train and watched it steam away, then walked towards the exit. As usual, it was raining.

The horse was thinner and attached to a cab; it did not speak to them; the crocodile seemed uneasy, hungry perhaps. It seemed scarcely worth while to take the cab as far as the hotel, especially as foreign cab-drivers are not only cruel but also avaricious. The rain still went on wetting them out of low clouds, undefined in shape or colour. They came to the hotel; a familiar smell seeped out towards them past the swing-door; it would be always like that whether between or during meals. The proprietress in dark with a dark shawl yet to darken her came out of the dark corner at the back of the office where the hotel smells were filed. She greeted them slowly. They had arrived at the Hotel Terminus.

It seemed that the room had been booked some time ago. Old letters which had been forwarded were waiting: a few circulars, a few small bills, negligently typed to Mrs. Bathurst. There was a palm in the hall, and on the stairs a plaster decoration much cracked. The smell followed them; in its cage the bird moved and blinked as though settling down to a familiar environment. The room also was as expected: the large pine wardrobe, the washhand-stand with the pink and gilt china, only a little cracked, the gas chandelier now fitted for electric light, the red and tasselled bed-covers, the mirror which had seen all. On the high mantelpiece was a clock which did not go, two vases, an ornamental biscuit box and a pot of gloxinias under a glass bell. The Boots laid out the suitcase at the foot of the bed, stared at them a moment, muttered and withdrew, shutting the door. The ticket-collector stood the parrot cage on the dark baize of the table. Skiageneia poked the bird with a hotel pen; it did not move. 'And now?' said Phoebe.

'This is the end of the journey,' said the ticket-collector, 'you've given up all your tickets.'

'You said I would have to pay at the other end.'

'Yes,' said the ticket-collector, 'that is in the Company's regulations.'

72

'How much?' asked Phoebe. The bird's beak made a grating sound against the cage; she shivered a little. The courage with which she had braced her fingers to hold firm had now ebbed, leaving her cold and lustreless.

The child answered solemnly: 'That's in your hands, Despoina Horón.'

'Is it?' asked Phoebe. 'Is it? Well, then . . .' She drew herself up. It was she, Phoebe, the wood-engraver, the craftsman, who had with her skilled hands and deep-seeing eyes held and vanquished the Creature. She said: 'It was I, Lady of Limits, who took the Creature at the end. I followed and chased through Etoile, the star, through all densities. It was you who asked me to help.'

'Yes,' said the ticket-collector, kindly and gravely, 'when you came to the barrier I asked you. And you did not refuse. You were alive.'

'And I *am* alive!' cried Phoebe, feeling her live heart pounding with a half fear.

'Of course you are, Despoina,' said the child, 'there wouldn't be all this fuss if you weren't. He'd be able to see to you sensibly. But Mother wouldn't have let me come away with you. And, by the way, Despoina, you'll have to talk to Father soon.'

Ignoring this last for the moment, feeling she'd got to ignore it, to fasten on the main thing, Phoebe said: 'You admit I helped you. Surely I get some reward?'

'Oh yes,' said the ticket-collector, 'you wrestled with the Creature. You made IT take this shape which now IT must keep for ever. So IT has become yours. To keep. For ever.'

'Keep *that*?' cried Phoebe. The dreadful little bird shook itself dismally; a slight powdery scaling showered from between its feathers. 'I don't want it and I won't have it!'

'I'm afraid you've got to have it,' said the ticket-collector.

'It's not so bad, Despoina,' said the child comfortingly. 'Lots of people have worse things, oh much worse. There's a very nice man who's got an eagle which used to peck frightfully and eagles take a long time to tame. And there's another man who's got a stone

75

he's got to push about. Why, Despoina, you won't notice this little bird after a hundred years or so.'

'A hundred years . . .' said Phoebe. 'But — Oh, I've got to get back, I tell you I'm going to! Where are we? Let's get on!'

'You can't go on now, Phoebe,' said the ticket-collector, 'we're at the Hotel Terminus. And that's at the end of the world.'

'It isn't!' said Phoebe, fiercely nay-saying him. And then she noticed that there were lace curtains across the windows and the lower halves were glazed with ground glass. She was across in three steps and struggling to get the sash up. And as she did so the bird in the cage lifted its throat and made a sound like a harsh echo of oboes.

'I don't advise you to do that, Phoebe,' said the ticket-collector.

But she went on. With a slight crash, the sash window which had been shut for so long, lifted, and Phoebe leant out and looked. She stayed there looking for a minute and there was no comment. She turned back into the room, slamming the window shut behind her. She was very white. She walked unsteadily towards the washhand-stand, and Skiageneia sympathetically snatched off the jug. Phoebe leant over and was very sick. She turned to the others. 'Yes,' she said, 'you were right. It *is* the end of the world.'

'You need not have looked,' the ticket-collector said, worried.

'No,' she agreed. 'I should not have looked.'

'And you are keeping the bird.'

'Yes,' she said, 'oh yes, I keep the bird.' She paced about the room a little, touching things here and there. She ran her hand along the mantelpiece. She lifted the glass bell off the gloxinia plant; she saw then that it was not real, not even a very good imitation. The trumpets were dumb and waxen, disconnected. She replaced the bell, carefully.

'Well,' said the ticket-collector, 'I expect we had better be saying good-bye.'

She looked up stupidly. Skiageneia, her child, was holding his hand. The divine beings prepared to go their aery way, leaving her only the crocodile. Small and empty, the crocodile touched her

76

hand. Not one ticket left. 'But I haven't paid!' she cried at them.

'But you will,' said the ticket-collector, 'in fact, you are.' And for a second, abruptly, his face was as it had been when he commanded the tiger.

'Nonsense!' said Phoebe. 'I demand an explanation! And I am going home. Skiageneia, tell me how to get back!'

'I don't know,' said Skiageneia, smiling gently, 'wouldn't you like to be alone now, Despoina, and have a nice long rest?'

'No!' said Phoebe, 'I wouldn't!' And she seized hold of the ticket-collector by the two lapels of his coat, her fingers closing over the badge of his Union. 'We've worked together,' she said. 'You can't just leave me like this! I won't let you go.'

The ticket-collector raised his own hands and laid them over hers, but did not tear hers away nor rise on wings out of her grasp. Of course, if you put it like that,' he answered, 'I'll do what I can, or what the Company allows. But you'll have to take fresh tickets, including one for the bird. And there will probably be a storm in the Channel and you haven't even got an umbrella. And there will be no one to meet you at Victoria. The Company can't be responsible, you know.'

'I'm going, all the same,' said Phoebe, 'but how do I get the tickets?'

'You'll have to see the Directors,' he said. 'I'd better talk it over with the horse.'

'The horse wasn't looking — quite himself.'

'Why, no. Nobody likes coming here to the end. I usually go back from the junction. The food at this place is really dreadful, pomegranate seeds in everything.'

Phoebe was still holding on to the lapels of his coat, still with her face close to his. She said: 'I don't understand. Are you partly human after all?'

He and Skiageneia both laughed, and a moment afterwards the bird gave a ghostly chuckle. Skiageneia said: 'I shouldn't worry, Despoina. He picks things up in the markets.'

'What — being human?'

'Oh yes. And fleas sometimes. And second-hand clothes and every kind of thing. But, Despoina, about your new ticket. Father's a railway director, you know, and you're going to see him anyhow.'

'She can't get back from here by Underground, Skiageneia,' said the ticket-collector.

'Why not? It's how she started coming. Anyway she can make a connection. Come along, Despoina, and we'll talk to Father.'

Phoebe let go the ticket-collector's coat; for a moment she felt only very tired, very unwilling to go to her interview with Hades. She would have liked a small sherry, perhaps, yes and dinner — pomegranate seed soup. She shook herself: 'Must I take the bird?'

'I'll carry it for you, Despoina,' said the child, 'it'll be nice company for Father's dog. I'm afraid you'll find he's a very affectionate dog, and as he's got three heads he's awfully sticky when he licks one. But don't mind him. You know, I expect Mother will be home.'

At that a curious sense of well-being came to Phoebe. If Koré was there, Queen Persephone, there would surely be nothing more to fear. The ticket-collector picked up the still unopened suitcase. Vaguely she wondered what it held, whether past or future. She called her crocodile to heel. The ticket-collector held open the bedroom door. 'We'd better have the lift,' he said, and rang for it.

All three of them stepped in with their various encumbrances. Skiageneia cried 'Oh do let me!' and pranced to the corner where she could work the lift stops. She fumbled with them and at last found the lowest, pressed it, and set the machinery purring. The lift sank uniformly from beneath their following weight. Stairs and plaster decoration sailed upward; they did not stop. We must be at the basement now, thought Phoebe, and then, we must be below the basement. But the other two were clearly not expecting it to stop yet awhile. No need for her to worry then. So the lift continued still with its smooth, its improbable, its clearly apprehended descent.

THE POWERS OF LIGHT

THERE were two of them. One was Fire Head, who had found she could do the same thing her mother had done. She could go to the hole in the wall behind the hearth and take out the yellow, smooth stones and rub them into her hair till the dancing of the fire came and her hair shot about and married the sparks. She had done this ever since she was tall enough to reach the hole in the wall. Her mother was dead now.

The second was the Surprised One. He saw things suddenly, and when he saw them like that it was different from ordinary seeing and stayed in his head till they came out. They came out when he drew them—best, in colours. Mostly they were animals, because other kinds of food stayed still, in the ground or on bushes, and could not be seen flashingly in the way he now knew and was always hoping to see. First of all he had drawn animals anywhere; in the smoke above the hearth, or in sand, but now They made him draw magic animals. They made him part of Their magic.

The rest of the men and women were They. It was They who decided things and settled things and killed anyone who broke the rules and said Why. It was They who knew when the moment was come to dance or hunt or move from the shelters to the big cave or back again. It was They who had made Fire Head's mother die in the winter, because her hair was getting too thin and old for the sparks to marry. It was They who said who was to find the flints, and who was to get food, and who was to feed the hearth and who was to chew the skins to make them soft. It was They who decided when it was time for the children to be made men and women and part of Them. As a child grew up it became part of Them. It did the right things. It lived in Their way and it died in Their way, either by accident when it was doing something necessary, or if it grew too old, it died when They wanted it to. They went on. The thing went on. There were always people in the shelters and the big cave, for a long time more or less the same people, but gradually different people, so that after fifty years every one was different. Only the new people were still They.

There was always the great fire in the cave, and the hole behind it where the women-part of Them kept the yellow stones and the shells and the pieces of red shining things, and there were always the little fires in the shelter. There was always food, or almost always. When there was no food it was terrible, because then They were threatened: then Always might stop, there might come an end to Them and the rules and patterns and what mattered, and heat or cold on the skin, and gladness or pain in the stomach and eyes and hands and everywhere, and the importance of being People. When there was no food the weaker ones died, but later there was always food again, and They went on after all, and every hundred or every thousand years, there were more of Them and They could do rather more things. As well as food, there was always warmth; there was always fire, and other bodies to get against, and old skins to crawl under when the frost bit and the cruel stars were bright. There was always, quite a long way off, the smell of coming back, the smell of being with the others. There was always the thin, dark, cold time of year when men and women slept close and did not go out unless they had to, and ate strips of smoked meat, and dry roots and berries, or sucked one another's nipples or lips; and there was the fattening time when there were birds' eggs and young, soft animals and sappy buds and grasses to bite. When the fat time came, the hot time of long days and little darkness, there were the moons and the dancing, and men and women went off in twos and rolled about in the long grass and did not remember to be They and did not remember the rules and the things that mattered; and sometimes they became so careless that they were eaten by beasts, but more often it did not hurt them much to forget the rules at that time of the year. They could make up for it later.

After the fat time was the time of the hottest days, and fruit and seeds and washing; they hunted and made things and mended things and smoked the meat. But then the nights began creeping back, whatever they tried to do to stop them, and soon they were all They again, remembering the rules. In the cold time the women got big bellies and then got pains, and then there were little new babies in the hay, too little to be part of Them yet; and while the little new babies squealed and sucked and whimpered and slept, magic went on above them in the dark of the shelters or the great cave, going in waves to drum-beating or singing, up and down as the fires roared and flared or were beaten back with wet branches. Everyone was frightened; everyone knew the magic was strong and cruel and would bring back the sun and the fat time. And They were part of it, and They liked to be gripped by it and hurt by it because then They were surer that it was strong and would do what They wanted. So They let the fire burn Them, and the singing frighten Them and the drum beats on the new hide pound at their hearts, and sometimes They cut off bits of their fingers or toes, and sometimes They made magic drawings, and sometimes They put the little new squealing babies into the fires to be eaten by the fires, and then They knew for certain that They were strong and that They mattered.

When the Surprised One was old enough to draw as well as to see, which was in the beginning of the warm time, a little after he stopped being a child and had been made part of Them, They took him to the long cave which was in the hill behind the shelter. There were other holes between great stones, twisting down into the earth, but this one did not smell of beasts. Nor did it smell warmly and comfortingly of man like the shelters and the big cave. It smelt partly of old smoke and partly of the earth itself, as though these things had been too much for man. He did not want to go into it, but he did not show what he felt because They were looking at him. He followed Them in. They had hollow bones full of fat with grass wicks. They climbed in, and up and down great rocks and through pools. Sometimes it was very narrow as though it were coming to an end, but They turned sideways and edged past, and the wet rocks scraped coldly against their skin. No one made any sound. He felt the earth above pressing onto the air in the cave. They came at last to a wide hollow where there were old drawings, and the Surprised One looked round cautiously. It was a very magic place and he was frightened. It was like the cold, thin time; it was like darkness and fear and women screaming and men dying and all the things he hated. And the magic beasts that were drawn on the walls were not seen as he saw beasts. He knew there had been nobody to draw magic beasts for half a life-time, not beasts that were certainly magic, only drawings that were meant to be beasts but did not look enough like beasts to make the real beasts come. There was not always one of Them who could see things suddenly and be so surprised that he had to draw them. So he frowned at these beasts, standing in front of them with the drawing sticks and the bones full of coloured earth. Across his shoulders and past his sides They pointed to the walls, and began to sing a magic song, and, step by step, the Surprised One, shivering and shuddering and stiffening, was bound to follow the

85

fingers and bound to go to an empty place in the wall and begin to draw.

They left him three of the lamps and then They went away and their footsteps still sounded in the hollow of the cave a long time after They were out of it, back in the sun. He had to stay, and fear was like a gnawing at his back, but still his eye and his hand could remember the surprise: the galloping bison on short turf seen for a tiny yet durable instant as a still thing. His eye and his hand remembered the shape of its back and the stretch of its legs. He smeared on the powdered red earth carefully, with pursed lips and a gathered forehead, and as the beast took shape it comforted him.

He was a little sore still because of the things They had done to him when he became a man. But he was glad to be a man. He was glad in the dark cave under the hill to be a man. The soreness helped him not to be too much afraid. He touched himself on the soreness with the powdered earth, and became part of what he was drawing. He knew he was drawing a real beast and the other beasts that were drawn in that cavern were not real beasts like his beast. They were no use. His beast was so real that it would come true.

After a time They came back, and They were pleased, and he and They drew the spears that would kill the beast when it came true. He was pleased because They were pleased. Their being pleased made him become part of Them again. He jumped up and down and shouted because he had killed the beast and it was his beast that he had made. His voice jumped and bounded among the rocks and wet hollows of the cave. It came back to him. It came back to Them and They knew it was the fastening down of the magic; for this was what people who draw beasts ought to do at the end. So now They were frightened and glad to be frightened, but the Surprised One was not frightened, and when They went out of the cave into the warm, dazzling, wide air, he made Them not to be frightened, too. So They were all glad and They were all men together and They boasted about being men, all the way back to the shelters. They told the stones and the plants and the birds and all the beasts that were hiding and afraid of Them. That was the first time the Surprised One had boasted. He was more and more glad of his soreness then, that made him a man and one of Them; it was still covered with the red earth he had put on it, so he danced. The others clapped their hands while he danced. The women who were digging roots ran to watch him dancing and clapped their hands too. After he had finished dancing They gave him a necklace of fishes' bones painted red. The bones were spiky, so that he could always feel them against his skin.

When his beast came true and was speared, he had the tongue to eat. That summer, in the fat time, the women played with him under the moon, the woman's light, and he went with one of them for all of the hot time. She was older than he was, so she taught him the things a man has to know. The young men went with the older women and the older men took the youngest women. So everyone learnt.

In the woman's light, in the white beating of the moon, Fire Head came out to play with the men like the other women. This was her first year too. She was fat and shining and beautiful. Her eyes were clear and her hair was firm on her head. She had been eating fresh meat and eggs and snails. The thing that had been done to her when she stopped being a child and became one of Them, had hurt her, but she had been glad to be hurt, glad to have childhood suddenly ended and the other things beginning. She and the other young girls had looked forward tremblingly to being hurt, and laughing when they were being hurt, as a woman should because she is a part of Them at last. Fire Head had laughed. And now she wanted the thing she knew of, the thing for which the pain was, which balanced it and made it right. When the men and women danced all the young girls knew what it was, although they had not felt it yet.

Fire Head and the young girls danced for the older men, the strong men who had killed many beasts, the men who made rules and gave orders, the men who had frightened them, the men who made the sun come back after the dark time, the men who were most of all Them. The girls danced to them and played with them, and by and bye they were chosen and taken away, clinging and shuddering, under the woman's light, the cold, maddening moonlight. Fire Head saw the other girls taken away, the girls she had played with and worked with when they were all children, and her skin tingled joyfully with the assurance of touch and pressure, soon, soon, while the high, dizzy moon was hanging above the rocks, and the whole of her was a sweet flower opening and sweetening and waiting more and more gladly, more and more hopefully and impatiently, trembling on the edge of what she wanted.

87

She could not see or hear for the knowledge of what she wanted. Time passed. And then it came to her, suddenly, like falling into water she had not seen, that the others had been chosen and taken, and not she. Not Fire Head. The oldest and strongest of the men had chosen, and so had the men who were full grown and hunters but not so powerful, and she could not go to the half-grown men because the older women drove her away. And then she knew that she was not to have what she wanted. What she could not bear the pain of not having. Because the men were afraid, even the strongest of the men. Because of her hair and the fire. Because they were afraid of the fire jumping out at them. But Fire Head, who knew the fire and was not afraid, knew too that the men were fools and cowards and she hated them.

There were almost always more young girls than strong men; but then the men took two and one watched while it was done to the other, waiting for it to be done to herself. Fire Head would have liked that. But she did not get it. She tried to go with one of the other girls, with the man who had killed the lion, following and crying to them desperately across the moonlight; but they hit her and threw big stones at her and laughed. She got up. She was bruised and cut. She went into the big cave. There were some of the women there, the women who had little babies from last year that they were suckling. But these women were happy, because they knew, they could feel with their bodies what was happening to the other women outside, and that happiness mixed with the happiness of their breasts being touched and sucked by the soft, strong babies. They were not separate. It had happened last year; it would happen again next year when they were done with the suckling of the babies. But when they saw Fire Head coming back they laughed. They knew what had happened. They had known before what would happen, but they had not told her.

Fire Head hated these women and she hated all the men. She hated Them. She went to the place behind the hearth and took out the yellow stones and rubbed them in her hair and talked to the sparks. She wanted the sparks to jump out of her hair into the night and put out the moon.

It was after that night that Fire Head found out, slowly and puzzlingly, because no one could show her more than one small part of it, what was to happen to her. The older ones of Them told her, the men and women who had power, first one and then another; only it was tiring for Them telling her and tiring for her trying to understand. She did not understand until the end of that year. What it came to in the main was that the Fire Heads could never be properly part of Them. It was bad for Them if there was not some woman who was a Fire Head, but it was bad for that woman to be a Fire Head. It was bad for her because no one would be able to think of her as a real woman; her being a Fire Head would stop any man; he would not dare even if there were no other women. So the moonlight, the woman's light, was not for her and never would be. The moon would never gave her a baby to suckle, because her fire hated the moon. Never would she get what she wanted, what all women want. She would have nothing but her hair and the yellow stones and the sparks.

Then for days Fire Head went about crying and sick, and then she remembered her own mother who had been a Fire Head too, but had got a baby in spite of the moon, and she tried to ask Why. Then They told her that if a man who was not one of Them came, he would not be afraid of the fire, and They would give him to her and she could deal with the moon. So she said: 'Are there men who are not You?'

And They answered, Yes, because of bringing the yellow stones, and the shells, most of all the great shining shells like moons, that will do instead of moons, and the little shells with slits like women, that are women. And Fire Head said: 'When will there be that man?'

And They answered that sometimes there would be years and years and lifetimes before such a man came, and sometimes such a man might come three times in the warm days of one year. If that happened she could have three men. But perhaps none would come all her life, or not until she was too old to have men. She asked what did these men do. They said that those men went on the next year after they had brought new shells and new stones, and perhaps taken away the old ones to be made new again, and anyhow having had everything given to them that they had asked for.

Then They told Fire Head what she must do for Them, though it was not much more than she had done when she was a child, for fun, for herself. She was to make sparks come for them in the dark nights of the cold time. She was to sit on the Tall Rock in the middle of the floor of the cave and make sparks for Them. And while she made sparks she was to sing. She was to do this every night they needed her in winter, but in summer she could do what she liked. But if she brushed her hair out against the moon or made her fire put out the moon, her blood would be scooped out of her with the moon shells and she would die.

That summer the Surprised One drew beasts in the cave seven times, bison and deer and horses, and always afterwards the beasts came true, and he was happy and one of Them. At full moon he and his woman played together and made little fires for themselves, and touched all the parts of one another, and touched plants and stones and the fur of killed beasts and his necklace of fish bones. By and bye the moon started a baby in her and made it move, and then she stopped being interested in him and touching him, but by that time too he was not so much interested in her. And it was time to dig pits and set stakes and hunt for the winter meat.

The Surprised One was not much afraid now of the long cave and the little lamps and the hours of darkness, or if he was afraid he had become like the rest of Them and happy to be afraid. He drew his beasts better and quicker. He drew them running and he drew their quarters sticking out from behind a rock when they thought they were hidden, but were really a good mark to shoot at! He did not like the first beasts he had drawn, so he altered them, but They did not want him to do that, because it was not likely that these re-drawn beasts would be as good magic as the new ones. But when he wanted to do a thing of that sort he stopped being one of Them and became himself. Still, for the most part it was well; he saw the kind of things They wanted him to see, the things that were necessary for the people, the things that would give life. That summer he was happy. But Fire Head was unhappy.

In winter Fire Head sat on the Tall Rock and her hair fell down all about her. It hung down her back and along her arms and in front it fell down between her breasts and down between her thighs as she sat on the rock. She held the yellow stones in her right hand. Sometimes the sparks came better than at other times. Sometimes she was tired and often she was angry. When she was asleep They would come and stroke her hair and sometimes pull it out if she was very deep asleep. She had some beads of coloured clay that she wore tied on to the ends of her hair, but they broke easily, when she played with them. She had to have something to play with.

Most of the other women had babies, this year's or last year's, or would have soon. She had none. She had been made by force into a child or an old woman past the age the moon would look on her. Even though it was the cold time, when men came near Fire Head, most of all the older, stronger men, the man who had killed the lion or the man who was Pit Digger, the skin of her breasts and belly and thighs tingled and grew hot towards them. But the men did not look at her in the way she would have wanted. So she went on singing and making sparks, and sometimes beating the skin drums, and she learned magic from the older women; but they would not teach her all the magic, because she was a Fire Head and so not properly one of Them. The only thing that comforted her was that when the food was being divided she got what she wanted, an older man's share, the share of a skilled man or woman. She did not understand this at first, but after a time she found out that if she looked angry They tried to stop her being angry; They stopped her being angry by giving her the food she wanted most. And when the women made the drink out of sweet roots which they drank in the dark nights in the middle of the winter, she could have it as soon as anyone.

It was when she had drunk this sweet prickling drink that she used to think that the man who had brought the stones and shells would come when the dark time was over—was coming now towards her between the thick trees, bringing her the moon, bringing her the shells that will do instead of the moon. He would walk between the thick trees without being afraid of them or of anything behind them. He would not be afraid of beasts. Her man would not be an Afraid Man. He could not be, because he would not be afraid of her when he saw her. He would make other people afraid; the beasts would be afraid to come near him; he would have a fire in him like her fire. When she saw him come she would not be afraid. The others would run away but she would wait for him. When he saw her she would lie down in front of him, in his path, and he would come. Then, that would be it. That would be right. She would think all that while she made the sparks come for the others, the ones who were afraid of her, and her singing would go slower and slower and almost stop and then suddenly it would go very fast, and her hair would shoot about and touch her lips and breasts and blind her fixed or swaying eyes.

In the cold, dark time, no one was so much interested in the

Surprised One and he did not see things so much, so he was sleepy and only did what the others did, and cared very little that he was not given the best parts of the food now, unless he was left really hungry at the end of the day. But sometimes he drew beasts in the smoke and They remembered him again. In winter They all played; in the dark They played games of touching and counting and fitting or rolling things with their hands, while Fire Head made sparks for them and sang.

As soon as the light time began They took the Surprised One to the long cave again. He wanted sometimes to draw his beasts differently, for sometimes he had seen them with a new surprise, but They did not like him to do that. Once or twice his beasts did not come true, or not for a long time. Then They would not let him be one of Them. They threw things at him and called him bad names and told him what They would do to him if he drew his beasts wrong. Then he was very frightened and he went back to the long cave again by himself and drew a bison the old way. He was really frightened of the cave then, not just wanting to be frightened like he had been before. That summer he had another woman because the first one was suckling the baby she had got from the moon. Anyhow it was more interesting for him and more interesting for the other woman that they should be each different from last year—so long as each was still one of Them, one of the people. But it was not such a good year for the hunting; the mammoths had moved away to some other grassy place, and the deer were wilder. The Surprised One was not so fat as he had been the year before, neither was his woman.

But again there was no man for Fire Head, and again she was angry and again the other women laughed at her and drove her away. But she did not dare to send her sparks against the moon, because They had told her what was to happen to her if she did that. She went far from the shelters. Sometimes she would be gone for days together, with her spear and snares. That was partly because she hoped to find the Unafraid Man who would bring the amber and shells to the others and bring the moon to her, and partly because she did not want to see the rest of Them. That way she got used to finding her way about and being by herself in the forest. She slept in trees. If she had done this in the dark time—only no one could have done it then—They would have been afraid and stopped her from going, but just now no one cared whether she went or not.

It was terrible that no one cared. Sometimes she even played with the children who had not yet been made part of Them, but the children did not want her much either. They would rather play with one another. She could remember being a child. She and the other children had been a kind of They too—a They of their own, apart.

In the dark time it was the same again. The Surprised One became part of Them and did and was Their kind of thing. But Fire Head had to make sparks and sing. Sometimes this winter she had not wanted to. Then They had frightened her till she started again. Sometimes They frightened people by telling them about hurting them. Sometimes They hurt by magic and sometimes with hands or stones or shells or fire. Sometimes They hurt people who would not do what they were meant to do, and sometimes They hurt people because They wanted to see what would happen. Sometimes the person who was hurt was one of Them who had never been anything but one of Them, perhaps a hunter or flint worker, someone They needed, a good eater, glad at the dances, one the women chose. He would not know what was coming. Nor would They, until the moment before. And then suddenly it would happen. They would all be seized upon by the desire to see something new, to try something They had not tried, to see the blood and the bones and the things which should be hidden in man or woman. The easiest way to try something new was on someone. And so They would all find that They had chosen one of Themselves, that They had taken him and dragged him to the ground and pegged him out. Then They would try things on him. Sometimes at the end he lived, and sometimes died. If he lived he would be apart from Them for a long time. They would drive him away.

Sometimes They found They wanted to do this to the children, and caught a child before it could get away. Sometimes the men wanted to do it to the women at the time of child-birth when they were touched by pain already, already showing the hidden blood. But the other women did not often let the men do it. Sometimes it happened, but not often, not once in a hundred years, that if there was a man alone in the great cave, all the women would set on him. These things happened almost always in the dark time. They did not happen often, only sometimes, perhaps not at all for years, then several times in one winter. Nobody knew why they happened or when they were going to happen. Once, when she would not sing, they began to do things to Fire Head with splintered ox-bones on the end of sticks, but Fire Head got away behind the smoke and held the yellow stones out at Them, and then They were afraid. Those who were not doing it, watched. The Surprised One watched. He wanted to know what would happen when the skin of Fire Head was cut through and the blood began to come. A little time after that it seemed to him that he must draw a woman.

At the very beginning of the warm time, when everyone was still thin and hungry, They took the Surprised One to the long cave, and the Surprised One drew a bison. He could draw very quickly now and when he had finished he began to draw a woman. He knew it was wicked. He shivered and shook with wickedness. But he had to go on until he had finished drawing the woman. He knew it was wicked to draw men and women because men and women are not food. Because men and women are not to be drawn to be magicked and hunted and killed. If they could be magicked that way—the food way—one must not magick them. That was wickedness. But he did not draw for magic. He drew because in the cold time and in the beginning of the warm time he had been surprised by seeing women, by seeing their shapes move, and he could not get the surprise out of him any other way, because it was not yet the time of the dances.

When They came back They saw he had drawn a woman. They pointed and Their lamps shook about, and They made all kinds of noises. They filled the long cave with the noises They made. They took hold of the Surprised One and some of Them held his hands against the walls of the long cave, against the red and black drawing of the woman, and They beat his hands with stones. They were beating the wickedness out of his hands. Then the Surprised One screamed and said he had not drawn the woman, that the woman had come there. But They went on beating his hands and those who could not reach to beat his hands beat the other parts of him which They could reach. The more the Surprised One screamed and tried to get loose the more They hurt him. He and They had shared and been happy until then, They had been the same thing, the same People. It did not matter; They had to break his hands up. When he stopped screaming They took the lamps and left him.

The cave dripped and dripped on him, and after a time he began to wake up. He began to wake into pain and darkness. For a time he did not know where he was; he did not know if it was real. Then he did know and the pain and darkness became solid and became part of him and he began to scream again. He screamed and screamed for light to come, for help to come, for Them to come—the ones he had been friends with—for his hands not to hurt him so much. He screamed the names of any of them who had names, the names of men and women. He could not understand at first that They had left him. He was thirsty; he turned over and licked the floor of the long cave. It hurt him to turn over. He screamed for Them again, and listened. There was no sound but the tickling and rustling of earth and water. At last he began to crawl.

He did not think he would ever get out; he thought the long cave would keep him and hold him, hold him for ever in pain and darkness, shut him in alone with pain and darkness and no help. He crawled for a long time. He could not put any weight on his hands, but he crawled on his elbows. His hands bled and he licked them. The darkness swayed and swung around him and sometimes closed on him altogether, but he always woke again, and always to the pain that was mostly in his hands and partly in all the other bits of him which They had hurt. He could not be sure he was going the right way. There were turnings off the long cave where no one had ever been, but he thought he was going right, for he could smell that there had been people. Only he did not think the long cave was as long as this. Perhaps it had stretched itself like a worm. Perhaps however far he went it would always stretch itself beyond him.

Then at last he began to feel warmth in the air and then to see a greyness. And the long cave let him go and he was crawling out between the rocks, blinking and dazzled. Although he was dazzled it was evening; the light was going. He looked at his hands and touched them softly against the grass. They were a wrong shape and a wrong colour. They could not do what he wanted them to do. He was so terribly surprised by the new shape and colour of his hands that he cried and cried. He tried to lick his hands into the right shape, to lick down the raw edges and broken nails. Even his own licking hurt them. It got darker. He wanted to go back to the others, to shelter and warmth and food, but he knew They would hurt him again, at least drive him out. He went back a little way into the long cave and laid his hands in a pool of mud and slept.

The next morning again he licked and cried over his hands. It was partly that they were so strange and surprising and partly that they hurt him so, and partly he cried because he was very hungry and he did not think his hands would help him to get food. He did not think that hands that shape and that stiffness would be able to throw stones or set snares. He was lame, but not too lame to walk. So he walked. He walked away from Them. And while he walked he cried and hated his wickedness and hated Them for finding it and hurting him and making him alone.

After a long time he heard someone and stopped and hid. It was Them. It was one of Them coming to hurt him again, to smash the rest of him as They had smashed his hands. He kept very still in his hiding-place. He saw that it was Fire Head and that she had a dead bird in one hand. Desire of that bird ran through him, fighting his fear of being hurt again. And then it seemed to him that Fire Head was not really part of Them. He moved, rustling the leaves, and Fire Head started and held her spear ready, smelling and looking. But when she saw it was man, instead of running away or into a tree, she ran straight to the bush. She thought it was the Unafraid Man at last. When she saw it was only the Surprised One she was angry; she stood there and went red. The Surprised One stayed crouched and held out his hands to her and whimpered. She came nearer and looked at them. She said: 'How?'

He said: 'They. They hurt the hands.'

Fire Head looked from the hands to his eyes; his eyes were grey-brown; his eyes were frightened. His eyes thought about Them as Fire Head's own eyes thought. Fire Head had been frightened too, and hurt, but not so badly as this. She took his hand in hers. The Surprised One rubbed his face against Fire Head's leg; now he was not alone. Her legs were thin and bony because it was not the right time of the year yet, not the fat time, the time of the moon and the dances. The Surprised One said to Fire Head's leg that he was hungry; he wanted the bird.

Fire Head knelt on her heels and plucked the bird. It would have been better cooked at a fire, but they never minded much. He looked at the bird and his mouth watered. Fire Head laughed, but she did not laugh to hurt, only bcause she liked to have power. She pulled off a leg of the bird and held it out to him. His hurt hands could not hold it, so he ate it from Fire Head's hands, pulling away from her like a strong baby pulling at the breast. Fire Head let him eat all the bird, although she had meant to eat it herself. His eyes were full of tears because he had been so hungry and so unhappy. He came close to Fire Head and touched the inside crook of her elbow with his nose and mouth; he had forgotten to be afraid of her.

Fire Head had not had a man to do this to her before, and she liked it, but he was not the man she was looking for, the stranger, the Unafraid Man. He was afraid still, afraid of Them. She put both arms round him and patted him, and unpinned the stiff horse skin she wore so that he could lie closely and softly against her. He felt with his fed mouth the shape of her breasts, and rested.

Then his hands began to hurt him again. He sat up and whimpered and said to her: 'Look!' He said to her: 'Make the hands right,' and he called her clever and good and powerful. So she took him to a pool she knew of and got moss. She washed the blood off his hands and straightened them between her fingers until they were the right shape again. While she did this he moaned and cried, but did not try to get away from her. She tied his broken fingers with grass onto sticks, so that they stayed right, and put moss round them. At the end he crawled to the pool and drank.

It was evening again by that time. Fire Head tried to make him get into a tree, but he could not climb. She was angry with him at first and hit him; she had not had time to kill anything for herself and she was hungry. She meant anyhow to climb into a tree and be safe, whatever he did, but when she began to climb he cried and called to her; he could not bear to be left alone again, out of touch of her. So at last she came down and stayed with him all night. There were beasts about and they were both frightened. They huddled together with their arms round one another, listening for beasts. He slept after a time, but she did not sleep till it was light and the beasts' hunting time was over. Then she slept for an hour or two. When she woke up she took the Surprised One's necklace of fishes' bones off his neck and put it on her own, and went to look at herself in the pool.

The Surprised One did not know what Fire Head was going to do, but he did not want her to go back to the shelters and Them, because then he would be left alone again. But he could not do anything to make her stay with him, now that she had taken the necklace herself, except to tell her again that she was strong and clever, good to look at and feel and smell, and that he was her child and her thing. She was pleased and killed a squirrel with a stone and brought it back to where he was hiding in the bushes. He could not do anything with his hands, so she fed him and laughed. He had been so glad to see her come back that he had laughed out loud among the spiky leaves. He had been watching for her, but he had been startled into laughter by the sight of her coming back with the beast she had killed for him. That day she washed the rest of the hurt parts of his body.

She never said she would stay, but she did stay. At night they were always frightened until she learnt to look for trees she could help him to climb into. They were both frightened in the dark night, because it was like the darkness that had hurt them, the darkness of the People's cave where They had made her do magic for them and had threatened her and nearly hurt her very much when she was too tired to do magic, and the darkness of the long cave where They had found his drawing and broken his hands and left him alone with pain. They wanted to get away from darkness and pain. Day after day they moved their ground, further and further from Them and the thing, the terror, that they were more afraid of than of beasts. After a time they found out from one another what had been the matter, and each dimly entered into the thought of the other, so that she could understand that he had not meant to do any wickedness and yet had to draw a person, and he could understand that she had been set apart and hated and laughed at.

After a time she took away the moss from round his hands and peered at them. They were thin and shrivelled looking, and very white; he cried when he saw them, for he had expected to see his real hands, the hands he was used to. She scolded him and hushed him and took the hands and tried to bend them and make them do things. The hands were stiff; they would not bend. Then he thought perhaps the hands had been so completely smashed that they would never be able to do any of the old things, never work flints or put the lashings on to a spear head, never hold or kill or fit things together, or break things, never draw any of the shapes which surprised him. He tried to tell her this; but she was interested in making the fingers bend, and so after a time was he. First she did it gently and then she hurt him. He tried to take his hands away when she hurt him, but she scolded at him and said she would go. And he knew that he was hers and must he hers while he could not feed himself, so he let her have his hands to play with.

They ate raw flesh mostly and not too much of that. Sometimes she would go two days without killing anything. She dug roots and they found snails, and a certain amount of buds and shoots that they could eat, and sometimes birds' eggs, but they were both very thin, so that their eyes looked big and blazing and their bones showed at the joints. Every day she made him let her play with his hands; she was set on making them work. She did not hurt him unbearably, but she hurt him a good deal and made him howl or sob with pain. He would try to do things that would please her or interest her, so that she would forget about playing with his hands, but, even if she had not thought of them all day, or been too busy getting food, the time would come in the evening when he would get sleepy and stupid, and then she would remember and catch his wrists and grin and begin to do it. After a time it seemed to them both that his real hands were coming back; he could do a few things, get a grip on anything big, a stone or a tree trunk. He began to understand that she was making the smashed things right, and, though he still tried to stop her doing it, yet when she did it he was much more interested himself and looked at his hands instead of looking away from them.

She still had to set snares and handle the spear, but by and bye he could begin to use a stick for digging roots. The days got longer and the sunlight warmer; the drenching rains soaked them, but they got dry again and went on. They were less frightened at night; they were getting away from the powers of darkness. The moon grew big and burnished and quivered overhead. They slept lightly in each other's arms, in the crook of a tree, out of reach of beasts; they both liked this increasingly, liked being so close to one another's skins, liked whispering and humming into one another's ears. All the same he did not have her yet; he did not want to. This was not because he was afraid of Fire Head now, but it was partly because they were both so thin and usually hungry, and partly because he was not yet quite a man, with these hurt hands which could not quite do a man's work. And she did not want him to, partly again because there was not enough food, but mostly because he was not a stranger and she knew that the man she was going to have in the end must be a stranger. But all the same they could talk to one another and sing to one another, and when she was away he made patterns for her out of leaves and twigs and stones, or if she killed early they made patterns together all the evening.

They did not see any other people or in any way become aware of them. But after a time they began to come on things which were apparently the work of people. They came on to one after another of roughly made shelters with a place for a hearth. They knelt by these hearths, snuffing the smell of the thin layer of old ashes, and at one of them it made them want a fire for themselves, so badly, that they set up a stick and turned it together. That was really women's work, and it frightened the Surprised One to have to do it, even though Fire Head knew the proper words to say. When the fire came she fed it, and, because they had nothing to carry it away in, and yet very much liked eating cooked meat again, they stayed in that shelter for some days. Between the shelters there were scarcely tracks and yet it seemed as though the best way through swamp or forest or over hills, led from one shelter to the next. Sometimes they would not find a shelter again for four or five days, but they always did find one in the end, and got to look out for them. Once it seemed as though a person had been in one of them not so very long ago, but they were not sure.

They wondered about it, separately. At last Fire Head said that these shelters had been made by the men who brought the shells and red and yellow stones, and she would not let the Surprised One think anything else. They did not know where they were going, except that they were going away from Them, going away from pain and darkness and the things they hated. It seemed right to Fire Head that they should also be coming on to the tracks of the strangers, the men she was to have in the end. Sometimes, if they were feeling like it, after a full meal, perhaps, or when they saw running water in the sun, they would tell one another where they were going, to a light place, a place of food and warmth and doing what one wanted, and not being hurt or frightened: where the Surprised One would draw anything he wanted wherever he liked, not only in the caves, but in the light: where no one would be frightened of Fire Head or make her do things that no one else did, or laugh at her, but there would always be as many strong and beautiful men as she wanted, always. A good place for them both.

After a time the Surprised One found that his hands could do almost all the things he wanted them to do. They were a little odd and knobbly to touch, but his thumb and forefinger could come together and pick things up, and he could press things tight against his palm. Once he found some red earth, and drew with it on a flat piece of dead wood that had gone white with age; Fire Head watched him. He could climb quite well. It was lucky that it was not until he was so nearly healed that they had the danger from wolves. The wolves went for them in the open when it was a long run to the nearest tree, and they were almost caught and eaten. But Fire Head had the spear and he had a long and heavy stick, and they threw stones. Fire Head was bitten in the leg by a wolf, but not badly. She cried and made the Surprised One tie it up with moss, and comfort her. After that he did not think he was her thing any more, but he kept the wound clean and let her hang on to his shoulder all the time when she was walking the first day, and stroked her and persuaded her to let him have the spear.

They had not been much in flint country, but lately they had found a few and began chipping them in the evenings. While the bite was still sore, he did most of the hunting. There were plenty of birds' eggs here, and later nestlings, and then they came on the wild strawberries. When they had eaten as many as they could hold they lay down and rolled in them. There were also wild cherries which they shook down and decorated themselves with and then ate, cracking the stones, and once they found a stream where they could catch fish with their hands. There was altogether more to eat, and the Surprised One said to Fire Head that when the moon was full again he would have her. She laughed and stroked him, and she was partly glad, because he had been kind to her and since they had been less hungry she had begun to want him and look at him, and partly bothered because he was not a stranger, and she had made certain that it was to be a stranger.

The evening of the wolf fight, when her wound was sore and throbbing, Fire Head said that the wolves were Them, following Fire Head and the Surprised One, trying to hurt them again. She kept on saying it all that night, even while the Surprised One held her in his arms up in the tree, sitting on his knees with her head pressed into the hollow of his shoulder, and by morning he believed it too. After that they kept on looking back for wolves. They were afraid they had not really got away from Them after all.

They came now into broken and hilly country with rivers that they could just wade across, and great out-croppings of rock, and they began to think they were coming near to people. They went very cautiously now and soon it became clear that there must be people very near them. There were familiar smells when the wind came blowing into their faces; once there were the ashes of a fire. At last they came to a real track with footprints, which they knelt down and smelt; it led uphill to the top of a bluff. They stopped and looked at one another. The same thing was puzzling them both. If they went along the track would it only be to find themselves amongst Them again? To find themselves again caught by darkness and fear and pain? Dared they? 'Not?' said the Surprised One, slanting his head forward along the track. He was afraid of coming to a place where he could draw and yet not be able to help drawing the wrong things. For he had been seeing things all this time—deer, horses, mammoths, elks, beavers, once from a tree-top a creeping lion, and then, very often, Fire Head coming back to him. His hands felt as though they could draw well now. They would have had to draw Fire Head dancing, Fire Head running, Fire Head holding a beast she had killed. And if he drew her—what? He scraped with his foot across the track. 'Not?' he said again.

But Fire Head hesitated. The track smelt of people, but not of Them. She thought of strangers, of that man whom she knew, in spite of the Surprised One, must be a stranger. They could get away again. She pulled his hand and said: 'Come!' They would go to the top of the bluff and see.

They trod along the track nervously; it was very early morning. Beyond the trees they came to scrub, a slope with big stones and sparse, prickly bushes. And between the stones there were pebbles and a great many bright flowers. Fire Head and the Surprised One both stopped and picked flowers and nibbled them and stuck them about one another. When they came near the top of the bluff they crawled, because they were not sure that they wanted to be seen against the skyline. They got to the top together and looked over, and then, first the Surprised One and then Fire Head, began to shake and quiver with excitement.

They were looking over a wide valley with a stream running down it; at their side and at the far side cliffs rose out of the woods or clearings, rather steeply and with bare expanses of rock cropping out and running along them, rock-face two or three times a man's height. In the valley were clearings and groups of shelters. Smoke rose up from the shelters and the smell of cooking. Meat, roast and boiled, meat with salt. They could see people, yes, men and women. Real men and women. They could hear them! Tiny, shrill voices

102

floating on the wind. And as though that were not astonishing and exciting enough, there was something else, something very difficult to believe in, something they shied away from looking at for the first minute or two. The whole of the rock of the cliff face opposite to them was painted in colours, with animals, hundreds and hundreds of animals, and shelters built in a way they had never seen, and weapons, and people—yes, people in rows hunting and dancing, people wearing feathers and hides, men and women you could tell apart! They were painted in colours, mostly red, but other colours too, and even from that distance the Surprised One could tell that in some places the rock had been cut, so as to make the drawings even better, to make them stick out and come real. He had never done that, only used the knobs and hollows of the rock as he had come across them in the long cave, but now it seemed the clearest and most beautiful thing to do. The Surprised One sprang to his feet and shouted, and plunged and leapt down into that happy valley, and Fire Head leapt and ran with him, crying out to the light.

It was all light. It was all light. The flowers were brighter than any other flowers. As they ran down the track, in an angle between two of the cliff faces, they looked round and the rocks were alive and magnificent with paintings. In that valley man had changed the face of the world, had done what he wanted and was glad. As they came down towards the river they ran slower and at last came to a stand, holding on to one another. People had come to look at them. People were all round them, whistling and calling to one another, coming closer.

The valley people did not speak quite as the Surprised One and Fire Head, but near enough. It was exciting for them to see the two strangers coming down out of nowhere. They shouted to one another to come quick and look.The two stood under a tree on the bank of the river. They had thrown down spear and stones to show that they were friendly. Men and women and children came running out of the shelters and clustered round. They made happy and questioning noises. They came nearer and touched the strangers. They stroked Fire Head's hair and pointed at the necklace, and touched the Surprised One's arms and legs to make sure they were real. No one was frightened, no one was going to hurt them. A woman brought meat and held it in front of them, held it out at arm's length until Fire Head tiptoed a step nearer and took it. Then another brought

103

honey, and another brought river mussels split open, which they were afraid to take because they had never seen them before. Fire Head tried to say things, and so did the Surprised One. They got hot and excited with trying to talk. Their hearts beat fast and they panted. The Surprised One kept on looking at the cliffs, and Fire Head kept on looking at the men who were standing round her. First one or two of the women and then after a little more and more of the valley people began to understand what the two were trying to say. They laughed and clapped their hands; their voices cooed at these two new ones who had come to them. They were kind.

Then suddenly the Surprised One picked up a small stick and jumped on to the edge of the river-bed where there was a clear space of sand between stones. He knelt down and began to draw on the sand. The valley people had made way for him, but when he began to do that, they began to crowd round him again, and one shouted, and then another and another, as they saw the drawing begin to come real. They shouted with pleasure, and the Surprised One became part of them.

Then Fire Head was standing alone under the tree where the Surprised One had left her. She looked down and began to tremble and she looked up and saw a man with strong arms and legs and a necklace of red and yellow stones. She had never seen anyone wearing stones before, only clay beads and fish bones which did not mean much, and she was very glad, because she thought that these people could not be afraid of the yellow stones, and she went nearer to the man and put up her hand to his neck and touched the yellow stones. Then again the valley people shouted because the new woman had chosen, and chosen well. So the man with the necklace took Fire Head at once, and she got what she wanted, and he was kind to her, and so were the other women. They took her with them and showed her everything and persuaded her to eat the river mussels and told her that the man with the necklace was a planner and had made the plan which killed the rhinoceros. They showed her the hide of the rhinoceros still pegged out to dry; she had never seen one before.

Fire Head and the Surprised One did not see one another again that day. But the next day the man with the necklace took Fire Head to the cliff and there was the Surprised One, and they were showing him how to make and mix the new colours. The man with the necklace was cutting the outline of his rhinoceros in the rock; when he had done this he was going to colour it. Fire Head had a basket of food. The man had given her a new and soft deer-skin to wear, and she put flowers into her hair. She rolled about on the flowers and sometimes the man stopped carving and came and played with her. Between times she sat among the flowers in the sunlight and ate great pieces of fat meat and watched her man and the Surprised One doing things to the cliffs.

By and bye the Surprised One came and sat down beside her; his hurt hands still got tired rather too easily, but that would come right. She gave him pieces of meat out of her basket. He looked at her man and grinned and asked her if it was good, and she said yes and asked if it was good with him. So the Surprised One told her that when he had made his bison in the sand, a woman had come and put her hand into his. She was fat and smooth-skinned and kind; she had rubbed him with sweet fat in the morning.

Fire Head and the Surprised One sat among the very bright flowers and held one another's hands and rubbed their cheeks together. They had come to a very different place, to the powers of light. They were not frightened any more. They were both so very happy.

THE WIFE OF AGLAOS

You are young now and I am not so young. You can look back continuously on your life and see it as a gradual change, a gradual drawing out and flowering. Although you have perhaps worked and seen more of people than I did as a girl, nothing very sudden or very frightening has ever happened to you. For it is not frightening to be married to a man as gentle as your philosopher. Nor was it really frightening for me to be married to my Aglaos. Old nurses cry and so do most mothers—because most mothers are bred to be fools and to look for bogies where there are none—when young girls are carried over a new threshold.

But sudden and frightening things happened to me, so now I find it very hard to remember—to remember, that is, with my blood and body, for I can remember well enough with my mind—what I was like before they happened, when I was a girl, or a young wife as you are now. It seems to me that perhaps, if these sudden and frightening things do not happen, it is very hard to grow up, very hard to become a wise man or woman. Of course men have called themselves wise—and been called wise by many followers—who have spent their lives retired and contemplating, in a windless grove, or who have been statesmen and generals at the head of a people which is, for the time, rich and victorious. But I doubt if we can really admit them. What do you think, my dear?

On the other side we've got Zeno, who from his childhood was tossed about by painful circumstances, driven from his city, earning his own living with difficulty and discomfort. Sokrates who was a stonemason and a common soldier. Plato—you see I'm not sticking to my own lot!—whose friends betrayed him and who was sold as a slave. Aspasia who as a young woman sold herself cheaply to many men so as to live with the idea of democracy. In our own time Sphaeros who was shipwrecked among savages on the Black Sea and shared the hardship of the Revolution with the Spartans, and Agiatis the wife of Kleomenes whose first love was dragged from her and killed, and who was married by force to a man she then hated, whose eldest son died, and who estranged herself from her old friends and gave up most of the things which you like and which I partly like during the Revolution. Do you know, I met her once when I was a child? She and King Kleomenes came to Mantinea on some kind of political mission and I with others brought her flowers; she looked very tired, but she talked to us and we liked her. Your man, after all, had a bad time before he came out here. And—well, I think even that I have a little wisdom myself.

Have you any thread that will match this? I have just not enough. Yes, that will do beautifully. Odd, isn't it, the way one's hands go on by themselves, when the mind's quite unshipped and looking another way! But what would one do in hard times if mind had always to follow body...

I wonder if I can say what happened with any measure of truth. I was so young. I had washed my hair only a few days before and now it was soft. It sprang up softly from my head. He had been rubbing it, stroking it with lips and finger tips as we sat together. I can remember very well the consciousness of my soft clean hair, which was a kind of symbol of everything I was then. Clean hair and clean linen, my mother's weaving.

So he said to me once: Kleta, Kleta—and then they pulled them away, him and my brother, and suddenly at my throat, touching me, there was the hard iron of a spear—something I'd never felt, never really imagined—and someone laughed, and I felt choked, as if something were bursting inside me, and everything blurred; and when I could see again, Aglaos and Arkas were gone, as far as I could tell for ever. I sat very still, feeling dizzy, trying to realize it, trying to know it was here and now, something which had happened to me, not to someone in a story. My mind knew that, but my imagination could not be brought to picture that I would never see my husband again, that he would be sold as a slave in Macedonia and I as a slave here. It seemed—silly. I kept on forgetting and then remembering with a worse and worse shock, until in an hour or two I was tired out. I suckled my baby and put him down again, clumsy and fumbling with tiredness, and then I went to sleep with my head in mother's lap; my cousin Nikotolea slept too.

You know, it was rather a horrible waking from that; I had begun to realize all over, with my body too, what had happened. We were all on edge waiting for the next thing. But that evening they left us alone; we cooked food for ourselves and the guards, even by moments quite gaily, and then we slept in the old room; the other women were there, and the babies; so I didn't have to think too much about Aglaos not being there. About his being driven farther and farther away every day, sleeping farther and farther away every night until he was so terribly far that one just couldn't begin to cross the distance in thought. And if he died or if—as seemed more likely—my brother died on that awful chained march, I wouldn't know. Arkas had been rather badly wounded. Mother, of course, was thinking mostly about him.

We were very practical in the early morning before it was full light making bundles of the things we thought we'd need most. They had already been through the house pretty systematically and had taken almost everything of value, but we each had a few small things. I, for instance, had still a ring which Aglaos had given me when we were married, an engraved amethyst; it was not worth so very much and they had perhaps been ashamed to pull it off my finger. I took what I could for myself and also some baby things for Drako'; he was three months old then, just beginning to be able to laugh—oh, deliciously. That morning I heated water and washed him with warm water and oil. He was my trust from Aglaos, all I had left, and a lovely baby too: a loved and lovely baby. As I was drying him one of the guards came in and told us to be quick.

We were taken to the market place; we promised one another if we could to keep in touch; and mother said that if any of us became pregnant by a Macedonian, to come to her and she would do what she could. She said that in a low clear voice and she did not look at me when she said it, and none of us said anything for a minute or two. It was getting too near.

Well, it is not very pleasant to be sold in open market; sometimes I shut my eyes and tried to repeat poems, but on the whole my anxiety kept me very wide awake; I snuggled Drako' up to me, trying to make quite sure that we were so part of one another that we would be sold together, and I rocked from one foot to the other to quiet him; once they let me sit down in some straw and feed him. Also I was trying to see who my friends were being sold to. Somewhere at the back of my mind I thought quite coldly that this would seem very shocking to many Hellenes in many cities, but that they would certainly not do anything to help us. And after several hours standing there with Drako' in my arms, I was sold to a Macedonian soldier who was taking up a settlement.

Well, he took a halter from under his belt, set it on my neck and jerked it. I just had time to pick up my bundle and to see mother, who was not yet sold, looking at me quite despairingly. And I, looking at the back and what I saw every now and then of the face of my new master, was very glad that Aglaos did not know and could never know now. We went out of the city and off the road on to a field track; I felt terribly unsheltered coming out of the city gate, and I was so tired, and the weight of Drako' and the bundle together, were almost more than I could bear, and I didn't know how far we still had to go, and I cried as I walked, and Drako' started crying too, and I wanted all at once for everything to go quick, for it all to get over and past, so that I would be an old woman and die before we got to the far side of the bean field—I who had always been so resentful of the passing of spring. My dear, after that it got for a time rather too horrible to put into words, and I take it that rape and all that is much the same wherever it happens. My mind had supposed that it was likely, but my imagination couldn't accept it, nor could my body, not then, not at first. I was strong too; I could have fought him, I did. In the ditch on the edge of the bean field. Only he said into my ear that it was my only chance of being allowed to keep my baby. Otherwise he would have made me just leave him in the ditch. He could have dragged me away by the halter round my neck, half choked. I wasn't sure he wasn't going to do that anyway, afterwards; he looked at me and my baby very cruelly. I believe that if I had met that look of his half way, if he had seen me accepting it and being afraid, he would have done what he wanted to. But that was all right. I hadn't really learnt to be afraid, yet. As for the other thing, I tried not to go on thinking of it, I tried to hope it hadn't really touched me, not me myself, only my body.

But one can't separate oneself from one's body, not if one's a slave woman kept at it all day, unaccustomed to really hard work; not if one's kicked out of sleep, the one possible, the one healing time, made to do all the cleaning and cooking and liable at any moment— during the first few weeks anyhow, later it wasn't so bad—to be made to lie down and have that thing happen to one. It was all very well to set one's spirit ranging off into a world of fine sounding words or ideas, but it couldn't stay there; it came beaten and quivering back to the body, whimpering and praying for Aglaos to come and save it. After a certain number of repetitions I could set my teeth to it. I came to know the grunting weight, the hot wetness of the thing on top of me, and the time of its satisfaction. I learnt to avoid immediate pain for myself, though afterwards I had an inside ache that kept on for hours. I learnt to avoid comparison, to keep my mind fixed, not to let it dart off after another image. As it began to happen less often I could accept it more easily. The first horrible, shuddering surprise was over. I told myself, reasoning about it, that if it had stopped I would probably in a way have missed it.

I did all the inside work, but there were two slaves who'd been sold with the farm; they had belonged to the former owner, and they made themselves useful to Koenos, telling him just how things went. They were pretty nasty to me because of my having belonged to the same class which had been over them before; and I was nasty back to them whenever I could be. I used to lie to Koenos about their having taken the store-room things, and when I did that I felt blackened—and yet I liked doing it. I did it because I wanted to, and very elaborately. I thought out new ways and I was cleverer than they were. My own pain jagged at me to make me do it; only when he beat them I used to think of Aglaos and what might be happening to him. Once after that I tried to make up for it by giving them some extra meat, but though they took it, it didn't make any difference. I couldn't feel I could ever like them, either.

All this time I went on nursing my baby, and I taught him to drink cow's milk too. Once or twice Koenos amused himself by barring me away from him, into one of the rooms. He used always to shut me in when he went to the town, and once he left us alone in the house like that, me barred into the weaving room and my baby in the kitchen. He did it to punish me; I'd let his porridge get smoked. I heard Drako' crying for hours, yelling and sobbing, and then he stopped. You see, he was old enough to crawl a little, and there was a fire. Besides, there were rats. And I banged and tore at that barred door till my hands and shoulders were bleeding and I was almost unconscious. It was all right in the end; he let me out; my dress was soaked with milk I'd lost; I found my baby asleep, only rather cold and whimpering a little as he slept. Koenos didn't do it again after that; perhaps he had looked at me with a little imagination himself when he let me out. The next week when he went to the town he brought me back a necklace of glass beads. It was the only thing he ever gave me.

It was winter now and very difficult to get news. When his friends came I used to hide away as much as possible. Otherwise—well, after a few times I got to know better. Only I did hear mother had been bought and was on a farm about ten miles away and further from the town. And I heard vaguely about my cousin Nikotolea; she belonged to a Macedonian called Andromenes, I think, who had been one of the commanders and now had a big holding along by the river. I heard her spoken of—appreciatively. As to news of the rest of the world—well, it didn't seem to matter anyway. One had gone dead. Dead like the prisoners. Like Aglaos. Like my brother.

Towards the end of spring I found I was pregnant. I suppose I was lucky to have avoided it for so long. But I was angry, angry, angry for days. Whatever else I could force myself to accept, I could not accept this. I refused to believe it for long after I knew it was so. Then my milk began to go. I did all I could think of and then I remembered what mother had said. Only I didn't know how to get to her.

By this time there were several of us on the farm. A couple of months after he took it over, when he really got down to the work, my master bought two more out-door slaves, a Carian man and woman; they spoke hardly any Greek and were both lousy. I didn't go near them if I could help it. They slept out in the hay shed. Once I caught the woman picking up Drako' and fondling him; I snatched him away and stormed at her; then they kept to themselves; she didn't even come into the kitchen if I was there. After that Koenos bought some sheep and a pair of plough oxen and a cow, and a beast-herd with them. I saw him come limping into the yard after the beasts and I just thought how I hated him, how he was another against me. Koenos told me to take him out a bowl of soup, so I had to, but I shoved it at him and walked away. He was sitting on the edge of the food trough looking about him, pretty miserable, I expect. Yes, I knew he was that, but I wouldn't do anything about it; I was jammed up with my own misery. Afterwards he brought back the bowl into my kitchen and spoke timidly, but I told him to get out. I was quite certain that day about my pregnancy; I couldn't think of anything else; only I did notice the man was a Greek of some sort. He was called Damis.

A few days after that I washed my hair and put on that necklace he'd given me, and—so on, and then I asked him if I mightn't go and see my mother. He asked me where, pawing about around my neck and arm pits. I told him. Then he laughed. I don't think he

111

meant to be specially cruel, he just thought it was funny. For him, mother was just any old slave woman, worth very little, nearly past work; he didn't think of her humanly at all. People don't think of their slaves humanly, much. No, I'm not going to tell you what had happened to my mother, it might make you sick. It did me. But not at once. Not with him there laughing. In the middle of the night I got up and was sick in the yard.

So now mother was dead and there was nothing to be done and I was very frightened and very alone. I had understood something new when he spoke like that of mother. This was that we—the Mantineans—were now just the same as any other slaves. People treated us and thought of us the same way. They were the rich people, the owners; we were the owned. It was only natural. We were in the same position that our own slaves had been in. I knew now. So I began to feel I ought to be with the others, to join them: against our master. I began to try and make friends.

Only it was no good. They wouldn't. I couldn't get near them. I tried to bribe them to be friendly with food from the store, but the two old slaves took it and laughed at me and got me into trouble with our master, and the Carians were frightened, and the new herd was mostly off with the beasts. And I began to be sick and wretched; I hated this live thing inside my body that I couldn't deal with, and I hated Koenos as I never had before. If I had accepted at all earlier, I accepted nothing now—nothing, except that I was a slave.

Then one day he said he was going to have friends coming, and I was to roast a lamb and make puddings. So I did, and they came, and two of them had women with them—wives; one woman was a Macedonian and the other was my cousin Nikotolea. I took them through to the kitchen while the men had their dinner in the big room. Nikotolea didn't much like seeing me. No!—she did in a way, she began to chatter hard about all sorts of things and people; she'd more news than I had. But she wouldn't wait for me to answer, she kept on looking at me suddenly, and then looking away. I gave them food, cuts of the lamb, and stuffing. The Macedonian was an oldish woman and kind; she pretended not to be listening. I didn't care much if she was. I wanted to hit out at Nikotolea. I said to her, you've sold the pass. And she said, I haven't, it was the only sensible thing to do, what about you—look where you are now!—and you'll never get out of it. Well, I said, have you? And she flared up and

112

said: Yes!—I've got as good as a woman ever gets, I've got things for myself, a house and servants, a man that gives me what I ask for, clothes and all that, yes, and knowing where I shall be next year, and as for you, Kleta, you could have had it all if you'd only—only ... She began to tremble a bit with anger and shame, because we'd been such friends, and I said to her, yes, if I'd been a bitch and taken dogs! Then we both screamed and ran at each other (my dear, I don't say it was the least bit sensible, and a good Stoic wouldn't have, but I promised to tell you the truth), and the Macedonian woman separated us, and I was trembling and crying so that I couldn't stand.

Now, of course, that day has gone into perspective, with other days. But while one is living through something, one can't get that. I think the pecular quality of my anger and misery and disgust was to feel myself again cut off. I had thought intensely of Nikotolea and the rest of my women friends suffering the same things as myself; I had never somehow contemplated any of them accepting. I'd always hoped that some day we might find one another and do something—at any rate *be* something together. I wanted help so much.

You see, there was this continuous struggle going on inside me between keeping myself a good Stoic, untouched by what was being done to my body, keeping myself separate from it all for Aglaos, or else giving up, accepting the Macedonian, letting my body take charge and my mind forget. The longer the thing went on, the easier it seemed to give up and forget, and here was Nikotolea shoving me into it, too! I hated her for that. She gave me money; I only took it because I suddenly saw how one part of her at least was deeply unhappy, too. I saw it in her eyes for just one glance before she went away again with her Macedonian husband, laughing and talking rather loud.

As summer went on, it got worse and worse. I was sick and my back ached and this live thing inside me would never let me alone, hitting at my heart, and pushing out the horrid taut white skin of my belly. As my milk dried my breasts began to sag like old slave women I'd seen and shuddered at. I began to feel it was no use keeping myself for Aglaos when this was the thing I had become. Besides, Koenos was angry with me; I wasn't much good to sleep with. He knocked me about a good deal, but he didn't kill this thing I was pregnant with. I couldn't think of it as a boy or girl, you see, only as a thing. Right at the end he was kinder and made the Carian woman come in and help me about the house. But I couldn't make friends with her then; I hadn't the strength to try anything new. Only I let her give Drako' his porridge; he used to scream that summer and struggle out of my arms and push away from my face trying to kiss him. I suppose he really hated the nasty shape I'd become, only it seemed the last bit of unfairness—when I'd suffered all I had to keep him alive.

Then one day my pains came on. I gave Drako' to the Carian woman and asked her to look after him; she said she would if I died; she stood over me with him in her arms looking at me calmly while I squirmed with pain at her feet, and I knew she was quite expecting me to die. Just because women often do die in childbirth. She said she'd come back later and then she slumped out of the room, taking Drako' with her, and left me alone. And I gripped on to the side of the bed and gritted my teeth, and the sweat ran down my nose, and my pain filled the room, and I was alone with it. It was as if that pain was a thing standing outside me and rather rapidly invading and closing in on me.

It went on and on and I was still alone and blinded by it, groaning to myself, and I wanted to die. I wanted an end. But I couldn't die all alone; somehow I just couldn't. My mind became occupied with the loneliness and the pain, confusing them. When Drako' was born there had been a lot of women all round me, and hurry and hope and importance, so that I didn't remember the pain, and I'd got that sense of importance, mixed up with my idea of birth, and now I was dully and horribly astonished at the lack of importance here. All this was happening and it just didn't matter to anybody.

I was dreadfully thirsty; that began to be a separate part of the pain. The Carian woman didn't come back. From a long way outside my own core, this tight grip that was slowly squeezing me to death, I heard the cows splashing through the yard, lowing into the byre. I knew vaguely that it must be milking time and evening. Pain swallowed me again between its sucking jaws, and the next time I opened my eyes it was because Damis the herd had touched me on the shoulder and was holding a cup of milk for me to drink. I drank it, my teeth chattering on the edge of the cup, and then I was sick, and I cried for a long time, helpless with shame and pain, and Damis wiped my face with a wisp of hay and dragged the hair gently back out of my eyes. I remember holding on to him after that, pulling violently at his hands, wrenching at them as I was being wrenched and twisted, and then I remember he was feeling about me. I didn't want him to, partly because I was ashamed, and mostly because I was afraid of being hurt more, and I doubled my knees up, pushing him away.

And then he'd hauled me up and over on to my knees, and I clung on to him screaming, and I knew I pushing something out, tearing myself open, and I thought waveringly that it was a wild beast coming out of me. And then he let me go and I lay back and he pushed on my belly with his fists to get out the afterbirth, and I knew somehow that he had done this kind of thing before to ewes and cows and bitches, and in a way that comforted me. I stayed still, aware of the cessation of pain, aware of the Carian woman helping him to wash me, dimly curious about the thing I had been hating all these months, and which I now saw was a boy baby, very hairy and with a nose like Koenos.

I lay there for a few days and once or twice Koenos came in; he seemed pleased; he handled the baby. Lying on the bed, I watched him from below, knowing that this had made no difference, no bond between us, that I was no nearer acceptance than I had been. He made me suckle it while he was there, looking on in a greedy kind of way. But when he wasn't there I used to pull milk out of my breasts into a cup and give it to Drako'. He liked it and it was good for him, for he'd grown thin, and the Carian woman didn't bother about his food. He might have started sucking again, but somehow I didn't want him to have to share even that with the other. Only I never did this for him when the Carian woman was there. I was afraid she would tell Koenos.

In a way it was rather hard for me not to accept the baby at all. He was so little and helpless and trusting, with those tiny, crushable hands and feet; sometimes I caught myself loving him, but then I used to look at him hard and see Koenos, see the baby's mouth and nose like the man I hated. All that was rather painful; it pulled me about. I fixed my love jealously, passionately on Drako', and was always wanting to touch him and assure myself how much nicer he was than the tiny thing. But Drako' didn't like it, he squealed and twisted himself out of my arms and even seemed to like the Carian woman. I was achingly jealous of that, yet all the same I tried to hide it; I tried to force myself to admit in thought and in action that she and I were only fellow slaves. But she didn't admit it, in fact she seemed now to respect me for having the master's son as she never had before; she brought me special food and combed out my hair.

As for Damis, I didn't see him again till I was up, though I rather wanted to. I remembered his kindliness and competence; I could have done with more of that. The first day I could I went out into the yard at sunset and watched for him after the milking. He came out of the byre, limping a little, as usual; he had black hair and a rough dark beard. I took one of the milk pails and said: 'Thank you for helping me.'

He looked aside and spoke shyly and aggressively: 'You chuck that!'

'Why?' I said. I was so surprised; I had thought he would be kind still.

He seemed pleased to have surprised me and at the same time on the defence. 'You aren't used to rough chaps like me,' he said.

Of course he knew I had been a citizen's wife. Hadn't I rubbed it into the slaves at first! But now I didn't want him to think of me separately like that; if he did it made me ashamed that he had seen and touched me as he had. I said: 'You're not a rough chap. You're a friend to me, Damis.'

He said: 'Don't you go thinking I'm that. I'm not your friend! You stick to the master! You don't get any more out of me.'

That hurt, but I smiled and said: 'I don't want anything from you beyond what you gave me, which was perhaps my life.'

He stared at me and half shouted: 'Don't be a fool! You can't get round me. Get back to the house. You don't belong with us.'

I nearly did go back then. I felt their not wanting me like something impossible. Yet equally I felt Damis was my first possible contact with them. I said to him quietly: 'Damis, do you think I want to go back?'

He said: 'Yes, if you're not a worse fool than you look. You'll get something out of him, even if it's not all you've been used to.'

I said: 'You talk as if I was a fine lady.'

'Well,' he said, 'so you were, for all I've had my hands where the gentlemen used to go so sweet and pretty! Here, give me that pail!'

I felt the tears thickening on my eyes and knew I wouldn't be able

116

to speak in a moment. But I just managed to say: 'Oh, Damis, you've been kind. Why have you got to hurt me now?'

He looked at me and it was touch and go; I didn't move. I suppose there was something about what I had said, something that put him into a superior position, the position of a giver. And he answered to that. He said heavily: 'I didn't want to hurt you.'

I said: 'Most people do want to hurt me.' For I felt like that then; I was sobbing a little; one gets easily tired, those first days on one's feet after a baby.

He put his hand out and touched my shoulder and said: 'There, lass, there.' He said it as if I had been a cow or a fidgety mare, and I felt like a beast being calmed. 'Don't take on so,' he said, 'if I'd known how it was ...'

He didn't finish the sentence and I looked up and asked him eagerly: 'Yes, what?'

But he smiled and shook his head and went on in with the pails. And I went in not too unhappy: I felt I'd found something human for the first time. And after that we talked a little, he and I, not much and not about anything that mattered, only I liked it. And it seemed like help. Pretty soon I began to see I might need help. Because, as soon as I was well again and able to get about, Koenos began pawing me, and I knew how it would be again in a few weeks, though I used his baby as a defence against him now. I was rather badly frightened. I just couldn't face all that again, especially I knew I couldn't face this business of keeping myself apart from him while it went on; if it began again I knew I should give in this time.

So I thought about it and thought about it and in the end there was nothing for me to do except to risk everything and run away with Drako'. I knew of course that even if I succeeded in escaping I should probably die of hunger on the hills and Drako' die too. I had to admit that. But all the same I knew I'd got to. So I got things ready as much as I could; I hid away some grain and some dried meat, a little at a time, and I rubbed myself and did exercises to try and get my body as strong as possible. And then, quite suddenly, I made up my mind to tell Damis. I followed him away from the house one day and talked to him out of sight behind a ridge; it was the end of winter and there was some pasture but not much. That day there was bright sun but often we'd had cold winds. I told him straight out what I meant to do; I just hadn't the strength to be clever with him

117

about it. He said: 'It'll be bitter cold in the hills; you'd best wait another month.'

I said: 'I can't. He'll get me if I wait.'

He said: 'He's had you already. What's the odds, girl?'

And I shook him, saying 'I can't, I can't!'

And then he said: 'Very well, I see.' And for a minute he looked at the beasts, and then he said: 'I know where you could go.'

'Tell me,' I said

He said slowly: 'No. No.' And as I stood beside him he put his arm round me and held me close to him, so that his beard was against my temple, smelling rather of sheep. I looked up at him, wondering, but he was looking away from me. Then he said: 'I'll come too.'

So, very quickly, we arranged it. I hadn't much time to think why he wanted to come or anything like that. Only I was very glad. For it gave more than a chance to me and Drako'. And suddenly I felt myself coming alive. Only I wasn't coming alive to the self I had been but to a new self, and a solider one, a woman who knew what she meant to do and be, someone—well, grown-up. I had never felt certainty like this before and I needed it, because one thing I had to do was to leave my tiny baby. And I thought that meant that it would almost certainly die.

The queer thing is, that I don't know if it did. And I never shall know. It would be horrible if it did die, but still more horrible if it didn't—if it were still there, that bit of me, that bit of Koenos, a little boy, his son—No, I just find that idea so disquietening that I won't think of it. One thing I've learnt is that it's no good bothering about things one can do nothing about. I suppose it died. Obviously, that doesn't matter now. Not to me, here, anyway.

I took Drako'. He was asleep when I picked him up in the dark, very carefully, wrapping the blanket round to keep him asleep in my arms for as long as possible. I had the food in another bundle on my back. I met Damis where he said and we went straight up across the pastures and began climbing, and the sky lightened to day behind us. When Drako' woke, Damis took him. Sometimes we stopped for breath or if one of us had stumbled badly. We climbed all that day, getting farther and farther into the hills; I suppose there was some sort of chase after us, but they never came near. It was very horrible expecting it, all the same. We were all on edge, whispering, angry with each other over nothing. But he seemed to know the way. At noon we stopped and ate a little. My breasts were heavy and hard. Suddenly I had the most terrible feeling about the baby I'd left behind, it seemed impossible that I should never feel it again nuzzling at me, trusting me. I'd smashed that trust in its eyes that knew only me. I didn't know what the Carian woman would do with it. Or Koenos might be angry and have it thrown out of the house on to the dung heap, for all it was his. And I didn't know. I began to cry and Damis turned and swore at me.

Drako' was hungry and I wanted him to suck; he could have got a full meal and there was some bread too. But he wouldn't; he wriggled his head away and when I pressed his mouth against my nipples he bit me. Then I had to squeeze the milk out into a little horn cup I had. It was very difficult with my breasts as full as they were, and very sore. It exhausted me to do it. Damis had been looking away, down the valley, watching for any sign of pursuit. But then he turned round and saw what I was doing. He knelt down beside me and took my left breast in his hands and began to press out the milk himself; it was much easier so. He handled me gently, as he had that other time. I looked down and saw my breast lying in the cupped palm of his rather dirty hand; it was white and blue-veined, the veins standing out now that it was so full, and hard like a fruit, a great fruit. And his brown fingers worked at it gently and the milk spurted in four or five little jets, and the cup filled and Drako' drank it up. And then Damis's fingers did the same thing for my right breast, easing me. I leant back against him a little. My thoughts about the tiny baby were dying down. When he had finished Damis did not drop the breast at once; he kept his palm under it, but the touch changed rather, and his other hand stroked in the hollow between. I did not know what to think about it, but somehow it seemed all right. After a time he jumped up suddenly, picked Drako' off the ground into his arms and said we must get on. I was rested and walked well; I wanted to carry Drako' but he wouldn't let me. In spite of the slight limp he went up the hills as easily as a sheep.

In the evening we came to a cave; we both wanted to light a fire, but we didn't dare: not yet. There was a spring and we got water; it was ice-cold. We found some fern and dry stuff to put on the floor of the cave. I said I wanted to give Drako' his supper and when I undid my dress Damis came over at once and helped me, settling me so that I leant comfortably against one of his knees while he bent over me, and again I watched the milk spurting out of myself. When my little boy had finished his cupful and I had put him down to sleep on my cloak, I said rather shyly to Damis that if he would like it I thought I had more milk. It seemed a pity to waste the chance of a warm drink, and I knew I should have plenty again by morning. He said: good. And I settled back again against his knee and watched, only I had a different and curious feeling now that it was for him. I felt that the other thing had been instinctive, what an animal would have done, but that this was a product of reason and intelligence, that it was a kind of deliberate action which mattered. I was giving and he accepting; he was accepting deliberately and because of his acceptance taking action. I cannot make it so clear now but it was clear enough to me there in the mouth of the cave with the moon up over the black jagged hump of the mountain and the cold air on my skin and his fingers warm against it.

The milk did not come so freely now; he tried first one breast, then the other; it began to hurt, his fingers pressed on the core of my breasts, the inner part, and on the sensitive edges of the nipples. Suddenly it hurt too much and I cried out. He stopped almost at once, but not quite, it was curious. The cup was three-quarters full. He asked me if I would like some myself but I said no. It would have made me sick. But he drank and I was glad to hear him drinking, though I could not see him very clearly. I covered myself and went into the cave. Drako' was asleep. Lying down in the fern, I thought I should have slept at once, but I was too cold. I began to wonder what would have happened to Drako' and me if we had been out that night on the run without Damis.

Then he came in. I said sleepily: 'Come close.' He lay down beside me and he was shivering too. Perhaps his shivering woke me more, for I began to be aware of something about him, something he wasn't saying; I sat half up, leaning on my elbow, and stared down at him; I couldn't see very well, but I knew. My heart began to beat very fast, but not fast enough to obscure my clear and lucid thought. I made up my mind what I ought to do and what I was going to do. I pulled my dress back, and I put out my hand and felt for him in the dark. He stirred under my touch and as he did I took his other hand and brought it over so that he could feel that I was naked. 'Come,' I said, 'this will keep the cold from both of us.'

He turned over then, taking me into his arms, holding me closely against him. He said: 'You are a good woman, Kleta.' He meant it. It was lovely to have that said to me. I was happy. I put my arms round him too, happy and sleepy again, and as I felt his quiet heart my heart quieted too and we both stopped shivering. He was gentle and competent. I accepted him completely, and as I went finally to sleep I knew that I was not separated any more.

In the morning we went on again; I had milk for them both; we still had dried meat and some bread. Nothing was different except that we were not so cross with one another, but that was perhaps because now we were not afraid of pursuit any longer. We let Drako' walk a little, but mostly he had to be carried. We got up on to a ridge and Damis looked rather puzzled. I asked him where he was going and he explained that he knew there were some other runaways somewhere up in the hills hereabouts. He knew the direction vaguely, somewhere between Mantinea and Laconia. We talked it over and at last decided which hollow we had best go along. It was lovely up there with the clouds going by overhead; we smiled at one another; we weren't slaves any more. Damis felt he was free, but I felt something more than freedom. I suppose one would call it brotherhood. It was very odd: for here we were, still in danger and with prospects of no more than a bare life among outlaws, and it was cold when the wind blew and I knew it would be bitter cold at night; but still I had an intense feeling of well-being all through my body, from my feet treading strongly down into the sides of the mountains to my head up in the air; I could feel my muscles smoothly at work and my lungs breathing easily and my breasts creeping with slow thick milk. I asked Damis if he had always been a slave. He said yes, he thought so, though he didn't know about his childhood—he had been taken away from his parents; he said that for a long time he hadn't thought anything else was possible. 'But now', he said, 'I will never be anyone's slave again, though I suppose I shall always be the poorest kind of man.'

And he asked me about my life and I told him, and suddenly I began to know how little I had to do with Kleta then, and how that Kleta would have died of shame and horror if she had foreseen what was going to happen. And I laughed a little and knew another thing, that I would find it hard now to be happy reading poetry and embroidering and making garlands, or having music and convers-

121

ation with other girls, or even going to lectures and discussions about philosophy. Often in these days I had got the sensation that it was all a preparation for something, some action. And now the action was upon me and I was taking it.

And then, at the end of the afternoon, we saw smoke and went towards it cautiously. Round the corner of a great rock we found our way barred by a man with a spear, in a sheepskin coat. He said: 'Who are you, strangers?' Damis answered that we were runaways and had been told of the stronghold by so-and-so. The man glared and told us to follow, and we went up the path to a cave, with out-buildings among the rocks and clefts, made of hurdles and mud, and a banked fire on the stony plateau in front of it. He shouted and three or four men came out of the cave, very rough-looking and wearing skins, armed with knives and spears. Damis said we had been slaves to the Macedonian colonist Koenos and had run away. He was a skilled beast-herd and I—he had asked me earlier—was skilled at cooking and weaving and all women's crafts. The head of the gang said: 'Well, you can come.' And then to Damis, slanting his head at me: 'Is that your woman?'

'No', said Damis, 'she's not my woman. She isn't anybody's. She is a free woman.'

The man said to me: 'Whose kid is that?'

I picked up Drako' and said: 'I was a married woman in Mantinea.'

He stared and stuck out his beard at me and spat and said: 'So you were a lady, were you?'

Damis said quickly: 'She's not a lady. She is a good woman.' And he put his arm round my shoulder.

The other man said: 'We could do with a woman here. We haven't got a woman. So if she's not yours we can have her.'

I felt only rather dazed, hearing that at the end of the day's walking, but Damis looked very angry and I thought he was going to hit the man and I thought if he did that we should all be turned out, and it wasn't fair. So I said: 'If you are good kind of men I will be anything you want. Only I don't belong to anybody and I am never going to belong to anybody again.'

The man said nothing for a minute, then he said: 'What's your name?'

I said: 'Kleta.'

And he repeated slowly, Kleta, and nodded and said: 'Come in.'

Inside the cave there was a sheep's quarter, skinned. He said: 'Cook that.' I said firmly that I had to feed the child first and he said: 'all right, you can do it after that.'

While I was cooking that meat and grinding up some barley meal to make cakes to go with it, I wondered what was going to happen. But I wasn't frightened, I was prepared to accept everything. My mind and body were new-born in a way, and receptive. As those runaways and outlaws came to the fire where I was cooking their supper, I greeted them calmly, and looked them over. I saw at once that they were going to be nice to Drako'. Some of them were definitely ugly and none of them were beautiful or in any way fine-featured, but most of them had something pleasant about them; the eyes would be alive even when the rest of the face was dull and sodden-looking. I asked the leader—his name was Komon—if there were no other women. 'No,' he said, 'they daren't come, the bitches. But you've come.' And another man said: 'You've come to us, Kleta.' They liked, I think, even to say a woman's name.

I said: 'Why didn't you raid girls for yourselves?'

The leader said: 'It's a hard life here. Cold. And food's scarce sometimes. They'd have run back, they'd have betrayed us, the bitches. But you won't.' And again someone said: 'You're one of us, Kleta.'

It was all curiously heartening; I felt as if I had some real value again. You understand that, don't you? What I want to make plain, you see, is what was going on in my mind. I slept with all those men, runaways, outlaws, hunters and thieves, with most of them during the first few nights. It was tiring, but not, I think, bad for me, though rather astonishing. I became one of them. I got their point of view. The things I used to do and think seemed silly, not connected with life. But I found myself wondering a great deal about Kleomenes and his revolution, and what had driven it to happen. Two of the outlaws had been helots, who were freed during the latter part of the Spartan revolution, but had run away after Sellasia when their old masters wanted to reclaim them. Yes, I remember, one of them had a sword sear on his shoulder, sunk and purplish and pulling at the skin round it; it horrified me at first—I always looked away—but later I didn't mind it at all; it was just part of him and I thought of him as a good kind of man, a friend. They gave me their point of view on it, not clearly, you understand, but bit by bit, in the evenings, as it came to them. And I saw why the Spartan revolution had had to come, because the system by which people owned things in Sparta had become top-heavy, and was bound to break up and if Kleomenes had not been alive then to lead it, someone else would have been. And I saw that the revolution had not really come from the bottom, from the people who were worst oppressed, as these two had been; these people were too squashed down to have been able to think of it and plan it; but because the revolution had come from on top, it was bound to fail just as it did fail, because Kleomenes could not get out of the possessor's habit of wanting more power for himself. He could not see that it mattered most to make a stable state where there would be no one under and no one over, but all equal. The Spartans used to get glimpses of that, they got the feeling of brotherhood sometimes; but it didn't last—it couldn't so long as Kleomenes wouldn't think out the difficult business of getting his state rightly based.

Of course the helots didn't say all that; they were hardly even thinking it; I got it out of them and put it into thoughts, for my practice with philosophic discussion enabled me to do that. Then they were surprised and glad to see it just as they'd meant. I knew a good deal of history and I used to tell it to the outlaws, who mostly knew very little; only three of them could read at all or even write their names. I taught the others to read and write, and I said them poetry and I told them history, but when they asked me questions about the history and poetry, I saw I had got it all wrong—I had only been seeing it from one side, from on top. For instance, I tried to make them see how important some battle or other had been, saving a state and giving honour to the generals and gods of the state. But I couldn't make them see the point and soon I saw that there wasn't any point for these landless, cityless men. They had to have a different kind of honour, and I had to think out what that was through all the history I knew, and pretty soon I saw that I really only knew one kind of history, which didn't touch the lives of people through all the ages who had been like my friends, in their position. They didn't like Homer much, either; Homer is all about kings and queens, people who acted as they did because they were rulers and irresponsible—free, the only free people in those days. I got to understand that when Aglaos and I had listened to the Iliad in old days, we had pretended to ourselves that we were kings and queens, because, being free, we were not so very far away from them; but these people were too far off to be able to do that sort of identification, so the Iliad was no use to them.

The Odyssey was better, and I knew chunks of it which I used to say to them, and tell them the rest, always telling it so that it was as much about Odysseus's crew as about him. What they liked best were lyrics; sometimes I used to say them little short things, those poems of Sappho, for instance, which are only an elaboration of what any girl or any boy might think. They used to love those, and got me to teach them, and they would go about saying them aloud to themselves. Oh, I was busy. Yet, I know that for everything I taught them, they were teaching me as much, and changing me far more than I ever could, or wanted to, change them.

Sometimes, when I had time, I used to think about this change in myself, and wonder whether it could have come about peacefully, without the horrible part before, without my time with the Macedonian, without being raped and abused and bullied and so much hurt. And I didn't think it could have happened without that, because till everything else had been knocked out of me, I don't see how I could have accepted and grown up as I had. I talked about this with Damis and with Komon, but they didn't quite understand, they hadn't had my earlier experience. I kept on wondering whether something of the kind mightn't have happened to Aglaos and to my brother. If so, even if I never saw either of them again, I could be in a queer kind of way, glad. But the others seemed to think it not very likely that either Aglaos or Arkas had got through the first year, the forced march north in the chain-gang, and the first breaking under a master. They told me some of the things that happened to slaves, which did seem to me so horrible that I didn't see how those other two could have got through. And now that I thought about it, I realized that these weren't extraordinary things, but just what I might have seen for myself any time, only I'd never looked at them that way. Yet the thing of all which would have been hardest for those two was not anything physical, not overwork or cold or tortures or being constantly rather hungry, but the business of not having any value, any worth to oneself. I suppose it is this feeling of nothing being worth while, not even oneself, that is what Homer means when he talks of a man's manhood going from him when he is enslaved.

During the first year two new men came to the gang, and it was queer seeing this sense of value coming to them. Because at first they were quite irresponsible; they didn't care how dirty and untidy and hateful they were—it seemed to them to be freedom to be as nasty as you liked. But then they began to feel they were some value after all; they owned themselves now and what they owned had to be decent. So they became decent. That seems simple enough, but it was curious to watch it. I could help them, of course, perhaps more than anybody, but it meant a violent effort of body and mind, as you can perhaps imagine. Once, when the others were out hunting, one of them amused himself by twisting my arms and making things generally unpleasant for me; it wasn't funny at the time. When the others came back they half killed him; I was afraid he would run away and betray us. Luckily Drako' was out of the way that afternoon; Damis used often to take him out.

I wondered whether they couldn't get some other women, and thought that probably some of the others from Mantinea might be in the same position as myself. But then I remembered Nikotolea and I didn't know what to think. It was so impossible to get in touch without getting into danger. But it would have been nice to have another woman. In autumn of that first year I became pregnant again; they were all terribly pleased and for several evenings they played dice games to find out which of them the father was. I didn't know. But I was quite pleased about it myself. I was strong again and I thought it would be good for Drako' to have a baby brother or sister. As it was, they spoiled him too much. Besides—oh, I was glad to know I was bearing a child that had started from one of them, I was glad to feel myself as closely mixed with them as that.

We had one scare at the beginning of winter when we thought there was a hunt up after us; we all left the cave and went higher up into the mountains. It was very cold and uncomfortable. But nothing came of it; I suppose the Macedonians were too busy and too anxious to bother about a nest of thieves one way or the other.

We got news now and then. We heard, about a year late, that Antigonos of Macedonia had died. We heard how things were going in Sparta. And we heard local news of this or that farm. But mostly we were just ourselves. They got me a certain amount of wool which I washed and carded and spun; I tried to make a loom, but it wasn't much of a success, and I only managed rough kind of blankets. Before the baby was born two of them went down into the plain and stole some cloth for me; I enjoyed having that and cutting it up and making things, and they liked watching me. When my time came, Damis and one of the others looked after me. It was bad enough, but they did make me feel that I was something very precious and that they were fighting for me. That was how Phanas was born, and they came in on tiptoe one by one and touched him and me very softly.

It was in the autumn that I was nursing him that there was a curious interlude. A new man came and joined us, and almost at once I found out that he was a Mantinean, a citizen; he had been too young to be fighting during the siege, and afterwards he had been sold to a colonist with his mother, who had since died. Now he was a young man, and very good-looking, the kind of thing I had rather forgotten the existence of. At first I was very glad to see him and talk to him. There had been something I had missed all this time, some kind of sublety in talk and relations, and I got it again with him: not that I think he was particularly intelligent, but after my friends, who had none of it, he seemed to be full of fine shades and irony and education. I knew his father by name—one of the magistrates—and his mother must have been a woman of intellect. He had read a great deal as a child, and could finish for me the half-finished quotations which bothered me sometimes. We used almost always to sit together in the evenings by the wicker cradle which Damis had made for my new baby.

At first I though Ophioneos, this new young man, was going to fit in and accept as I had; he seemed to me to be a proof of my argument. He had obviously had a fairly bad time, especially in the last year since his mother died. And then I began to feel he wasn't fitting in, and I saw that the gang were jealous because I talked to him so much, and then I saw that he was rather pleased about that and was using it to feel superior with. At first I had been rather angry with them for being jealous, but when I saw how he was taking it, I was angry with him. I began to find the subtle conversation less interesting; it tended to repeat itself. And it seemed to me that he was trying to get me to re-accept certain values which I had definitely decided were not worth having. For several evenings I avoided any close talk with him; we all sang, or played games, or made plans for the winter. Komon said to me: 'Good job you aren't so thick as you were with that lad, Kleta. I couldn't have stood it.' I said: 'Nonsense—what's wrong with him?' and laughed, but I was rather bothered all the same.

And then one day when the others were out Ophioneos came up to me and looking round to see we were alone, suddenly began urging me to leave the gang and come away with him. I was so astonished that I let him go on. At last I said: 'But don't you like them? Don't you feel they're real, they're good people?'

'Oh, they're good enough,' he said impatiently, 'but not for you, Kleta, they're killing you, they're dragging you down to earth. For all they're free they can only think of slave things, they do slave things to you. Oh, I can't bear to think of you sleeping with them, being pawed about, like an animal, Kleta, like a slave woman. Come away with me and I'll be gentle, I'll be subtle with you. Look at me, look at my body, for you, Kleta, and your's for me.'

That woke me up: 'No,' I said, 'I won't be anybody's again. I know you're beautiful, Ophioneos, much more beautiful than they are. I know—oh, you put the taste of anyone less beautiful right out! But they're my people, and you've got to understand that.'

I felt a good deal shaken; he was, of course younger than I, and, as I said, very good-looking. I had not slept with anyone since the baby was born, but I knew they'd want it again soon, and that I must not refuse. And he was offering me something that I rather wanted. But I didn't like what he said about the others. He tried something else then—he began to try and make me remember Mantinea, remember being a lady, full of delicacies and finenesses which I knew I had lost now. He tried to rouse my pride, not only in what I had done and felt, but in what I had been part of, lovely Mantinea, the city that my father Podares and his father had lived and striven for, the city of my husband and brother, the city where I had felt myself close and secure and certain of everything. I couldn't listen, I jumped up and began breaking kindling wood; I wished one of the others would come back. I asked him what he thought he could do with a woman with two small children, and then suddenly he said he would try to find Aglaos and bring me back to him.

That made me feel very queer; I told him quickly to stop. He said he had friends in Sparta—his mother had told him about them, men who had known his father. He was going over the pass and down there. And then he would find out—He had heard that some of the old Mantinean citizens were beginning to get back to Greece. Why not Aglaos? 'And if he sees you like this,' Ophioneos said, 'what is he going to think? Oh, Kleta, have you never tried to imagine what he would feel if he could see you here, letting yourself go among these slaves, these thieves, forgetting him and all that we meant by Mantinea!'

'Go and find him,' I said, half sobbing, half menacing him—I remember—with a sharpened stick, 'tell him to come and find me here! Tell him to come!'

And then Ophioneos looked at me and he said slowly, 'I will,' and he walked away. And he didn't come back. I told Komon and Damis more or less what had happened. They were rather upset, because they were afraid he might betray us, but I knew he wouldn't do that; it wouldn't have been the kind of thing he would do. But it had stirred up everything about Aglaos, and all the things connected with him, and I was gloomy and cross for several days. They all noticed it and tried to give me things and comfort me; which, of course, made me worse. Then Damis told me I was a stuck-up bitch of a fine lady and he would have to do something about it. And he did.

How odd it is to think of all that now! The others stood by and laughed. I bit Damis. He hurt me rather, too, and I thought he'd shamed me and humbled me so that he'd spoilt everything. But he hadn't, of course. Everyone seemed to think it was very sensible, as it probably was, and left it at that, and the next day they asked me to say them poetry, and all sat round while I did, with their mouths open and their rather dear eyes fixed on me.

The next year I had another baby, that is, of course, Pheidike. Drako' was four and a most bewitching brown creature with yellow hair and green eyes. Phanas was nearly a year and half old; we used to try and see likenesses between him and any of them, but one couldn't be sure. It was a good game, though. I had an idea that this one was by one of the Laconians, but I really didn't know. I was pleased to have a girl and so were they; they made jokes about her all the time. During all those years there had been only one other woman up with the gang; a runaway had brought his girl along with him, and I was delighted and yet in a way embarrased; I hadn't seen another woman for so long; I wondered what she'd think of me. But I never could find out or make friends with her; she was shy, and

129

probably very stupid too, and she stuck to her man all the time. Perhaps I would have been able to pierce through if she had been with us for longer, but she fell over a precipice and broke her neck. It was a pity. I wanted to see myself with a woman; I wanted to be sure I wouldn't be jealous—very likely I would have been. But it would have been funny!

Those years seemed to pass very quickly; there was so much to do all the time; very often there was someone to nurse; they hurt themselves on rocks or got bitten by sheep-dogs if they went down raiding. We were always making things or repairing things; we were always hunting for food. I remember berries and nuts and dew-cold mushrooms. I remember wild honey, and salt they had stolen from a farmhouse, and sour cheeses I made from the goats' milk, and birds' eggs in spring.

I remember all that. And then Aglaos came back.

It was winter then. I was in the back part of the cave with the babies. I was making a reed basket and humming to myself. I heard someone coming up the path, but I didn't bother much; I thought it was one of the gang. Then there were voices; I didn't exactly hear them, but something began to startle me, so I stopped humming; I still didn't quite know what it was, but I got up and came to the mouth of the cave. And there was Aglaos. He was quite ridiculously like he had always been, clean-shaven, in a red wool tunic like the ones he usd to have. He was so unchanged that I thought he was a ghost. I must have screamed. He said: 'Kleta...' in a queer way as if he wasn't quite sure. So I ran into his arms; I was dizzy with a pelting of sharp small physical memories; I buried my face in him; he smelt the same. He felt the same. It was really him.

Then I began to stammer questions at him, not really noticing the answers, only his voice, only the fact that he was there; I hung on to him, for my knee muscles had gone soft and weak. He said he had been a slave on board a ship, but had been rescued and helped by some Stoics at Olbia—I didn't know where Olbia was—and that he'd come back to Greece and he had heard from Ophioneos that I was here. That woke me up a little. I lifted my head off his shoulder and said: 'What did *he* tell you?'

Aglaos seemed very uneasy and said: 'About your life here. And—and—' But he couldn't finish it.

I understood and said: 'Aglaos, I have had two children by these

130

men, but Drako' is well and so lovely. You'll see him soon.'

I didn't want just then to tell him about Koenos and that other baby.

'Oh, Kleta,' he said, 'my darling, has it been too awful for you?'

'No,' I said, 'not here. It was awful at first. While I was a slave. Was it for you?'

'Yes,' he said, 'worse than you can imagine, Kleta.'

'I can imagine a lot now,' I said, 'I'll tell you what happened to me some day. What are we going to do?'

He said: 'I've heard from Arkas.'

I cried out at that, asking if he was alive and well, suddenly seeing his image sharp in my mind, the brother I'd been so fond of.

Aglaos laughed and stroked my hair and said, 'We can go to him and we will. At once, Kleta. He has land in Macedonia, gold, cattle, slaves. He's done well. A big farm.'

But everything began to go round and round for me. It was, I suppose, the idea of Arkas slave-owning. You see, slave-owning by now meant something quite different to me. Only I saw it didn't to Aglaos. I shivered and asked him, rather sharply, to come into the cave. He followed me. I saw that two of the gang were just outside, standing by the fire, watching me. I brought him over to the big sleeping-bench at the back and sat down a little way from him. Phanas came toddling and laughing up, and caught on to my knees with his fat bare arms. Aglaos said: 'Is that one of them?'

I said, 'Yes,' and nodded to the cradle where Pheidike was asleep under a lambskin. He said nothing, only looked away, then in a low voice, he asked me: 'You didn't like this? You didn't mean this, Kleta?'

I didn't know how to answer. Only I did know I'd got to speak the truth with Aglaos—as we had agreed always to do with one another—and I knew I mustn't deny my thieves and runaways who had accepted me as their own kind of person. I said: 'I did mean this, Aglaos.'

And he: 'Then it was true what Ophioneos said.' And he drew in a sharp groaning breath.

I said: 'He never understood. But you should, Aglaos. You've been a comrade of slaves.' And I took his hand in mine and said: 'That's true too.'

But his hand did not answer to mine. He only said: 'It took me

131

three days to find this place. I was out on the hill-side. It was so cold; my blanket froze at night. I get pains in my bones since Olbia. And at the end: this. I used to think of you, Kleta, every day. My little Kleta with your soft clean hair and the smile you had for me when I came home, only for me, and the way you put your hands up like nestling birds on to my shoulders. My own girl. My own wife. Oh Kleta, your fine quivering smile and your wise innocent eyes.'

I remember very well those words, one after another beating at me, and when he had finished I found it hard to speak, hard to answer that pain which yet, I knew, had got to be, as a part of his growing. I said: 'Look my dear, aren't my eyes perhaps wiser now?'

But he shook his head and I saw that there were grey hairs on his temples, and this moved me so much that I was nearly weeping. I picked Phanas up and hid my eyes in his soft, cool little shoulder.

Then Damis came in. He said at once: 'So you're that Aglaos. We heard a lot abour you.'

Aglaos stood up and shook hands; he tried to say something but couldn't.

Damis saw, I think, and meant to make it easier. He said: 'Well, I suppose you've come to take her away. We knew you would sooner or later, if you were alive. She's too good for us to have always. Kleta, lass, where are we going to get another of you?'

I felt then, in the most curious way, how much I loved them, more, perhaps, than I loved Aglaos; yet somehow I also knew that I could leave them without hurting them much—I couldn't hurt them as I could and might hurt Aglaos. I didn't want to hurt them, and I knew that perhaps I had got to hurt him. They talked a little constrainedly. I could feel that each of them was wanting to be nice to the other, but they were both uncomfortable. I couldn't help them. They'd got to work it out between them, only I kept on wanting to touch Aglaos, to touch his fingers and over his temples where the new grey hairs were. I wanted to be his again, and he mine. And yet I knew I couldn't be, I knew I'd grown up out of that; it just couldn't be easy like that to either of us again. If we started now on those terms we should waste all that had gone between, all the pain and misery and growing-up. We'd got to think of something better, at least I had, for he wouldn't be able to; he was still thinking of me as if I were someone else, the girl I had stopped being for so long now that I'd half forgotten how she would have acted to her husband. I didn't hesitate, of course, about going away with him; I was prepared to go anywhere he said and do anything he wanted me to do; he was my husband, and besides, I loved him. There'd never been any doubt in my mind that if he came back he'd tell me what to do next and I should do it; I knew I wasn't wise that way; I'd been out of the world a long time, too—I wouldn't have been good at that sort of decision.

So he and Damis went on talking and by and bye Komon came in; they didn't look at me much, only I kept on passing them and overhearing them as I went about my jobs. They didn't seem to be talking about anything much; I was very impatient with them, I wanted to hurry them up, I wanted, among other things, to know where and when I was going. And then I thought, perhaps, that's how men have got to do it, smelling around one another like dogs. If only they could just couple and have done! And I wondered if I'd be like this with other women. And I thought if there are to be difficulties and misunderstandings and tensions, how much better if they're between men and women who can deal with them so much more simply without taking all this time about it.

Drako' had been out with the men that day and by and bye I heard voices. I saw Aglaos stiffen a little and I said: 'Yes!' And my Drako' came running in all wild and beautiful in dirty sheepskins, with his hair curling gloriously away from his green eyes and cold-nipped cheeks. He rushed up to me and I said to him: 'Father's come back.' He let Aglaos pick him up and kiss him, but he had gone very grave and quiet, and came back to me afterwards and held on to my hand and whispered about what he had been doing out with the others, instead of shouting it. Aglaos wanted to be left alone with him, but Damis and Komon were slow to understand and before I could get them away the others had finished penning the sheep and goats and had come into the cave.

One of the helots had shot a young fox, which, though it was not good eating, I was prepared to cook in winter with plenty of seasoning; he skinned it and pegged out the skin. I was just claiming the beautiful red fur for Pheidike, when I realized that probably I and my children would be gone before the skin was fit to use. And perhaps this man was Pheidike's father. It would be very odd, I thought, just sleeping with one man again, though lovely to sleep with Aglaos. I kept wanting to take his clothes off, the heavy wool that kept me away from his skin. I wanted to see and touch his body, to know it again. And yet, as the evening wore on, I became more and more bothered. I began to see that, in spite of what had happened to him, Aglaos hadn't really got the sense of being the same as my gang. He was out of it. He wasn't thinking of things in the way they thought, or feeling as they felt, touching as they touched, he was still in the same attitude of mind as he was when he was a citizen of Mantinea, an owner, on top. He was being as friendly as he could—I saw that—but in the same way that he might have been friendly to his own slaves at some festival. For he had always been kind to them; during the whole year we'd been married I don't remember ever having seen one of the house slaves whipped. He might easily have said that they were his brothers: that's good Stoic theory. But these outlaws of mine were a long way from theory and stoicism; they had the real thing.

And they felt quick enough that he was really still a master. They didn't hate him for that because he was my man and they loved me, but they were squashed. They shrunk together, as it were, and hardened themselves against him. If he wasn't going to give himself at all to them, they weren't going to give themselves to him. And that worked round again, and stopped him from seeing the good in them, above all from seeing why I had accepted them. He could only see them as they were with their defences of deliberate stupidity and insensitiveness up against him. Yes, and it made me see them at their worst too, as underdogs and slaves; they seemed somehow dirtier than usual, they sang their stupidest and most indecent songs; they were dulled. He made them feel inferior and they lost their balance towards me, so that they were either cringing or rough. And when they were rough Algaos felt that he was rescuing me from them and I felt that I wanted to be rescued. And when they were cringing I despised them for it, and he felt that. Oh, it was horrible!

The torches at the mouth of the cave died down; there was nothing but ember light—we couldn't ever get enough wood to keep the fires burning high all night—and the light of my one little lamp over the sleeping-shelf. The children were all three tucked in under blankets and warm skins. This was the time we used to go to bed in winter. I wondered what it was best to do; my heart was beating violently with excitement. But it was taken out of my hands. They all went off to the pile of cut fern and stuff, nodding good-night to me.

Aglaos said loudly and deliberately to Komon: 'I'm taking my bedding over to the side,' and he spread his cloak over it and lay down with his back to me. None of them kissed me that night, and long after they were all asleep or pretending to be, I lay awake and alone on the sleeping-bench, still keyed up with anxiety and wonder and anger against them all.

But I went to sleep at last and only woke up to Pheidike's early morning stir and whimpering. I picked her up quickly, so as not to let her disturb the others, and her soft greedy mouth fastened on to me. It was only just light enough to see her. Sucking, she became completely part of me, as a man might have been, but for longer and softlier. We two women, my baby and I, were warm and living and gentle together in the grey cold light, we two awake among the sleeping men, we two alone functioning and aware. I alone thinking. I whispered into Pheidike's tiny crinkled ear: 'This is nonsense, my little girl. I can't let it go on. I'm the strongest here, I can surely put my will across them. I won't be shaken or angry or hurt. I shall make it come right.' And I soothed myself to certainty, lipping and smelling about her soft brown head and delicate sleepy face.

When I put her down into her warm blanket beside me, it was almost light and I saw Komon watching me. When he saw I'd seen he slipped out of his blanket and over, very quietly and cleverly, not rustling the dry fern. He settled down beside me and said, half turned away: 'Looks like you're off now, Kleta, you and the kids.'

'Yes,' I said.

He said: 'You were a good one. You smelt like irises.'

I said: 'Komon, my dear, you'll have other women as sweet as me. Others who'll be better to you. Half a dozen, not just one for the lot of you!' And I laughed at him a little, gently, so that it wouldn't wake anyone and told him he ought to go raiding, and stroked his knee, the way he liked to be stroked.

He said: 'We don't want half a dozen squabbling bitches. We only wanted you.'

'Nonsense,' I said, 'you knew I'd go when my man came back.'

'Hell!' said Komon sharply, 'that's it. A rotten chap. Don't you go with him, Kleta!'

'Don't speak so loud, Komon,' I said, 'you'll wake someone. Why, you stupid, you're shivering.'

I sat right up and put an arm and blanket round him. I could

135

quiet him, I thought, like that, with my cheek still and steady against his rough cheek. 'Why,' I said, 'what's he done to make you say that?' I was determined not to be angry with him for saying it, though.

'Coming the gentleman over us!' said Komon, 'making me feel as if'—and he hesitated, stiffening against me—'as if I was back, being a slave, as if you didn't belong to us any more. The dirty bastard. As if you was a lady, our Kleta!'

'My dear,' I said, 'my dear, don't you know he's been through it all too? How can you say that?'

But Komon went on, and louder: 'Much good it's done him! I don't want him to have you, Kleta! He shan't.'

'Yes he shall,' I said, 'because I want him to and this is my business. Isn't it my business? Isn't it?'

He wouldn't answer, but I thought I must make him answer. I pulled his head round towards mine and repeated the question, and at last he said yes, and I kissed him on the mouth, and then he dropped his head down on to my breasts, and I felt him breathing hard and short and troubled, and then, looking across the cave over his bristly dark hair, I saw Aglaos propped up on his elbow, watching, and I saw he was hating Komon and me in one look, and I did not know what he had overheard. I raised my hand with the blanket over Komon's face to keep him from that hate-look till he had stopped feeling so bad, and I motioned Aglaos to keep quiet.

But at that Aglaos jumped up to his feet making a great noise, and called me by a name that even the worst of the gang had never called me to my face, and which I won't repeat to you. And Pheidike gave a start in her sleep and a squeal of fear, and everyone was awake and getting to their feet, and Komon shoved himself out of my arms white with anger, and before I could do more than snatch up Pheidike out of their way, they were fighting and out to kill. I put Pheidike up on the sleeping-bench and shouted, 'Stop it!' And Damis was helping me, and then the others, and we pulled them apart. Luckily they'd had no knives, but Komon's nose was bleeding and Aglaos's eye was swelling already, and they were trembling with anger and looking like devils. And of course the three children were yelling at the tops of their voices. I hated Drako' to see this—I knew he'd remember it; I expect he does. I was holding Komon's arm, ready to twist it hard if he tried to break away. Damis and two

136

others were holding on to Aglaos. He stood slack in their hands and spoke with an awful kind of quietness, spoke to hurt. He didn't call me names this time; but I won't tell you what he said all the same. You see, I don't mind it a bit now, I can laugh at it—and it must all have been quite funny. I've washed all the hurt out of my mind. But I can't help remembering the words, though I've tried hard to forget them, and I don't want to say them over again. In fact, what he said was that Ophioneos had been right about me, that I'd made myself—oh well, you can guess well enough the sort of things he said about me and them!

Damis said to me quickly, 'Shall I stop him?' But I shook my head. I just stood, waiting for it to stop, like a wet sheep in a thunder storm. I remembered being so sure I was strong and wise, and I couldn't see just what had happened; somehow all this didn't seem true. And at the end he began to struggle hard and quietly, and pulled one arm loose from Damis.

'Let me go!' he said, 'I'm getting out of here! I'm leaving that woman with you and I wish you joy of her.'

Komon said harshly: 'Let him go!' And Damis and the others dropped him.

He took a couple of paces and stood in front of me; I hoped he would hit me because that would have meant his touching me again, that would have been a possible new beginning. But that wasn't in his philosophy. He just said nothing and hitched his cloak over his arm and walked past me. 'Oh,' I said, 'oh you can't go like that without your breakfast.'

But he went. I heard him stumble on the stones at the head of the path, in the way most new people did, before I moved at all and before anyone moved. Then Komon said suddenly, loudly: 'So we've got you for keeps!'

Then I looked at him, I looked round, I looked at his face flushed, his mouth half open, his hands out towards me, and I watched the eagerness drop out of his face as I stared back at him, not answering as he wanted. Because I knew this wasn't good enough. I hadn't been set free of the old way of life only to get re-entangled in this new one. I saw that Komon was wanting to own me and keep me separate and for himself, just as Aglaos had wanted to, and as I looked round I saw the same thing lighting up the others, and I knew that something was broken and that now they might even fight

137

one another for me. Something had got loose among them which made them stop being comrades and feeling themselves together. I was rather frightened, but not very, because I felt free in myself; in a way their wanting me like that had set me free of them. And I suddenly knew that I had to go, that the kind of thing we had all been together was ended and they couldn't have it again with me, though they might with someone else; and I knew that I had to take on to some other place the thing I had learnt among these men, and above all I had got to show it to Aglaos and to my brother, at whatever pain and difficulty to myself. Although for the moment I knew I rather hated my gang, yet I did feel an intense gratitude towards them, and I knew I'd got to repay them somehow, through others. Of course at the time I didn't intellectualize it so much, yet my mind was working calmly and coolly. As I looked round I saw Damis and it seemed to me that he was less changed than the others. He looked as if he was nearly laughing.

I planned very quickly. I couldn't possibly follow Aglaos myself; I'd have done that alone, but not while nursing a baby. The goats were giving very little milk just now, not nearly enough for her, so I couldn't leave her, and I daren't take her out on to the hills in winter—besides carrying her would have hampered me so that I could never have caught him up. I said to Damis, 'Please get him back. You go.'

Komon gave a jump and caught at my shoulder roughly, swinging me back against the wall of the cave and shouted No! It hurt quite a lot and I didn't hear what Komon and Damis were saying to one another. For a moment I felt nearer despair than I'd done for a long time, but I knew I mustn't show it, I mustn't break at all. And then Damis came to me and asked me if I was quite sure. He looked into my eyes, puzzling, breathing close to me; meeting his eyes, I could only nod, and say in a whisper, 'Hurry.'

Then Damis said, 'I'll get him back for you somehow, Kleta.' And he beckoned two of the others to come with him, one of the helots and a Phrygian, rather a nice man who used to help with the cooking sometimes. And they went out, and I heard their feet quickening to a trot, and Komon came and stood in front of me with his fists clenched, and after a time he slapped me over the cheek and ear with his open hand, hard and stingingly, and if I hadn't been standing against the wall I would have fallen. And some of the others laughed. Then I got their breakfast ready. I wished Damis hadn't gone with nothing in his stomach, but that couldn't be helped now.

None of them said anything to me while they ate, but I didn't really mind; I felt deaf and stupid, partly from being so unhappy and having failed in what I'd meant to do, and partly through being hit. They went out, and I attended to the children. Drako' asked questions for a long time, but I didn't answer him; he got as cross with me as the men were. And the next feed upset Pheidike and made her cry; I expect all that had turned my milk sour. The only one who was nice to me was Phanas. I cried quite a lot that morning. And then about noon Damis and the others came in, treading heavily, carrying Aglaos between them, with his head bleeding and lolling and his eyes shut.

Damis said to me quickly, 'We haven't killed him, we had to knock him out. Heat some water.'

So I did, and Damis and I washed the wound on his head, and bound it up, and by and bye he began to groan and twitch, and then he opened his eyes and vomited. While I cleaned up he watched me; I knew he was watching me, but I didn't want to meet his eyes yet, I wanted to gather myself together to show him everything in one look. But then I heard him in a sick whisper asking Damis for water, and I heard Damis answer him with such definite kindness in his voice that I thought something must be happening; as I turned I saw Damis lifting him to drink, with an arm under his head, and I knew I'd got to let them alone.

It was one of the hardest things I've ever done, going out then. I so wanted to stay and see! I was full of the most violent curiosity about those two men. And also of course I wanted to be the one in the middle of the picture, the one who was to do the healing and joining. But—well, I took and shook my silly, vain she-self, and I picked up my cloak and went right out of the cave, not looking back. The children were all right. Drako' was playing with Phanas; they'd got some sticks and grass, and Pheidike had cried herself to sleep. Anyhow they wouldn't have interfered in the kind of way I would have. I walked up the hill behind the cave and I prayed aloud. I'd rather forgotten the gods; we hadn't really had much use for them in the gang; they weren't our gods—they were lady-goddesses and gentlemen-gods and we used to laugh at them; we had our own living together instead of gods, except that we sometimes tried to get round Luck some way or another. So I don't know quite who or what I prayed to; perhaps it was just that I got my mind fixed and intent and calm. But I walked about the hill for quite a long time, till I knew by the feel of my breasts that I must get back and feed my baby.

When I got to the cave mouth I heard her crying a little, and then I saw Damis walking up and down with her, and Aglaos, lying on the bench with a doubled blanket under his head, was grinning at them. When I came in he turned his head a little and grinned at me and murmured something that I didn't catch, and when I took Pheidike he motioned me with his hand to come and sit beside him while I suckled her. So I sat very close to him, and he didn't say anything, only when Pheidike had half finished and I was shifting her across, I felt certain enough to stoop my head over him and just kiss him very lightly. He whispered my name then and moved a hand; so I touched his fingers with mine and his fingers crooked themselves and held on. And I knew it was all right.

Shall I go on and tell you the rest? Pheidike's not back from her class yet, and you've still got half your seam to finish. For, you see, that was the end and the beginning between Aglaos and me; there wasn't any going back on it after that. But of course it wasn't all. For I hadn't given up my gang or what I'd learnt from them, even when my cheek was bruised stiff from Komon's hand. I wasn't going, just for the sake of that, or just for Aglaos's smile and clasped fingers (though they meant in a way everything lovely to me) to side against them or become only one half of a couple. That wouldn't have helped Aglaos, either.

When the others came back, Damis met them, and he and Komon argued louder and louder in the cave mouth, while I sat beside Aglaos and saw him growing uneasy, frowning and twitching at the quarrelling voices. Then they all came in. I'd cooked their supper. But Komon wouldn't speak to me, nor would some of the others; they talked at me elaborately, meaning to hurt. But I didn't mind much, because Aglaos had gone to sleep and didn't hear, and Damis and two or three of them were friendly. I remember I had rather a bad night of it, because Pheidike was sick and cried, and Aglaos woke up with a touch of fever and a had headache, and the only thing he liked was for me to sit by him, and stroke his face and hands.

The next few days were really very curious. Komon still stayed angry with me and most of them still disliked Aglaos and were suspicious of him. And Aglaos, because he was weak and in pain, was frightened of them and somehow accepted the idea that they were right to dislike him. I found myself shielding him from them just as I'd shielded Komon from him before. But he was beginning to explain himself, to show himself to them, through Damis. He had seen why and how Damis was a good sort of person, and he tried very hard to see it in the others; he made the effort to get inside their skins—and it was an effort. Perhaps he couldn't have done it if he'd been well and strong and confident with all his physical barriers up between him and them. But at last, five or six days later, when he was better and able to walk about, Komon suddenly came up to me and took me by the wrist and half pulled me out of the cave and said, 'He's not too bad after all. You take him if you want to, lass!' And he gave me a great rough hug and a friendly sort of smack behind, and I knew that was all right too.

After that Komon went in and told Aglaos he'd be a fool not to spend the worst of winter with them. I didn't want to influence Aglaos in his answer—in a way I hardly knew which I wanted myself, to stay with them or to be alone again with him—and I pretended to be doing something and didn't look up. But I was very glad when Aglaos agreed that he'd be a fool to go; coming from him, that was what I wanted. And, of course, it was really much better for the children. We had this long journey ahead of us, and we wanted to go part of the way by ship if possible.

Aglaos was shy of the others for quite a long time; it made him very uncomfortable when Komon and Damis laughed at him for not sleeping with me, they said it was a shame if nobody did. But that wasn't difficult to put right. No, it was all rather lovely, nothing badly done, nothing to hide, nothing to be ashamed of. We stayed with them all winter, and in spring we said good-bye and took our bundles and started north with the three children.

FIVE MEN AND A SWAN

THE boys were all sitting round the table in the cabin of the *Highland Mary*. They had their cups of tea and the thick pieces with red jam, the pips of the rasps gritting on their teeth and the tea strong and sweet. They were talking about women. The engineer, who had been in a collier, was telling them about yon place in Cardiff; but they had heard it before. Black Rob was was telling about a girl at one of the bars a wee bit up from the Broomielaw and the man she was with said that was all right, but he had been frightened to do much. You never knew with the Glasgow girls; or maybe you did, and that was the worst.

Willie the cook was not listening. He was reading a piece about the Rangers on the bit newspaper there was on the table. It was an old paper and there were jam stains on it here and there; he could read through them. If he could ever get over to Glasgow on a Friday then he would get to one of the big matches on the Saturday afternoon.

But Black Rob, Johnnie the Ghost and Alec the engineer, who was mostly called Alec Shop, the way his father used to keep the shop at the crossroads after he left the fishing, all went on talking about women, though it was little enough they knew when it came to the bit, and less they had done. For they were mostly all shy in the big towns where people spoke differently, and perhaps it would be an English girl talking quick and rough, and they would not understand her at all, for all they might let on that they did. Johnnie the Ghost had got married to Effie MacDonald in August, and time too; he was not saying much for himself, in case the boys would be laughing at him, and Effie expecting her bairn a while before the New Year. But indeed she was a nice enough girl, though a wee bit homely.

Outside it was rough late afternoon, and the light beginning to go. In another half hour they would need to be starting. The *Highland Mary* had not been a lucky boat at all these last weeks. There had been little herring in it, and the one time they had a good shot, the net had torn below on a reef, and their neighbour boat saying it was their fault. Their neighbour was the *Annie MacQueen*; she had been a Tarbert boat to start with, named after a Tarbert skipper's wife, a fine red-haired woman that had eight bairns and all the boys brought up to the fishing.

The skipper of the *Highland Mary*, who was mostly called Hat, just sat at the end of the table, and first he ate a good lot of bread and butter and jam, and then he told Willie to get the cheese and he ate a good lot of that, and he put four spoonfuls of sugar in his tea, for all this happened a few years back, before the war, and he swilled it round. But he said nothing for a bit. He was a big man and when he left off shaving for a day or two you could see it was a red beard he had on him. All of a sudden he said: 'Stop it, boys!' And they thought that was queer, for Hat was not one to get annoyed with this kind of talk, except it would be a Sunday, which it was not.

So Johnnie the Ghost asked what was the matter, and Hat let out with a great deep groan, the way he might have had a knock on the head. And he put his hand in his pocket and he took out a stiff white feather and laid it down on the table between the jam jar and the cheese. Now the boys all looked at the feather, and it was clear it was a swan's feather, the like of those you might find on the edge of the West Loch when the swans are in. But there was something queer about it, for each one of them had a quick feeling as though what they had been saying was just bairns' talk and blethers and the truth away brighter and bonnier, and nothing at all to do with the girls that could be dirty girls in the bars by the Broomielaw. And even wee Willie the cook stopped his reading and listened, and they all believed in the thing Hat told them he had done.

For it seemed he was walking along by the point one night in the warm weather near two months back; he was coming home from seeing a man that had a cousin in Gourock with a winch he was wanting to sell. The two of them had been late talking, but there was a full moon in it, and Hat was walking back slow looking at the bonny sight the moon made playing on the water, and a sweet south wind coming in gusts now and then and ruffling the tops of the waves the way they would be catching the light. And then in the moon track he caught sight of a girl swimming and it was the long hair she had on her, the kind you are not seeing much these days, and this long shining hair was not shut in a bathing cap, but hanging loose into the water. And as he watched her, he saw she had no bathing dress on her at all and she was playing about in the water, rising her long white arms out of it, the like of a bird.

So first he thought she must be one of the summer visitors and he looked for a rock to hide behind, the way he could watch her closer when she came out. There was a rock and he knelt down, but as he knelt he put his hand onto a thing that was warm and soft, and he thought ah, it was the clothes of her he had and maybe he could be tricking her a wee bit. But when he held them up in the moonlight to look at, he saw it was no woman's dress, but the feathers of a white swan, a woman's shape of feathers.

Now, Hat was a man that took things as they came, and he had been a skipper fifteen years, and his wife died a while back, leaving him with one lassie that was away training to be a nurse and another lassie at school yet; but the school lassie would be asleep in the back room now. So Hat took up the swan's dress and away with it to his house, and when he looked over his shoulder, there, as he had thought, was the Swan herself coming up out of the water wet and white, and her black hair dripping behind her, and cried on him to drop her dress.

There are plenty of men who would have found that an awesome thing, and so it seemed to the boys round the cabin table; and plenty would have dropped the shape of feathers there and then, and run for it. But not Hat.

He took a tight grip of the feathers and walked on, and every time he looked back the Swan herself was nearer and calling to him, and oh it was a bonny sweet voice she had. And when he was at his own door she was just by him, and he tucked the feathers under his arm and opened the door with one hand and pulled her in after him with the other.

He laid the feathers down on the bed and he lighted the lamp and held it up and looked close at the Swan. She was in every way like a young girl, he told them, but only this, that where women mostly all have hair growing on them she had the wee white feathers. And when you put your fingers on them one way they were smooth and cool, but when you ran your fingers under they were warm and soft the way swansdown is. She was dry now and she kept looking at the feather dress and asking for it back in thon sweet voice that almost melted the heart in him, for she seemed as young as his own lassie, younger than his wife had been at the time they were courting and away bonnier. And indeed, said Hat, he had only meant to keep the Swan a short, short time to look fully at her and maybe to have her on his knee for a while, but not to be spoiling her. But when he had

144

got her on his knee right, he needed to be holding her there, and one thing led to another and he went just a hairsbreadth too far with the Swan. And the third time he went too far with the Swan that night, he was that sleepy afterwards, and when he woke the Swan was away and her dress with her and it was cold morning.

But the Swan had told him that once a month on the Saturday of full moon she was under a necessity to swim in the water off the point, and she must leave her feather dress among the rocks. So he knew he was bound to go back for her in a month's time.

The skipper stopped speaking then, and Black Rob asked quick had he done that, and Hat said Aye, he had gone, but this was the way of it. He had gone down that Saturday night to the point and he had heard her laughing and he had smelt the smell of her that was partly the smell of a woman's body and breath, and partly the oily queer smell of a swan, and maybe that sounded not just right, yet it was a thing that had stayed in his nostrils ever since. But he had seen neither her nor her dress, and it was borne in upon him that he would never see her again.

Then Black Rob said: 'It will be time again in three days.' For it was near the October moon. And he looked at the skipper and his tongue licked at his lips.

'It is not myself will stop you from going,' said Hat, 'but it is no luck she has brought me.' And that was true enough surely, since it was in these last weeks that the *Highland Mary* and the *Annie MacQueen* had been getting the bad fishings when other pairs were doing well enough. And Hat said low to the rest of his crew that it was because he could not think right now. Any time when he should be looking at the land for the marks, or asking himself was it a right bottom where they were, there would come a thing like the flap of a swan's wing across his mind, and he would be left all in a maze and not able to ack quick as a skipper should.

By now it was dusk. Alec Shop went off to start up the diesel; wee Willie got the tea things washed and redded up in the cabin. Behind the grey of the low clouds the moon was after rising. Dougie shouted over from their neighbour boat where the engine was starting up too. But on the *Highland Mary* the boys were all thinking of thon woman with the wee white feathers on her, except for Willie the cook, and he was thinking that it could not be fair how they worked the football pools, for he had been going in for them these three years back and never once got anything out of them, and if you added up the sixpenny postal orders he had sent off it was fair staggering.

Again that night they had poor fishings and so for the rest of the week. If they had a ring at all there would only be a scatter of fish in it, and the herring boat giving them bottom prices, so that there were only shillings to share out at the end of the week. But Black Rob was caring little. He washed and shaved and put a bit brilliantine on his hair that was wavy like a black retriever dog's, and he put on a clean white shirt and his best Sunday suit, and off he went on the Saturday night to the point and whatever was there for him.

There she was, sure enough, and there behind a rock was the shape of feathers, and the October moon white on it, and Black Rob warmed his hands in it, and it was more than his hands were warming, and when the Swan came up out of the water Black Rob caught hold of her, for he was never one for beds and houses when there was bracken on the braeside. And the more the Swan cried out, the more Rob was not caring at all what he did with her. And he made her promise he would see her again at the next full moon.

Not one of them said a thing on Sunday and who would be asking Black Rob what kind of thoughts he was having at sermon time. But on the Monday they all asked him, and he said Aye, it was so, and laughed a bit. But Hat was angry all the week, and an angry skipper makes poor fishing, forby a white wing blinding his mind at the time he needs his judgment quickest.

So another month went by, and in November Black Rob put on his best suit again and off to the point. And he saw the Swan indeed by frosty moonlight. But that was all there was to it. For he could not anyway lay hands on her feather dress. Black Rob came home with his good coat torn and himself cut and bruised, the way he was running about and bashing himself against the rocks, and that Sunday he was not at the morning service nor yet the evening.

Now it was mostly Rob who was at the wire in the *Highland Mary*, and he had a quick and certain feel of it, but now it seemed he had lost that altogether, and though they might be ringing, it was for nothing but a scatter of herring or a ball of mackerel, and the rest swearing at Black Rob and he swearing back at them. And the noise they made would be skipping across the water until one of the Lamlash skippers who was a gey religious man, bid them be quiet for fear a vengeance would come on the whole fleet.

But when it came on to December, Alec Shop had a thought of all this. He said: 'You will all be taking her the wrong way. How were you not saying you would marry her? It is this marrying that the lasses are always after.'

'Who would be marrying a swan?' says Black Rob. 'It is eggs she would be laying on you!' And that was not all he said, for he had a great hatred and anger at the Swan for the trick she had played on him.

But Alec wiped his hands that were all filed with the diesel oil, 'I would be marrying her,' says he, 'for I am thinking breakfast would be easy come by with only the bacon to be got!' And then he says: 'The first time I was after seeing yon feather it came in my mind to marry the lass, and I will have my witnesses waiting, and I am telling you this, Black Rob, she will be keeping my house for me and never a thought in the head of her but for the way she will be pleasing me best. And I am telling you another thing, it is not you will be speaking to my wife of anything that may have passed!'

Now Black Rob made an answer to that, and it was none of the best, and Alec gave him as good as he got, for he had found the trick for it, working in the south. And the skipper laughed, for he was cold angry at Rob over what had happened, though he was not saying it, being an older man. But Black Rob answered again, and Alec caught up a spanner, and there were the two of them fighting. And before the rest could get them out of it, they were cut and sore, and Alec had his shoulder knocked against the corner of the wheel-house, so that he could hardly get lifting his arm for four days afterwards, and Black Rob's hair full of blood from the spanner. And Hat was going from one to the other saying he would need to give them their books if they could not be behaving themselves.

But the way it worked out just before the full moon, the engine had a breakdown and, Swan or no Swan, Alec needed to stay by the boat and work on her, all the more because Dougie and the rest of the boys on the *Annie MacQueen* were not pleased at all with the way things had been going, and indeed there was talk of them looking for another neighbour. So Alec was cursing and swearing, but stay he must, and wee Willie the cook stayed with him to help work on the engine. But he had a packet of Wild Wests with him, for next to football what Willie liked best was a book with six-shooters and all that in it.

Effie MacDonald was near her time, and there was her mother and her aunties for ever in and out the house, and it was no place at all for Johnnie the Ghost and they casting their looks at him. So the night of the full moon he slipped out, but before he went he took a wee nip, and after he got clear of the houses he took another. For he was a man that had a trick of seeing some kind of frightening appearances, and that was the way he got his by-name.

When he was half-way to the point he took another nip, for he was feeling the wee-est bit shoogly about the knees, and by the time he was there he had all the courage in the world and had forgotten there was ever such a girl as Effie MacDonald. And he seemed to have everything right clear and arguable in his head and shooting up from one moment to the next the same as a fountain. And he was asking himself how could the Swan not be saying sweet words to a man as personable and noble as himself? But what at all happened when he saw the Swan and what he was doing to her, were not clear any longer, and there was a blackness cutting into his mind, and there was a screeching and groaning that first seemed to be the Swan and then all of a sudden was his wife Effie with her time come on her, and he standing in the door of his own house looking over at the bed. And as he stood he grew cold and vomited, and Effie's mother gave him one push out that landed him in a rosebush, and when it was morning and Effie's bairn come into the world, he found himself covered with scratches and vomit and ashamed to go into his own house and wash.

So he went to the spring behind and took his coat off and washed. And there were white feathers and swansdown in under his shirt and every place, and whenever he saw a bit of it a deep sadness came on him and he took the bottle out of his pocket and drank again, the way he could forget that he had forgotten all he needed so sore to remember. He was not back on the boat that week, and he was not sober one day of it. And that was the hardest for Effie, and there are plenty skippers would never have taken him back at all, but Hat knew fine what had come to him, and at the end of the week Johnnie went back. But he was an ill man to have to do with for long enough after that, and Effie was right glad always when he went off on the Monday.

Then it was New Year, and those were the days that folk kept it as it should be kept. And after New Year Alec Shop began to make his plans. He lived in the shed at the back of his mother's house, where she and his aunties were; and he asked his two witnesses to be at the shed that Saturday night. And one of them was his own brother and the other was his skipper, for Hat was thinking that they needed to deal with the Swan some way, or there would never be any luck at all for the *Highland Mary*, and if this was to be the way of it and Alec to be the man, well then, he would rather be helping than hindering, and maybe when the Swan was another man's wife he would be able to give over thinking of her and could turn his mind to the fishing again.

Alec got in a cake and a bottle of sweet port wine, the kind that they were telling him the ladies would like, and he put a new red cloth with fringes on the table and a mug with some snowdrops, and he put his budgie-cage into the window, with the two budgies that his aunties looked after for him during the week. And he redded up everything in the shed, and he got sweeping up the cigarette ends and throwing them on the back of the fire, and forby that he took out the dirty photos that he had got in the south and that he had in the foot of one of his old sea-boots so that his aunties would not get seeing them, and he threw then onto the fire without so much as looking at them again. He was doing all this in a regular and quiet kind of way, the way an engineer would be getting on with a job, and then it got to be evening, and he polished up the lamp and put a new wick in it: and he had bought a pink shade for it with kind of lacey trimming, the way he thought a woman would have her eye pleasantly caught by it.

And then he started to wash and he whistling to himself, and the budgies chirping and rustling. And then all of a sudden he caught sight of himself in the bit looking-glass over the basin. And he fell to wondering what will the Swan say to me, and will the Swan have me at all? And he had never-ever thought of it that way in all his life, for the girls in Cardiff or Glasgow are taking a man's money even if the man is dead ugly, and the dirty photos will look back at you the same way whoever you are, and when it comes to a dance you are mostly all thinking more of the music and of the dancing itself than of your partner, anyway in the hard dances and those were the kind Alec liked best himself.

But now he stared hard at the face in the looking-glass and

149

thought what is this odd face I have on me that I have never studied it at all? And he could not tell what a woman would be thinking of it, nor whether a woman would like the colour of his eyes that were grey blue with a darker ring round them, and he wished now he had his teeth white and not all stained with the smoking. And he thought maybe she will not have me in marriage at all, maybe there is only one thing to be done with the Swan and that is what Hat and Black Rob and Johnnie the Ghost have done, and it is not a lucky thing at all, but if it is bad luck she is bringing on us, then that is the luck we must take. And yet, he thought, the way I am thinking on the Swan now, it is not that way I want her, but somehow else. And he fell to studing how it would make all the difference if he and the Swan were married, but he could not see right yet how it was, and his heart beating at full speed with the difficult thoughts he had.

But while he was on that, and putting the comb through his hair so it would stay flat down, in came his brother and his skipper. His brother was wearing his kilt, for he was in the Gaelic choir, and the skipper was in his best suit, with the hat he had for weddings and funerals, and a Bible in his hand. So Alec said: 'You will wait in the back room until the time I am calling for you,' and he set candles for them there.

Then he put on his coat and he was shaking a bit, and Hat looked him over and then took up some few of the snowdrops and put them in his button hole. And by now the moon was risen, so he went on his way to the point.

For a little he had the feeling that there was no truth at all in any of this, that there would be nothing at the point but air and moonshine and the cold beating of waves. And he wished he had a bottle with him, for he was dead sober and shivering. But then he came to the rocks and looked out, and his heart turned over on him, for there she was, and in a little he came on the shape of feathers, and he took it up and began to walk back, looking over his shoulder for her to follow. And follow she must, wet and shining and sweet-voiced, and he saw it was all true, and for a short time he felt himself near to doing what Black Rob had done, for she was so bonny, and he needed to touch her and have her, the same way a sad man might be needing the whisky, for it would mean the breaking of a black and hard and terrible thing in himself. It would mean light and life and an escaping. But he walked on and she at his elbow, and he trying not to look at her too often, and she asking, asking for her feathers back. So he said: 'Marry me, lassie, and you shall have your dress again.'

And she said: 'Much good it would be to you, Alec, to have a wife only at the full moon!'

And he said: 'I would rather a night of you, lassie, than four weeks of any other woman in the whole of Scotland!' And then he said: 'It is only week-ends I am home, anyway, so I would be seeing you one time in four, and maybe,' he went on, 'if we were up north at Mallaig or Castlebay itself, or on the East Coast, you would be coming to me on your wings?'

'You would need to keep faith to me, Alec,' says the Swan, 'and never-ever to lay hands on me to be hurting me, for indeed I have been sore hurt the way it was with the rest of your crew, and I will tell you, Alec, what it was your skipper did to me, forby Black Rob and Johnnie—'

'You will not be telling me!' says Alec quick and hard. 'For I could not bear it at all. And indeed and indeed, lassie, you will keep yourself quiet and you will not be looking at me too much until after we are married, for I cannot know what I will do and you are over bonny for the like of me or for any of us poor souls, but if you will have me I will do anything in the wide world for you.' And a great shame came over Alec, thinking how they were only poor fishermen, with no education beyond the age of fourteen and no chances at all, and some years there would be little herring in it and if any pair did well then the rest would be angry at them and jealous, and if at any time there was plenty of herring, then the buyers would get together and force the prices down, or maybe they would be needing to dump their catch at Ayr, and there was no way out of it at all for the fishermen, and what kind of man was he to think he could be marrying such a bonny one as the Swan? And he wiped his sleeve across his eyes because of the shame he was in, and the tears that had come on him so sudden, and there was the Swan with her arms round him and her long wet hair and her cheeks yet cold from the sea, but softer and kinder than anything Alec had ever known. But he sprang away from her, for he saw the light of the lamp in the window of his shed, and he was remembering the clean cloth and the cake that had not been cut and the glasses that were dry and polished and the bed that had not been rumpled; and when he came

151

to the door he shut his eyes and he lifted the Swan in over the threshold and took his hands from her quick. Then he said: 'I will call my witnesses and we will be married now at once, and later on I will be going to the Sheriff's Court to pay the fine on it, but all the same this will be as lawful a marriage as any in Scotland.'

And she smiled at him and said: 'Are your witnesses to see your wife naked, Alec?'

And he said: 'I would not like that at all, but if I give you the feathers back, you will not fly away on me, lassie? For if you did that I am thinking I would lie down and die.'

And she did not answer, but she smiled at Alec again. And it went dancing through him like an electric current running through wires when the starter makes its contact, and he gave her the feathers without a word and she held them to her, and she began to change into a bird, and he cried at her: 'Stop, stop, lassie!'

And she stopped, the way her face and hands were clear of the feathers and as for the rest of her, there was a kind of swaying in that room, so that sometimes she was a bird with the high cold breast of a swan, and the great wings starting back, and sometimes she was a woman in a white shining wedding dress. And Alec called in his witnesses and took her hand and said aloud before his brother and his skipper that they were man and wife. And the Swan was saying the same in thon sweet and bonny voice she had.

There was a kind of daze and enchantment on them all, and Hat was standing stiff and staring at the Swan, with a tight grip on his Bible; and Alec's brother was looking on the floor where the lamp light was running shadows in the cracks between the boards, and his hands fidgeting at the chain of his sporran and a singing in his ears. And then Alec and the Swan had their hands together on the knife, cutting the cake, and Hat opened the bottle of port wine, and for a little there was the circle of lamp light on cake and glasses and hands, and the white clean feathers reaching up the back of a girl's fingers, the way a long sleeve would, and moving with her. And then Alec said low to the witnesses that they could be going and he would surely see them in the morning on their way to the kirk, and he with his wife on his arm. And they went out and they said nothing to one another, but Hat could not get seeing in his mind at all how yon swan-winged and snowy woman could be walking the kirk road with Alec, and all the old wives staring at her.

But Alec turned to take the Swan in his arms, now they were married and alone, and there was a fire and a hurry in him, and his hands were seeking for the flesh of her under the feathers. But it was not a right woman's shape he was holding to, and as he caught at her she swept out with an arm or a wing and the lamp went over. He jumped at it and threw the rug on the burning oil and tramped on the flames and had it out before it had set the shed on fire. And then he pulled the curtains back and the moonlight came lapping in. And then he saw that the feather shape had closed over the face and hands of the Swan, and it was a great bird he had with him and no woman at all.

Then Alec let out a great screech and seized hold of the bird, and the long supple neck of it came down beside his own as it might have been her arm round his neck when he had wept coming back from the point, and he knew fine it was her somewhere and he cried out: 'Lassie, lassie, where are you at all?'

And he battered with his face and fingers against the bird as though it were something between him and his lassie. And it seemed to him as though she must be within the feather shape, and all at once he pulled out his knife and opened it with one hand and his teeth, holding all the time with the other hand onto the bird's wing where it joined the shoulder, and he struck with the knife to open a hole in the feather dress and tear it away from her. But when he struck, a terrible skirl came from the Swan and the wings beat at his head and knocked him clean over, and he was left on the floor in a flurry of feathers and blows and broken glass where at last the Swan had burst her way through the window and out.

All night Alec lay there on the floor and the fire died on the hearth and in the early morning rain blew in through the broken window, and he turned about and moaned and opened his eyes in the dark, and he was alone and hurt. And when it was right light he sat up, and there was the open knife and blood on it. And Alec went to the table with the cut cake and the glasses and he leaned his forehead on it and he wept, and there he was when Hat came back and knocked on the door of the shed.

Alec told Hat the way things had been, and old Hat nodded and said he had best be taking a good dram, even it if was Sunday morning. But Alec said no, no. And then he said he must look for another berth and maybe not in a fishing boat at all and not among the kindly folk of the West coast, but on the East or maybe in England itself.

Hat said would he not wait for the next full moon, but Alec said: 'No. I have broken my promise to the Swan and I cannot see how she will ever forgive me, and maybe I have killed her, and there is no good in me at all.'

'There is not that much good in any of us,' said Hat, 'and I will be sorry to lose you, Alec, and I wish I had never set eyes or hands on this damned woman or bird, for she has brought bad luck on every man of us!'

'She is my wife,' Alec said, 'and I do not even know what name she has. I was thinking to find all that out after we had been to bed.' And he fell to shivering, and his head ached from the blow he had got from her.

So on Monday Alec went off to Greenock to find a new berth, and Hat was needing to see about a new engineer for the *Highland Mary*, and it was a heavy heart he had on him. The fishing was no better at all, and Dougie on the *Annie MacQueen* saying he would try to get another neighbour. None of the boys said a word in front of the new engineer, and when it got round to full moon again, none of them said a word either, and it was a wild night that was in it that Saturday, and Johnnie the Ghost and Black Rob went off in the bus to the pictures and the whisky, though it was little enough they had got on the share-out, and Johnnie should have been letting Effie have the lot of it, for she was needing to get credit at the shop and that is not the best for a woman with a wee bairn. And Hat sat at home with his school lassie and she learning off her psalm and he reading in the Book of Revelations to try and take his mind off what it was for ever on.

Then on the Monday afternoon the new engineer was down the hatch oiling the engine and wee Willie was making the tea for the rest, and when they were all sitting to, Willie says, 'I saw the Swan on Saturday.'

'You!' says the lot of them.

'And what for no?' says Willie.

'Well,' says the skipper at last, 'how did it go, Willie?'

'It went fine,' he said.

'How?' says Black Rob and Johnnie together, and their voices snapped like two dogs wanting to fight.

154

'Well,' says Willie, 'I met her down on the shore the way all the boys did, and I went off home with her coat and she after me as bare as a plucked hen.'

'And so?' says Black Rob.

'She asked me what it was I wanted of her,' Willie says and goes to fill up the tea pot.

Just then the new engineer came down and Hat began quick speaking with him about the weather and the way the herring were shifting their ground, and the other two were eating their pieces and glaring at wee Willie. He stood up with the kettle in his hand. 'I told her I was after filling in the names of the football pool,' says he, 'and would she get helping me; for I thought maybe she might have some kind of knowledge and would be bringing me luck, and at least she could not be bringing me worse luck than I have been having, and she said Aye she would tell me the right names to put down. So that was the way the two of us were spending our time.'

'Are you telling me the whole of it?' says Black Rob low.

'Aye, surely,' says Willie, 'and it took us all of two hours, what with the information she was giving me about the teams, and indeed I am thinking she knows more than the newspapers themselves. And I have the forms in the post now!'

The new engineer said women were no good on football though he had known some could pick a horse. But it worked out the way wee Willie had said, and it was five hundred pounds he got out of the pools, and his photo in the paper grinning, because the Swan had given him all the names right. And Hat said this had changed the luck and he was praising up wee Willie. And indeed things went better for the *Highland Mary* for the few weeks that were left in the season.

But it was not that good for Willie himself. His father took the half of the money and had it invested the way Willie could not get touching it; but with the rest he took to the betting. Maybe the Swan could have guided him right there too, but he had no skill in it himself, and he was off at Glasgow the next full moon. Then he started to lose the money and the next thing was he was away spending what was left of it all April when the boats were lying up, and he got into bad company. And if it had not been for him losing the money so quick he would have ended up in the jail. But he came back to the *Highland Mary* the next season and there was no more talk of the Swan one way or the other.

So a year and a day went by, and months and weeks, and Alec wrote home to his mother and his aunties, and sometimes he would be one place and sometimes another, but never coming back. And the truth was he was homesick enough; he did not like the food or the weather in the south; there seemed to him to be neither seriousness in the folk nor yet a right gaiety. But he could not come back, because it was not in him to forget the Swan and, whatever way you looked at it, he was married to her by Scots law, and both his brother and his skipper agreed to that. And if he went with a woman now, he could not do it sober, and there was little pleasure he got out of it, and nothing but shame and sorrow on him afterwards.

But at home the fishing would be worse and then it would be better, and then came the war. Wee Willie was the first to register, and then the new engineer who was a young chap. Then the *Highland Mary* was requisitioned and Black Rob and Johnnie needing to get berths where they could until the time came for them to register. But Alec volunteered as an engineer, and he was put into an east coast patrol boat. He liked it well enough, better than he had done anything for all this last while. They were mostly all English and Irish in that boat, but there were two Scots forby himself, and the pay was good enough, and he had his photo taken in his uniform to send home. But one of this aunties was dead by then. And it was new budgies they had in his old cage.

Then, on a clear day and out of the eye of the sun, a bomber came down on them. Alec was below most of the time and it sounded the way hell sounds. Then a bomb came through one of the hatches and there was Alec trying to do a dozen things at the once, and in the middle of it he saw his overalls were on fire, and he beat them out, and someone shouted to him to come up, and he saw that his right hand was bleeding all over the iron rungs of the ladder though he could feel nothing at all in it yet, and first he was in a boat and then after the next explosion he was in the sea and swimming, but he did not think he would be able to keep it up for long, the way he was.

And then there was something under him, holding him up so he could rest himself from swimming, and he seemed to let go, and life went dark on him for awhile. Then he woke clear up, and he was in pain, but most of all he wondered where he was, for he was not lying

156

on any plank or raft or hard thing. And he put his left hand down to feel, and it was feathers was in it, and he knew he was on the back of a swan. And after a bit he said: 'Are you nor wearied, my darling?'

'Aye,' said the Swan, 'but we are near land, Alec.'

And soon enough they were in shallow water and a sandy bottom, and he waded to shore, steadying himself by the Swan's lifted wing. But when they had made their way beyond high tide mark, Alec shook at the knees and he could not get any further, but he lay down on the sand and said to the Swan that it was dying he was.

'It is only cold you are and hurt and hungry,' said the Swan. 'But take you off your wet clothes, Alec, and let them dry.'

So Alec sat up and began to strip off his things, and his hands and everything covered with oil and blood; and he saw that the bonny whiteness of the Swan was smeared here and there with it, and he said, 'I have dirtied you, my dearie.'

But the Swan said—and oh, the sweet gentle voice she had on her and not like an English voice at all: 'You are my man, Alec. I am thinking nothing of it. And do you not be so shy to be taking off your things in front of me, Alec, for we are married by Scots law and there is no getting out of it.'

So Alec said: 'My darling, did I hurt you that time?'

'Aye,' said she, 'I bear the mark of it yet.'

By now the Swan was beside him on that English beach, and she brooding over him and he burrowing with his hands and face under the smooth top feathers of her and into the warm down that kept the sand and the hard English air out of the hurts on him. 'I did that to you,' he said, 'and I was not faithful to you. I broke my promise all round and every way.'

'Aye,' said she, 'but it is over and I am your wife, Alec.'

So they lay quiet for a time and he half asleep and happy the way he had forgotten one could be happy. Then the Swan said to him: 'I am hearing the Home Guards up in the dunes, Alec, and I must be leaving you.'

'No!' he said, and held onto her.

'You will get six weeks' leave out of this, Alec,' said she, 'and there will be two full moons in it.'

'And after that?' said Alec.

'Ach,' she said, 'it is the war now and which one of us can see more than the two moons ahead?' And with that she rose out of his arms, and a few minutes later the Home Guards came running, and one of them asking Alec had he seen a parachute, for they had seen some great white thing flapping in the sky and were minded to shoot at it. But Alec laughed a bit and said: No, no, and then he said to the man that was helping him: 'How much leave will I get out of this?'

'You will get six weeks easy,' the man said. And Alec laughed again, and they all thinking that the Scots were a queer lot entirely and no-one in the south could ever see what they would be after at all.

THE HUNTING OF IAN OG

AFTER the long spell of wet weather there was, it had turned fine at last. The mists were lifting and the sun beginning to bring out the smell of everything, honey-sweet on the high hills, but bad enough round the castle rocks: the smell of human dirt: the smell of bait and old sheep-skins and what the women had thrown out in the hopes the high tide would take it, and now above everything the choking, burnt smell from the out-buildings and byres. You could forget it a while in the wet weather: not now. Young Ian was suddenly and horribly sick of it: the smell of the old burning and the faces of the women who had been there that time, and the draggled way they walked and looked now. There had been no dancing all the summer and little enough of the food and drink itself, with all the beasts gone. So young Ian was walking out across the scorched ground to where he could smell the heather, and then he said he would be off to the hill to bring them back a stag.

'We could be doing with that meat, Ian Og,' his mother said, 'but do you be careful now.' And she looked up at the hills, and her body twitched under the plaid and her face screwed and crumpled. She had been an island MacDonald; one's own island had been safe. Ever since the first years of her marriage, this other thing had been hanging over her. After twenty years it had come. And her man and young Ian and the rest had been away in the boats, down at the great feast there had been at Dunaverty, and she had been alone with the old men and the women to face it, and she had not been able, either by luck or by courage, to do one thing to stop what had happened. And it had happened to her own Isbail as well as to the other lassies. And it did not seem likely that there would ever be the chance of doing anything that would wipe it all out in blood. Though she knew well enough what she would do if she had one of them, even, where she could do it. He would be sorry. In front of the lassies she would do it with her own hands. Waking and sleeping, working and praying, she had thought about it; she had spoken her mind to her man and to young Ian and they had agreed; she would have the right to do anything at all.

She rocked herself about; she shuffled her feet on the blackened stones. Young Ian knew what was in his mother's mind; she kindled his own anger. Some day he would get to the other side, he would

159

come down on them, those others of his own clan who had done this thing, and he not there. Aye, that would be fine. A sober and satisfying and steady killing it would be. And the burning of that castle of their's and the driving of their cattle. But it could not be yet: not this year anyway. And the full shame to come on the lassies when the months were up. Ach, it did not bear thinking about at all. He wondered if he would know one of those others at first sight. There were times they had met. At the gathering on Islay two years back, but the thing had not ripened to bursting then, it was still a matter of angry songs and words used the way of arrows. Donal Bàn had been there, older than he was himself, stronger, richer, cleverer at the twisting of words. Thinking of Donal Bàn, his mind darkened as though a heavy rain cloud might be coming up over it, his hand fretted at his sword. At least he would kill a stag now.

He shouted to his sister for a clean shirt; she gave him one anxiously, asking him not to tear it; there were not so many in it now, and no wool at all for the making of new ones. He put it on, and twisted the plaid round his body, pleating the end round his hips into a kilt, belting it into place. He crossed the strips of soft deer skin round his legs and laced on his own brogues. His mother and sister and the rest were watching him. 'When I have the stag killed,' he said, 'I will light a fire, and you be looking out for it.' He had meal in his sporran; he could make a bannock with that and deer's blood. Some of the boys wanted to come with him, for there was little enough sport for them now; but he needed to be alone.

The river was low. He crossed by the stones, lightly. In the field beyond, the barley was tall and green, yellowing just that much already. The burning had been too early in the year to hurt the crops. But it was when you came to think of the sheep and cattle and the little horses, and they not in the fields any longer, nor yet in the summer grazings above: then the black anger came, jagging at you, making you glad you were armed, making you sorry it was not more than a stag you were after.

The women, watching him, saw young Ian leap the dike between field and wild hills, the way a deer might have cleared it. But the pride they should have had in him was all scarred with their own shame and hate, that the bonny weather of midsummer was only making the worse. Isbail looked after him awhile with the dumb envy against her brother going lightly up the hill, and then with a

160

sick hunger on her for the red meat he would be bringing. But young Ian did not look back. He went on up. Some day he and his men would be going this way, on a wild night it might be, and silent, and up across the marshes and the flat, high hummocky land with the peat holes, the wee dark hell-mouths, ill enough to walk among, and then down; and then they would be doing that thing which would clear the sky again; and there would be the pipes and the blood and the hot anger loose at last; and he would bring back fair Donald—tied with the bow-strings—for whatever his mother would do on him for her own avenging and the avenging of the lassies—and an ending of fair Donald's pride and boasting! Thinking this way, young Ian began to sing, their own song that they had not had the heart for these last months. And, as he went on and up, he was singing all the time, and all kinds of songs, for he was a good one at the singing. And now he was far up from the river and the sea itself. The glen was away down on his right, deep green with the rounded heads of the oaks and the thick hazel between them. But where he was, it was all heather and the hot honey smell of it and the sound the bees were for ever making, the swinging sound that would set you singing low in time to it.

Now he began to watch for the tracks. He went quietly. The singing had eased him. What he wanted the death of now was no man but a stag, a piece of meat, good eating. The yew bow in his hand made him feel its need of an arrow; he whispered now and then to his bow—soon, soon it would be time. Soon he would be dropping quick to the moss, crawling and hiding, the sweetness of the heather closing over him, keeping him secret until he was close enough, until the bow could speak to the stag. He watched for signs of birds moving, listened for slight ripples of sound, the stamp of a hoof or the tearing of grass. He came cautiously and soft-footed between rocks to the opening of a corrie, and up on the sky-line saw birds wheeling, and stiffened, and asked himself what was it, maybe a deer hurt, and thought he would go softly and see.

The corrie led up to the tops, to the march and the peat holes. Already there were wide black cracks in the heather, sometimes to be crossed, very cannily, and making sure the foot would not sink too far when the weight came on it, and sometimes to be worked round. The lips of heather and hard deer grass overhung the black peat. If one were in the peat and sinking one would see that edge with the

161

blossom and sun on it, the very same way the edge of heaven can be seen out of hell. Young Ian was near the head of the corrie now. He went on hands and knees. He made for a mound of rock and heather that there was and looked round it. He saw no deer, but a man lying beside one of those cracks, and the brogue off one foot of him and the foot and ankle swelled and bruised looking, and smears of black from the peat on his arms and face and everywhere, the way it was clear he had fallen and hurt his leg and could not walk. Young Ian stood up and the man saw him and shouted a gathering cry on him, and it was a MacDonald cry surely, but not their own cry—it was the cry of the far side of the march, Donal Bàn's men's cry.

Young Ian took three steps forward and he answered with their own cry, and his voice was as cruel and mocking to the other one as the voice of the wheeling birds had been; and the other one, who had for a moment thought he had sight of life again, now knew it would be death, the way things were between the two sides of the clan, but he got his sword drawn and he twisted round onto one knee and one foot, and the anger that was in him swept out the pain in his leg, and at least it was better to die this way than the other.

Young Ian laid his bow down and laughed. This was his stag then! And he was wondering which of them it was, for it was a fine shirt and kilt the man had on him, and the brooch at his shoulder with a yellow stone in it, so that it was no common man he was, surely, and ach, the fine sword he had—I will have that, young Ian thought, it is a better sword than my own, it is from the south it comes, I must knock it out of his hand cleverly, so that it will not be broken. So that was how he went for it, to give the hurt man a knock on the wrist, the way he must drop the sword. And the hurt man knew that too, and he was guarding against it, and the dagger was in his other hand, for neither of the two of them had their targes on them. The hurt man was the better swordsman of the two, but what chance had he at all the way things were, and the pain and sweat he was in, and the other dancing round him, and soon enough young Ian got in the heavy crack on his sword arm so that he lost all feeling in it for a moment, and the sword was loosened from his hand and Ian's sword twisted against the guard on the hilt, twisted it away from him, and then they closed and in another minute it was all over, and the dagger knocked away from him too.

Young Ian stood up and stretched in the sun, and the smell of the

162

heather went right down into him with the deep breaths he was taking, and he had that bonny great sword, and the dagger with the silver mounts. He picked up the sword and looked at it; and it was the way he had thought, it had the mark of Ferrara and the running wolf on it, and it was the great pleasure he had holding it and running it through his fingers, and the man whose sword it had been watching him.

He took the spare bow string out of his sporran and went back to the man, and the man struggled and tried to fight with his bare hands, but young Ian hit him across the eyes and the man let out a screech on that, which was another great pleasure to Ian, for it was the first sign he had got out of the man. So Ian got him the way he wanted, and tied his wrists behind him with the bow string; and again it was the great pleasure for Ian to feel the man's body under his knee. The man was bleeding here and there and Ian had a cut on his own arm that he noticed now for the first time, but it did not hurt him at all. He stood over the man, the way he could kick him where it would hurt most, and the man doubled his one knee up to stop him, but his other foot was dragging, and suddenly Ian was angry that the man was not whole, but had this hurt foot, so it had been no fair fight. If it had been a fair fight it would have been away better. And then for a time he did not know what he was going to do with the man now he had him tied, and he wished he had killed him, and his thoughts churned and tumbled in him like a rough sea over rocks.

The hurt man looked up at Ian; bad it had been and worse was to come. And the years of living he would not have now! But the pain of his torn muscle and sprained ankle, and the steady bite of the bow string on his wrists, and the hurts on his face and body, were putting out all thought and he wished he was right dead and out of it all. Often he was making up to himself proud deaths in battle and the skirling of the pipes and the keening of the women. But it would not be like that.

Ian went off and found water and got himself a drink and washed his hands and face. It was mid afternoon now and the water was not right cold; it was a green trickle amongst brown slime and thick mosses, creeping under the sunlight. Ian lay and played with it for a time. He saw a blue hare slip between two rocks a bit below him and thought he must find some beast to shoot, and then he thought of the stag he had got, the man with the sword that was away finer than any stag's antlers. And he thought I will go and look at him again.

So back he went and the man was still lying there just the way he had been, but his eyes were shut. 'What is the name you have on you?' said Ian suddenly. The man opened his eyes and said nothing. 'Speak!' said Ian, and went over to him. The man said nothing; if the man could do it at all, he was going to stop the pleasure Ian was having. Ian saw that and he saw the only way to make the man speak was to hurt him. But he did not want to do that, now he had been away from him, playing with the water. He did not want to spoil his stag.

He sat comfortably in the heather, regarding the man, and the sun beat down, and the man twisted his head about because of the sweat and the flies. 'There is a wee burn yonder where I have been,' said Ian, 'cool it is, and fresh.' And almost at once the man's lips drew back from his teeth and he whispered 'Water'. 'Tell me what name is on you,' said Ian. But the man said nothing.

Ian went to the water and took his horn cup full of it and brought it back. 'Look,' he said. The man looked, surely, he wriggled his body towards the water. 'The name,' said Ian, and began to spill the water in sight of the man. He threw the last drops in his face. Still the man was not speaking, but he might speak yet.

Ian walked off whistling. He was going to try again. When he was back, the man had rolled over onto his face; he was half in the peat crack again. It was as though he were trying to burrow away into the ground between the roots. Ian took him by the shoulders and pulled him out; his face was mostly all peat stained now and he was crying; he could not stop; he sobbed under Ian's hands. He put an arm under the man's shoulders and held the cup for him to drink. Then he took a handful of moss and rubbed it over the man's face, wiping away the mud. The skin was hot and red under it. Ian fetched another cup of water and the wet moss that was all along the trickle. The man was bruised round his eyes; the bruises were rising; he was blue-eyed. Ian washed the mud out of his eye-lashes. The man's teeth had blood on them where he had bitten his lips; the blood was brown and red; there was a still, secret smell of blood and heather honey together that young Ian could not somehow bear. He wiped the blood away from the man's lips, resting his head against his own knee. The hair was full of twigs and moss and mud, yellow

164

hair tied back for hunting with a red thong. 'What is the name on you?' said Ian again softly. The man gave up. 'Donal,' he said. 'Donal Bàn?' said Ian. The man moved his lips in assent. 'I was beginning to think it was you,' said Ian, and he remembered sharply that time in Islay. But this was different. 'I am Ian Og,' he said. 'I was thinking that too,' the man whispered. His head still lay on Ian's knee; there was a live spot in his throat, twitching. Ian reached down for his knife.

They were watching one another. There was something about this that Ian did not like at all. He turned Donal Bàn half over and cut the bow string round his wrists. It had been so tight that now Donal Bàn could not move his arms. Ian began to rub his arms, the way he would get blood flowing back into them and the muscles working. Ian avoided looking at his stag now. He did not know at all what he was meaning to do, only that it was the stag of all stags on the hills that he had got. Donal Bàn was moving the fingers on his hands now. It was hard to say which bit of him was giving the most pain. He had never been in any man's power before, and he knew it was Ian Og who was bound to have the most hate on him of any man in Ceann Tir. He did not know why his hands had been loosed. Nor did Ian Og know that. Only it had seemed the first thing to do.

'How long were you here?' he said. 'A day and a night,' said Donal Bàn. 'You will be hungry.' But Donal Bàn shook his head; he was not hungry any longer, only thirsty still; the clegs had bitten his face and neck a good bit; he could feel the blisters now, a sharp wee top to all this other pain he was plunged into. He did not want to say how thirsty he was still; but when nothing happened, at last he said so, shutting his eyes. He did not want to see what the other one would make of it.

Ian Og went over again to the water and drank again himself and brought back another cupful and another handful of the wet and healing moss. He laid this about the face of fair Donald. As he did it, for a moment his fingers and fair Donald's fingers were touching and catching, he pulled his own hand away. It would not do at all, that.

The sun was sloping over now; it was late enough. 'Wait, you,' said Ian Og and went over for his bow. Donal Bàn's sword was there too, lying like a woman with the sun on her and the steel warm to touch. Ian came back with his bow. 'When I am away,' he said, 'you will not be crawling to the sword,' But the other said nothing. 'If you will not promise I will tie you again,' he said, 'and tighter.' Donal Bàn muttered that he would not move. It would be no use anyway. And he could not stand being tied again.

Ian went off singing a little; it was the bonniest evening and the heather sprang under him, so that he was half dancing. It was hard enough to stay still, but he did not need to for long, so many blue hares as there were racing and stopping through the soft light. He came back with his hare, singing again, and he cut heather tops to make a bed, and so back to the hollow where he had left his stag.

When he came to the edge of it, Donal Bàn's eyes met his, and it seemed to him that this man was wanting him back, and he could not help smiling a little. He came and stood by Donald, laughing, the hare in one hand. But Donald was not looking at the hare, he was not hungry; there was something else in his asking eyes. 'What is it?' said Ian suddenly. 'It is this leg I have hurt,' said Donald low. 'Can you not stand on it at all the way it is?' Ian asked. 'If I had been able it is not here I would be now. I think there is something torn maybe.' Ian stooped over it; the thing was hot and swollen; he did not think there was a bone broken, but it would be best to get it tied up, the way it would not get worse. He fetched the end of his plaid full of the wet moss and packed it round and then bound it on with the deer skin strips from the other's leg. Donal Bàn moaned a bit and young Ian found himself trying not to hurt him now. He was angry at himself for that and jerked at the leg and jerked a cry out of Donald and that was no good at all. So he finished with it quickly and stood up, and put fair Donald's bow over with his own, and it was a beauty too, with the red wood and the black polished tips to it.

The hare was still warm, but soon it would be too cold if he did not hurry. He opened it and made a paste with its blood and the meal. He brought some of that over to Donald, but Donald shook his head. Ian was angry. He said in an angry voice: 'You will eat this!' and he saw how the other's pride had crumbled down to nothing at all, so that he could be frightened like a baby would be, by hard words only. Some way, Ian did not like to be doing that, so he came close to Donald and put an arm under his shoulders again and said to him gently that he should eat, it would help him and make him strong. He was eating the paste himself, because he was hungry enough, and Donald ate a little and then more. Ian was pleased he was eating; he did not want him to die. He ran his finger round the boss of the brooch on Donal Bàn's plaid. Donald looked up at him and said: 'That is your own now.'

'Ach no!' said Ian, and drew his hand away quickly, 'I was not thinking that at all, Donal Bàn!'

'You can be thinking it,' said the other, 'for it is true.'

Ian did not want to consider this for the moment. He said: 'Is your leg easier?'

'It is now,' said Donald.

'What were you doing at all to get here?' Ian said, 'and why were you alone?'

It was hunting we were,' fair Donald said, 'and the other way entirely, not out from among the trees. We had killed our beasts and the rest going away down, and then there was a stag I saw, oh a bonny one with a great head on him, and I followed him to the march and across, and I lost him. It was near evening then, but when I saw where I was I said to myself that I would go over that far onto your side of it.'

'How?' said young Ian.

'To see—what like it was,' fair Donald said, and his eyes shifted.

'To see what harm you had done us?' Ian said in a cold way.

'Aye, that was it, and I am not lying to you. I went in the pride of my heart, Ian Og, and all at once I slipped on an edge and there I was with my ankle twisted under me, and myself on the wrong side of the march.'

'It was the worst kind of cry you gave,' said Ian.

'I was thinking for a moment it was one of my own people. But they will never be looking for me here. They will think I am still among the trees.'

'If they did come,' said Ian, 'I could kill you easy before they could get at either of us.'

'That is certain,' said fair Donald, lying still. Then he said: 'What is it you are going to do with me, Ian Og?'

'There is something I do not rightly know yet,' said Ian. He still had his arm round fair Donald's shoulders, and the thing was he had no wish at all to kill him nor even to hurt him, and now there was a star showing over the hill and the short night beginning. 'I will be lighting a signal fire,' he said, 'and you will sleep, Donal, and I must get carrying you over.'

'You had best leave me here,' said the other one.

167

'I will not,' said Ian, 'I have the heather cut for us.' So, one way and another, holding him up and giving him the bow to walk with, he got fair Donald over to the heather bed and the plaid well happed round him. Then he went to the tongue of rocks, below at the mouth of the corrie, where he had thought the fire would be seen from below. There was little enough dry stuff up here and he was some while getting it together and another time lighting it with flint and steel. It was only a small fire that was in it when he had it going, and the skinned hare that he had spiked over it was little more than toasted. But young Ian enjoyed it fine, for the raw bannock had not been enough for him. When he left the fire it was right dark but for the many stars and a wee glow still in the north-west, and he was needing to take care or he might have done the same thing to himself as the other one. And indeed he was not too sure of his way, and he stumbled on water again, and thought he would be bringing the full of the horn cup for Donald, in case he was not sleeping. So he did that and Donald was awake and thirsty and pleased enough to have the water.

Young Ian lay down beside him, but he was not sleeping either. The great excitement he was in had set his heart beating the way he could not but be shaken by it. And the dreams he had were not right sleeping dreams, for he was aware of fair Donald on the heather beside him, but some way in the shape of a stag, and in the dream everything was going wrong because the stag was not fully dead and in another dream because after all the stag was dead, but should not have been. Ian woke clear of the dreams, and then it was no stag at all beside him, but the enemy of his house, and how had he not killed him, and what trouble was he not bringing on himself? And now it was in the north-east that the sky was pale instead of starry, and young Ian asking himself could he kill this man now and telling himself what this man had done and seeing his mother's face before him and hearing her voice. Suddenly fair Donald had his eyes open looking at Ian. He whispered: 'What is come on you? What are you dreaming?'

Ian said: 'I am thinking of what you did to my folk. I am thinking of how you will pay for that. I am thinking of the thing the women will do to you when I get you down to them. You will not be laughing then.'

'I am not laughing now,' Donal Bàn whispered back, 'and it was

168

an ill thing we did, though maybe it is too late to be saying that.'
And then he said: 'Do you need to give me to the women, Ian Og? It
is your own I am on this.'

Ian Og did not answer. The thought of the stag had come back on
him. Yet the stag was everyone's meat. They had half starved in
Spring because of Donal Bàn. There had been no dancing nor
singing, and his own sister the way she was now. Yet he was not sure
that he wanted to see that thing that had been planned done to
Donal Bàn. And it was likely that Donal Bàn had guessed already at
what it was, for he said: 'I am wishing you would kill me first, Ian
Og.'

'Maybe they will not want to do it when it comes to the bit,' said
Ian Og.

'If there was any other way I could pay,' Donald said, and then
fell to shivering. Already the long dawn had begun to lighten a little
and a cold grey in it. It would be warm enough when the sun came,
but meanwhile there was a heavy dew falling, and for all his plaid,
young Ian shivered too and moved himself closer to the other, the
stag. And now he fell to considering how, if they had met on the hill
and Donal Bàn without the foot twisted, it was not likely at all that
himself would be the winner or that it would be any hands but his
own would be tied with the bow string. And it was hurting him to
think that, so that he turned about in the heather. It was lighter now
and the stars beginning to be swept out by the soft hair of morning.
He could see the other one's face and his eyes open still. He said:
'Are you not sleeping at all, Donal Bàn?'

'How would I be sleeping,' said the other, 'and this the beginning
of the last day I will have? I will be asleep long enough after this.'

'It is the way you are cold that you are not sleeping,' said Ian Og
firmly, and took half the plaid off himself and put it onto the other.

Fair Donald shoved it away: 'There is no sense in that,' he said.

'There is no sense in plenty of it,' said Ian Og. He could see the
bruises round the other one's eyes and he wished it had not been
himself put them there. He said: 'It was laid on me to get a stag
yesterday. I will call you Donal the Stag and maybe they will not
know it is you.'

'They will know it is me down there,' said the other, with a kind of
proud anger, 'and your father will know me surely, Ian Og. He will
know me from Islay.' Then he said: 'I wish the Chief had settled this

thing for us that time.'

'You would not have taken it if he had,' said Ian, and that was the truth and they both knew it. Now it was all over grey and the heather a pale colour, and the mists here and there among the hills. Ian Og was wondering if his fire had been seen. When the sun rose and began to dry out the stuff, he would make a smoke.

The other was lying still enough. At last he said, with a kind of grip on his voice, the way he would not be thought, even to himself, to be speaking as a man should not: 'Is there no way out of this? Is there no way else I can pay for what has been done?'

'I do not know at all,' said young Ian, refusing to take responsibility.

'If you will set me a ransom, I will not bargain and I will see it paid. We could end this thing. There would be sense in that surely, Ian Og. Will you be thinking of that now?'

'Well, I will try to be thinking,' said Ian Og, and indeed there would be great sense in it—if the others would be thinking so too— and there would be an ending of this hate—but then what at all would they be making their songs and their pipe tunes about if this was over? There would be something gone. And indeed, at the beginning it was two brothers that had started it, away back; it was over an inheritance they had quarrelled. So that he and Donal Bàn were cousins some way. 'I will do my best for you, Donal the Stag,' he said, and now it was in his voice as though he were meaning it, and the other one turned himself half over and got him by the hand, and their hands at least met in a kind of amity.

When young Ian went over to make his smoke signal he could see that there were a few coming up, though they might be an hour yet. He did not tell fair Donald at once, but tried to make him eat some more of the hare that was left. At last he finished it himself. He was taking the twigs and caked mud out of Donald's hair and fingering the fine stuff of his shirt; he was talking to Donald as though he were the stag, making a kind of game for himself, with the great sport he had got. He was wiping over the two swords again; the night dew was on them and must not be let spoil them. It was a bonny sword, this new one, he could not give over his play with it, pointing and slashing. He looked round and could see fair Donald watching him, and his face dark and eyes bright with anger: 'Well?' said Ian.

Fair Donald caught his breath back and his lips drew away from his teeth, and then he said: 'It is your own,' and he hid his face in his elbow.

Young Ian laughed and said: 'Was it your father's?'

'Aye,' said the other one, his voice muffled by his arm across it.

'And his father's?' The same answer. 'Now it is on our side,' said Ian, 'and it is myself will be well served by this sword, will I not? Speak, you!'

Donal Bàn raised his head and said: 'If my leg were whole on me I would try to kill you now, I with my bare hands and you with my sword. And I think I would do it!'

Ian looked at him queerly and said: 'You are hating me the same way my mother is hating you.'

Donald felt suddenly sick at this, because he remembered that Ian Og was the only one who stood between him and what that woman would do, and he tried to speak differently to Ian Og who had his life in his hands, but he could not bring himself to do it, and his foot and leg ached and burned with the great anger he was in.

But Ian Og said: 'It is a low spirited man you would be not to be hating me for this: but look, Donal the Stag, I have laid your sword down, and you had best not be angry, for I see my father coming, and you will need your wits about you.' Then suddenly he came nearer and said: 'I was meaning to make you angry, I was meaning to tease you. I wanted to see you so. Do not be minding now.' And then he brought the sword over so that Donald could get touching the blade of it, but not the hilt. Yet indeed the touch of it and what Ian had said were in some way healing, and the pulling ache went out of Donald, and when Ian sat down beside him on the heather, Donald turned over his way, and so they were when Ian's father and the men came up the corrie. Then fear came on Donald like the drenching of a thunder storm and he had not even words to speak to Ian nor to ask for help, but he thought Ian knew how it was.

Ian went down to meet his father and said that his Stag was a prisoner and worth something to them maybe, and hurt, and would they carry him down. Two of the men had hunting spears, so they got the spears worked through the sides of a strong plaid, and the man could lie there; but when they asked who was it, Ian only answered that he was Donal the Stag, and Donald himself said that he was the Stag, but he said little enough. They put the sword onto the plaid beside him, hilt towards his feet, and there was much talk about the beauty and rareness of it. Ian took turns with the others at carrying his stag, and it took them long enough to walk down, and Donald mostly with his eyes shut and his leg paining him.

At the river Ian was walking behind the others with his father. The old MacDonald said: 'Why do you call him Donal the Stag, Ian Og?'

'That is the name he has on him,' said Ian.

'I do not think so,' said his father. 'I think the name he has on him is Donal Bàn. What is wrong with you at all to be shielding him, Ian?'

Ian said: 'Well, Father, if you know you know. But I am thinking he is worth more to us alive than dead, yet I am not sure my mother would be understanding that.'

His father looked at him under his brows and said: 'I was not thinking this of you, that you would be a bargainer. But I have no doubts you will give him to your mother freely. She will only be thinking of her honour and of my daughter's honour and how she will make it clean.'

'Well,' said Ian, 'I will not give him up and that is that.'

'And if I bid you do it?' said his father.

'Still I will not,' said young Ian.

They had crossed over the stones now. 'What is the matter with you at all?' asked his father.

'It was no fair fight I got him in,' said young Ian.

'There is no need to fight fair with a wolf,' his father said.

Ian was suddenly very angry with his father. 'You have no sense at all!' he said: 'If this is handled the way it should be handled, we will end the quarrel for ever and get the cattle back and the byres builded again and all be the better for it.'

'Are you wanting to end the quarrel, Ian, my son?' said his father: 'You cannot be wanting it, and you sister and the other lassies the way they mostly all are. No, we will go on with it, but it is his folk who will be sorry and shamed now and their leader libbed by a woman! They can buy him back after that if he lives.'

'He will not live,' said Ian, 'but whether he lived or died and that that done to him, it would mean a worse destruction on us in another twenty years, when you are dead likely, and it will be me has to spend all my days guarding against it, and most like be caught in the end the way you yourself were! I am telling you, Father, I was thinking the same way you do at the first, but I had a long night to consider it and I am come to another conclusion. And he is mine and his sword is mine and I will not give him up at all!'

'It will be a wonder if your mother does not guess who he is,' said the old MacDonald.

'You will not be telling her,' said Ian.

'I will not be needing to, likely,' said his father. Then he said: 'I have my own tally with Donal Bàn. There is a wee small part I will be settling.' And he called to his men to lay down the prisoner. They were amongst the burnt byres now and the forlorn smell of the ash that rose when they dropped the plaid with the heavy man on it. Old MacDonald stooped over the prisoner and said: 'Look.' And Donal Bàn looked indeed, but he said nothing. Then the old man took up a handful of dirt and ash and jammed it into the mouth of the other one, and would have put his heel on the top, but young Ian pulled him away. 'You will not blemish my stag on me, Father!' he said, then to the men: 'Will you be laying him down on my own bed now!'

Then he waited, trying to show his father how he saw the thing, for it was becoming plainer to him every moment now, but his father would not heed at all; then he hurried after the others and hard and quick he was thinking. They had carried the Stag, and he with his hands up over his face, through the hall and up the twisting stone stair where they needed to get him out and lift him between two of them, and so to the square room in the tower, with the small narrow windows in the thickness of the stone, where Ian Og and the rest of the young men slept.

The women in the hall had all come scuttling over like hens to corn, to see what was here, and two or three of them asked Ian, who said shortly it was a man called the Stag and he with a hurt foot. The only one he said more to was his sister Isbail, and he took her by the hand and asked could she not be bringing up cold water and cloths to lay on a sprain and a torn muscle, or indeed it might be a bone broken.

Isbail came at once; she was glad to be doing something new, and glad to be with her brother and away from the rest of the women and they always reminding one another, whether they would or no, of the thing that had happened. She and another lassie who was a foster-sister of her's, brought up the water and the cloths, and both

173

of them wondering who it could be. When they got there, Ian was leaning over the man and wiping his face and mouth with an old shirt, and the other men standing by the window; when Isbail came over, Ian chucked the shirt down so that it covered the man's face and he made no move to take it off. The sword was laid in by him, the hilt at the foot of the bed. Ian was busying the two girls with the hurt foot and they set to work on it: the ankle and above were swollen to a great size now and the bruises angry looking. Then Ian went to the window and said low to the oldest of the men: 'Do you guess who it was you were carrying, Neil?'

The man said: 'There is only one man that your father would be treating the way he did this one. But it is a queer thing you are doing, Ian Og, to set your sister to wash that one's foot and I would not like to be in your place when it is found out.'

Ian Og said: 'I am thinking once the lassie has been healing him, she will not likely want to kill him.'

'Why would we not be killing him?' said Neil, and sucked at the hilt of his dagger. 'I am sure your father and mother would both like that.'

'If he is killed he will get back for us neither sheep nor cattle,' said Ian.

'You are right there, Ian Og,' the man said; 'and if we have plenty of meat all winter I will not be complaining for one. But he will make his promises now: will he keep them?'

'He will not go from here till we have our beasts back. And indeed it is likely he will pay that with a light heart to keep himself safe from the thing the women would be doing.'

'That is sense you are talking, Ian Og,' said the man, 'and I will back you against the women.'

Ian Og saw that the lassies had the shirt pulled off the face of the Stag; they were talking to him and he answering softly and gayly the way he might be pleasing them, but with his hand over his face, and indeed he was bleeding a little from the scratches he had got from the fistful of ashes. Isbail turned and caught at her brother's arm: 'Who is he at all, Ian? It is the great weaving in his plaid, and the sword by his side the bonniest sword ever I have seen!' Ian was thinking how best to answer, but she went on: 'It is troubling me, Ian. There is something I know about this one—' And then their mother came in from the stair. She was a tall and thin woman. The

174

white plaid was gathered on her breast under a great round brooch of bronze with snouted and lengthy beasts on it, and the children who had sat on her knee knew it and feared it a little, for it was very old. She said to Ian: 'What is this stag you have hunted, my son?' And she went to the bed and pulled back the arm of the Stag and looked him in the face for a long moment, and suddenly he cried out as it might have been a hare and the dogs after him. And that was a horrible thing for the young men in that room, to hear a man crying with fear that way before a woman. 'Aye,' said she, 'you have brought meat for my knife, Ian.' And she looked over her shoulder to the other women who were standing in the doorway and on the stair with the light plaids over their heads and the big eyes of them, and she said to her cook: 'You will bring me the great knife out of the kitchen.'

'Who is it?' said Isbail, 'I do not know yet!' And she stood between Ian and the Stag, looking from one to the other, and a high colour on her and the black hair on her hanging down, but with no ribbon on it, the way she was neither maid nor wife, the poor lassie. 'It is Donal Bàn,' said her mother and laughed. Then Isbail threw her head back and shut her eyes and let out one long screech, the way she remembered everything suddenly and the smell and heat of the burning and the bleating and lowing of the driven beasts, and the men coming in on the lassies. But young Ian could not think what to do, only he had his sword drawn and he was shouting their own gathering cry, and there were a few of the men with him.

The scream went out of Isbail and she opened her eyes again, and there was the man whose foot she had bathed with the cold water and whom she had spoken with pleasantly, but she knew now why he had his hand over his face. For a moment she could not make him in her mind into one and the same man as Donal Bàn whom she hated, and she took a step towards him to make sure, and the man caught at the edge of her plaid and said: 'Isbail MacDonald, marry me!' And he looked up at her and there was so much fear and need in his face that she did not know what to do, and when she looked round her brother was between herself and the other women. The man had a tight grip of her plaid now. He said: 'Is it my bairn you carry, Isbail?' Her lip trembled and she said: 'You are not remembering me!' He said quick: 'Whether it is or not, I will father it, Isbail, and we will both be proud of it, and indeed I remember you,

Isbail!' She said: 'You do not, so!' But she did not tear her plaid out of his hands and he was sitting up on the bed now and close to her and he said: 'Marry me and save me and you shall have everything that's mine!' But she was thinking of the bairn and could it by this be turned from a terror and a punishment into a glad thing, and there was a sickness and dizziness on her, and the man holding to her hand and it sweating.

But Ian Og was not hearing any of this, and he saw the women behind his mother laughing and passing her the great skinning knife out of the kitchen and she saying to him: 'Stand back, Ian!' And he was frightened of her, the way he had been as a child, and this terrible look on her face. The sword was loose in his hand and the point dropping. But then suddenly there was a change in the noise the women were making and he looked round quick and there was Donal Bàn with the sword in his hand and there was no way he could have got it except from Isbail. And Isbail was standing at his left shoulder and he with his arm on her to keep his balance as he knelt on the bed and the hot dark fierceness on his face.

'Isbail!' said her mother, 'come back!'

'I will not,' said Isbail, and she looked at Ian.

'Shame on you,' said her mother, 'going like a bitch to that bed!' And her foster-sister cried at her: 'Come away, Isbail! What will be said of you! We will not be speaking to you, Isbail!'

But Isbail said: 'He will get husbands for all of you—will you not, Donald?'

'Aye,' said he, 'I will do that for any woman who was wronged yon time, and you shall have the beasts back, and the best of weddings it will be surely, and we bringing over the red wine and the white, and the pipers from both our houses all playing at the once, and five days of dancing and singing, and an ending of this quarrel, and all of you saying it was the great hunting that Ian Og had!'

The women began whispering on that, and the mother of Ian and Isbail looked round on them with anger and bitterness, and worse anger against her own children; but there was that in her lassie's face that she had not seen all these months, for there was pride again and decision, and the girl cried out to her foster-sister: 'Get the priest, Seonaid, and we will get a letter written and sent off!' And she felt the arm of the man tighten round her and she knew he was proud of

176

her quickness and sense, and she leant back that much against his shoulder and he whispered to her: 'I will dress you in silk, Isbail, and the fine wool, and gold on your hair—' And then he said to her brother: 'I am not letting go of my sword, Ian Og, but take you out the brooch of my plaid and ask your sister will she wear it.'

Ian Og looked from them to his mother and he saw the anger was smouldering down in her now, so that at least she would not strike yet, and he went to Donal Bàn and took out the brooch, so that the plaid slipped off his shoulder, and Isbail said: 'Let that be the fastening of my own plaid, Ian, and give my man the pin that I have been wearing.'

So Ian took out the iron pin that fastened the fringed plaid of white wool with the fine lines of red and green in the sett of it, and fastened it instead with the round brooch that gathered up the folds in a far bonnier way, or maybe it was only that Isbail had not troubled that morning with the hang of her plaid; and he pinned the dark plaid on Donald's shoulder with the iron pin. Isbail said over her shoulder: 'I had as bonny a brooch as this last winter, Donald, but it was torn away from me, and it's likely you will know where it is.' Donal Bàn said: 'You will have it again, Isbail,' and he put his head down into her plaid, for he was deep ashamed and the truth was he did not remember her at all and it might have been any one of his men, but he could not be saying this to the lassie.

By and by Seonaid came with the priest. He was saying nothing, for it was from old MacDonald that he had his house and his bit garden with the bee-hives in it. But he had pen and ink with him ready to write. Donal Bàn said: 'I am ready to draw up this letter with any of you.' At that, old MacDonald who had been below in the hall, at the beginning, came through, and he looked at his wife and she shrugged her shoulders and handed back the knife to the cook. Then Donal Bàn gave his sword to Ian Og and was unarmed again among his armed enemies, but he was not afraid of the men.

So they drew up the letter, and Donal Bàn was not bargaining. At the end he signed it, and sealed it with the cross-marked stone on the hilt of his knife, and old MacDonald and young Ian signed it to show he was truly in their power, and one of the men offered to take it over. 'We would have the answer sooner if you had left us any one of our horses,' said Ian Og.

Isbail was tired suddenly. She went out of the room into the hall.

She would have liked now to go to her mother, to cry and be praised, but her mother turned away from her, and so did the older women. But Seonaid and some of the girls came softly and said first, how could she do such a thing, and then, well, she was the clever one, and was it true they would have everything back, the cows they were each of them used to milk and all, and there would be a wedding for every girl that chose to marry this way? And she said Aye, it was all in the letter and they would be righted surely, but ach, she did not want to be thinking about it all. So she went out and across the burning and into the fields, and the lassies with her, but by and by they were picking flowers, the way they had not done all that summer.

It was two days after that, the man who had taken the letter came back, and with him the mother's brother of Donal Bàn, and he was a proud and high-handed one, and angry enough with Donal Bàn, and saying they had been looking for him in the hills these four days, and indeed they could have done well enough without him if he had been killed, and how was it anyway that Donal Bàn had let this lot get round him and a poor kind of marriage it would be indeed and everyone laughing and making up the songs about it! But Donal Bàn knew well enough that he was more use and value to his side of the clan than ever his uncle was, for he was a grand swordsman and a clever one at the planning of raids and defences and sports of every kind besides, and the young men of his own age would not care to be without him. And forby that, he had come to like Ian Og, and they had slept next to one another for three nights now, and it was Ian Og's shirt that he had on him while his own was washing. And there was the kind of pride on him to see the glad looks of the lassie, and she bathing his foot the way it was far easier now and he would have it on the ground again in a few days, and he speaking to her every time with the great courtesy he would have had to a Queen. It was only old MacDonald and his wife that he was not caring for, but he was not minding that, because Ian Og would get all the credit for this with the rest of the men all up the glen, and the power would be going more and more to him. And the mark of it before all the world and the whole of the Clan Donald was that he would not take his sword back, but he would give it to Ian Og, and later on Ian Og would give it again to his sister's son. This they had promised to one another, speaking together softly after midnight, and the rest of the

178

men asleep in the room with the thick walls. And the next time they were going to Islay, he and Ian Og would go as brothers indeed, and it would not matter at all what the old ones on either side were saying.

So all this was going on in Donal Bàn's head. But the uncle was for bargaining over the sheep and cattle, and he said too that none of their own men would be wanting to marry these girls. But Donal Bàn knew he would be able to deal with that himself amongst the young ones, and the time of the wedding coming and maybe a song to be written about it that would make the men soft-hearted towards these lassies of their own clan. So at last when they had talked about all that and had it settled up, the uncle took a thing out of his sporran and said with an ill enough grace that his sister had asked him to give it to her son. Donal Bàn was glad indeed, for he had hoped his mother would send some gift when she knew what it was her son had escaped from, but he had said nothing in the letter, for he could not be asking for it as a right or indeed for himself. But now he took it, and it was wrapped in a square of white silk; he could feel the shape and weight of the silver links and the square stones through the soft stuff, and he held it in his hands, waiting for the next time Isbail would come into the room again, and she saying it was on some errand of her mother's she had come, and lifting the lids of the chests and shifting the linen about, but she knowing well enough in her heart and he knowing in his that it was all to find the Stag her brother had hunted for her and whom she had saved from the knife.

THE HILL BEHIND

In the Valley without Water they cried for rain. Oh let it rain, rain, a soft and comforting day-long rain like a girl's skin, the skin of her face, her neck, her breasts that would some day sweeten into milk, the long smooth skin of her thighs. Wet rain. Without rain they died a little every day. The small children died first, not playing, going slack on their mother's knees. But also the big men who wanted to be ploughing, they died partly. They sat in the shade, not speaking, their hands and heads drooping over their knees. Heat hit them out of the dust, their toes curled up like dry leaves. The herd boys took the cattle further and further to drink, but they might go three, four days without water. Some of them lay down and died. A man's pride, a man's riches, fell day by day as though one threw gold into a bottomless crack in the ground. Even if the cattle died beside paths it was no use to skin them; there was no meat on their bones. The women walked many miles to carry water from the wells which still held a little deep down. When they came back, weary, they could have drunk the whole pot themselves, but it was for their men and their children.

Out beyond the Valley it was worse. In dry miles of sand and thorny bushes Tsaxau uncovered the nest his mother had made and took out one ostrich shell full of water. One egg of water is not much for a family, but his mother and grandmother had both died; they had become too tired to move their legs on; they had been left in the shelter. Nobody would come back for them, ever. It was so. Always it had been so. He thought of his mother when he lifted out the egg of water. Tsaxau gave some to his little brother, but most to his father. His father might kill something. When he had drunk the water his father prayed that he might find something to kill.

The people of the Valley without Water went to their King. 'Make rain!' they said, 'we need rain. Our cattle die. Let there be rain, Kgosi, call on all the Kings so that through them you may speak for us to God.'

Kgosi answered them, 'I hear you, people. But my cattle too are dying. The sky is unkind. The smell of rain is far. I have tried to speak for you, but it is useless.'

They began to mock him. The women beat him with branches. They brought a black ox and stayed silently watching, in case he was moved to sacrifice and open a way to the ancestors and through them to God.

He went away from his people. He went into his house. It was not the large, goldenly-thatched round of his wife of the first house, which had many pleasant things in it, cooking pots and sieves, fine leather skirts and necklaces of beads and gold, blankets and soft furs, and over all a smell of women that would stir like a snake in a man. He did not go to the houses of any of his wives, although they stood in the doorways watching. One had been pounding grain. Another was plastering a piece of her wall which had broken. She used even water from far off for this, but a King's wife, although she is not the great wife, should have all things seemly round her. He had married them for many reasons of family-binding and an ending of old quarrels; he had given them much pleasure. There were small children. As they looked his way, eyes glowed or were cast down. They would have given him what water they had, although they too had little. But he went past them to his own house and sat there in stillness and darkness.

For indeed he had done all that should have been done for the Valley without Water. He had made the *tshitlho* for rain, using the herbs which had been shown him and told him, and also parts of water-beasts and birds, the frog and the fish-eagle, whose wings are like thunder-clouds. He had secretly sent to the roads out, and laid the sticks and beaten the earth in case some sorcerer from another place had laid a curse and stopped the rain from coming. Early, before first light, he had sent children with new, small pots to sprinkle the lands with water into which the *tshitlho* had been stirred. And he himself had strained and sweated in hard prayer, knowing that to be a King is nothing if he cannot help his people.

So now he thought there was perhaps one more thing to do. He slept alone and his dreams could be made clear either one way or the other. Very early in the morning he sent for the Princess Naledi, the star. Now stars can be bright and lead people to their homes, or they can be darkened by clouds and shifting in the sky, and so it was with Naledi. She did not wish to come when she was sent for nor yet to understand what was asked of her. She looked away from her father; her toes scuffled at a small crack in the floor, her fingers twisted her beads. Her father became angry, but a King must hold his anger in, even as he must hold his pain. Yet it became as though his words

181

were a whip striking her and her eyes went dark and she held her head up and at last she listened. She was afraid but also not afraid, since it was something new. Her father saw this on her. 'Come,' he said, and walked out of his house, she following.

Now all this while Tsaxau's father and Tsaxau himself were looking for a thing to kill, since hunger was at them all and the small one cried almost all the time. They left him and went hunting, silently. They looked also for the wild melon which is a little bitter, but full of almost water. Far off across dry grass and thin bushes they saw ostriches, and now they separated and ran like shadows, each with his bow. Tsaxau ran faster than his father, but he had not spent so many years sighting and thinking along the flight of the small arrow with death smeared on its tip.

A beast slipped through the rustle of grass ahead of Tsaxau, but it was not a beast one could eat; it was a beast of sharp claws and tearing teeth, though a small one; its flesh was not good for a man. Tsaxau did not bend his bow, but as he came nearer to the ostriches that was what he did. The male ostrich was very big; he was taller than two men. His wives must obey him and run when he called to them. This was the one his father would shoot. And as he thought that, the arrow of his father came through the air. But the ostrich had jumped and the arrow hid itself in his thick tail feathers without touching his skin. Yet the ostrich was disturbed and started to run with his great naked legs, calling to his wives. There was only one shot for Tsaxau, who was now also running. This was a female, not very big, she had become confused. He shot her. She ran for a little, then lay down.

Now they were pulling out her feathers. Before, it had been his mother who had done this and Tsaxau cried without making any noise, because he thought of her so much that she seemed to be there, but when he turned his head she was not. He and his father did not do this so well as his mother and grandmother had done; the feathers stuck to their hands and they shook their hands about. Inside the ostrich were eggs which were tender to eat; he would keep one for his little brother. About and about the feather flew. The wind caught them.

The people of the Valley without Water watched the King and the Princess walking through the dust, past the shadow of the high dark branches under which the counsellors and elders sat and where

182

there had been good talk and grave laughter and the coolness of water or beer. But now the heat beat through it. Some, seeing Naledi wearing the beaded kilt half way to her knees and the necklaces and bracelets which were her due, shook their heads. 'She is wilful,' they said, 'she will not do what Kgosi tells her.' For some of them had guessed what it might be.

'She should have been beaten,' they said, 'even as a child she wanted too much.'

'She is not beautiful,' said another, 'she is like a boy.' And they spoke of the way she held her head in the air, so that the golden earrings bobbed in her ears, instead of keeping her eyes cast down and her smile unseen. She had slapped the hand of a boy who had gently touched her on an evening of dance; it had been a hard slap; he was her cousin. It could have been suitable to let his hand rest for a moment. At the time of her marriage there would be feasting for all the people of the Valley without Water. Fat beasts would be killed; there would be meat and beer and porridge in the great pots.

But the King and the Princess walked away without greetings, only the small click of the tongue from one or another. He carried his gun, which was a muzzle-loader with a date inlaid with brass on the stock, and also two spears. He had a cloak of soft fur slung over his shoulder. Naledi carried the bag of powder and the bullets, and also a small bag with water and a handful of meal in a little cooking pot. They walked out beyond the sad unploughed lands, the hard, sun-baked earth where only a few thorns showed, breaking through. It was hot, hot. The dry land breathed nothing but scorching hotness at them.

A certain hill had seemed in the dawn a violet shadow. Now it was near and steep with great rocks piled and poised and trees and bushes growing between, which seemed greener and more full of leaves than the bushes at home. It was a hill that the King knew and that the Princess had heard many stories about: a hill of ancient stories that was called the Hill Behind. And it seemed to Naledi that she was beginning to know what was laid on her to do. They stood under a tall tree and the King looked carefully at his young daughter. He thought, Yes, she is a brave one, and she will need to be. He said to her, 'We have finished the journey on plain ground; our feet are dusty. Now, for you, my daughter, begins the magic journey.'

183

She laid down the bag of powder and the bullets and looked at him and asked, 'Shall I come back from it, my father?'

He said, 'If you are brave and clever you will come back. If you are worthy of the ancestors. I will wait for you a night and a day.' She seemed to straighten herself. 'And another night,' he suddenly said; and then, 'You will pass to the great clefted rock and there leave your clothes and your necklaces: everything on arms and legs and ears. Then you must climb.'

'May I take your spear, my father?'

'No,' he said, 'but you will not need it. You will see wild beasts. You will see many small snakes. Do not fear them, above all do not hurt any of these small snakes. They will be there to strengthen you. This you will feel in yourself.'

'To strengthen me for what, my father?'

'At the end, at the very end, behind everything, behind the rising of the moon, you will meet the rain-snake, Kgwanyape.' Now it was said. He watched her take a deep breath and her breasts, which were still so small, quivered; the shining beads moved on her soft skin.

'And then?'

'Truly, I do not know. This is something very old. It is from the ancestors. But you will be strong. You are a princess, my daughter. Do not fight the rain-snake. Even if he is also the terrible storm-wind. This is all I know.' And he stood there and saw her walk to the split rock and in the last light take off all she was wearing and climb naked up and over the split in the hard, towering rock. And the moon was not yet risen.

Naledi began the magic climb. She looked up at the sky. Was she, too, a star? One of the big stars low down that seemed to change colour, or one of the high, quiet, small stars which stay in their patterns and together make the starlight in which she could see this and that? There seemed to be a very small and narrow path between the rocks, although here and there a thorn bush had grown out across it and tried to catch her. She felt a little trickle of blook down one arm. She saw a small, thin snake and stopped; but she did not pick up a stick or stone to hurt it, and it slipped away. And then she moved and laid her foot on the little twisting spoor of the snake, and she felt a kind of strengthening beginning. There were noises all round, night noises and smells with them, which she could not quite name. Was this the place of leopards? She made up her mind that she was one of the big stars. How can a leopard leap at a star?

And now the moon was rising, very large, golden turning to silver. It seemed she was walking across a shoulder of the hill which one did not see from below, a kind of platform of worn and flattened rock, and here indeed were beasts of the night. One with a sloping back, dog legs and shining eyes, passed her, and other shadows, big or small, slipped from rock to rock. There were snuffles and cries and breathings. But especially there were small snakes, and these she did not touch to harm them. Once she heard far below her a lion roaring and then she found herself afraid for her father, and this was strange. She was not afraid for herself and before this she had not felt love for her father; until now they had shared nothing. But now she was sharing with him in the deepest need of the people and she knew far down in her heart that he now felt love for her and his spirit would have tried to be with her on the magic journey which yet she must do alone.

And then in the moonlight she saw that there were hollows in the flat rock bed and that these reflected the moon. Water. Hollows, deep pools, of water. How? She went to one and knelt by it, seeing her own quivering moonlit reflection. She dipped in her hand, her wrist, her arm. It was deep, deep. She felt something twining and when she lifted her arm there was a small, shining water-snake which slipped off her and back into the pool. She stood up with her body wetted from her cupped hand. There was a tree growing, and as she passed it many large moths came and sipped from her damp skin. They were beautiful, with markings of grey and brown and silver. She brushed them away gently, moving along and always up between the dark pools. All belonged to the Hill Behind. Then something larger than a moth came circling round her; it did not seem right to her, it was alive. She brushed at it more sharply and it fell into a pool of water. As it fell she seemed for a moment to hear a voice inside her head, calling 'Mother'. Yet although she understood this, it was yet not a known word but perhaps only a thought loosened from her mind. The thing was swallowed by the dark water. It had travelled far, whirling on the winds, up and down and up. It was a feather from the she-ostrich. It had blood on it.

The moon was high now, above the crest of the hill. As she walked, she began to feel sleep coming on her in short waves, so that between one tree and the next, although her legs carried her, it was as though she had lived through a whole life. Once she leant against a rock and it seemed to melt and take her into soft darkness, but in only a few breaths she was awake again. She watched the shadows of her own moving body, moon shadows darker than sun shadows. But she could see colours; here and there were very small flowers, blue or yellow. Flowers of the Hill. Their roots must have known water.

Now she was coming up on to the moonlit crest above the shadows, and dawn was nowhere. Then Kgwanyape, the rain-snake, was beside her, was mounting her, coil upon coil, throwing weight here or there until she staggered on her feet but yet he held her up and his pointed snake face with its bright cold eyes looked into her face and his forked and strange tongue that had licked her body all over in his climbing now flicked into her ears, her nostrils, her eyes and her mouth, bringing a sweet darkness and the thought of rain.

In that sweet dark of dreams many lives happened to Naledi. She was a warrior, a leader of men; she was a horse galloping, all four hooves ringing on the ground; she was a fish slithering among white roots and green weeds; she was an eagle quartering the land, guarding: and again she was a water-creature, a dragonfly with all-coloured wings skimming and touching. So that when she awoke it was no surprise that she felt drops of water on her skin. And now the morning star had risen. There was no moon but it was time to go down the hill, to go down with rain.

It was easier going down. When she passed the shoulder of flat rocks it was beginning to be dawn and she could see that the great holes were now brimming over and flowing together into twists and trickles of water. The rain was not cold, nor yet dusty; it had not come with a harsh wind, but straight from the clouds. As it grew light she went more quickly and came to the clefted rock. There was her kilt and there her necklaces and earrings, her bracelets and leg ornaments, all a little damp. Cool, cool the morning, and looking across, there was her father, his head on his knees, his spears beside him, the gun under a fold of his cloak, and, when she was dressed she came running and calling through the beautiful rain and everywhere there were soft grey clouds bending low over the land and from the rocks and stones of the Hill Behind small springs bubbling and twisting with clear water.

Her father lifted his head. He stood. He saw her. He came towards her and there was great happiness. 'Greetings, my daughter,' he said. 'I see you. I see you with rain!'

'I come with rain,' she said, and now she was a little cold, but he put round her the half of the cloak which was warm from his own body. Then both of them drank from a small new pool under the rocks.

'When you did not come in the morning I was terribly afraid for you,' he said.

'But I came in the morning,' she answered.

'Not the morning after the evening when you began the magic journey.' At this she fell quiet and she thought of Kgwanyape, the rain-snake, in the night and the snake eyes like shining stones and the licking fork of the tongue and all that had happened in her long dreams. 'So you met the snake in the end,' he said. 'You met Kgwanyape and you were brave. And he gave you rain. Through you I have rain. Through you, my daughter, the people have rain. We shall be saved alive.'

She said, 'That is good, my father. But tell me a certain thing. I heard lions roaring, and I was afraid for you. But all was well?'

'There was roaring,' he said, 'but, as I caught up my spears it was for you I was afraid, you naked and alone.' And then both of them laughed a little. He said: 'You are somewhat changed, Naledi my daughter, star of the people.'

'And you too,' she said, 'my father.' And then she busied herself with making a fire where the rain had not yet come through the thick branches of a tree, and on this she put the small pot with the meal and water from the new, fresh pool. While she had been on her magic journey he had not eaten. It was well, and in a while they shared the porridge, while the rain began to come in big, pleasing drops through their roof of branches.

The King and his daughter walked back in the light soft rain. The ground was no longer hard and scorching under their feet. Here and there long brown pools were gathering. Soon, soon the grass would come. When they came through the lands and nearer the people, it was seen that such oxen as were fit for ploughing were being taken to the wagons and sledges, on to which already the ploughs had been loaded. As soon as the people saw Kgosi coming, and his daughter alive at his side, they rushed to greet him with words and songs, and the women shrilled at the backs of their throats, and all at once it was said that the Princess Naledi was indeed beautiful.

High up on the magic hill the ostrich feather was drinking life out of the pool. It was drawing to itself the features of an ostrich, a she-ostrich asleep and still small.

In the desert, Tsaxau and his father and his little brother chewed at the tough ostrich-meat. It had been partly roasted over the fire, and there was a little salt, also Tsaxau had found a root that could be eaten. They wished it had been meat of buck or wild pig. Yet it was food. And then a small dark cloud came over them and it split with a roar of rain. Tsaxau filled again the ostrich-shell from the hidden nest and other rain was caught in melon rinds and the meat went down better. But Tsaxau still thought of his mother.

So it was that the people of the Valley without Water were saved. For a time, even, the stream that ran through the valley once and that had seemed to be dead, began to run again, pleasant to the feet. The grass came and the cattle ate and the flesh came back on their ribs and hip bones and knotty backbones. There was ploughing. There was milk. For a time death would keep away. And for a time Naledi was quiet at her mother's house, or else she was making songs. Her small breasts grew; her bracelets and leg-bands looked well on firm flesh. She went away out of the Valley for the raising of her *mophato*, the time of learning how to be altogether a woman. But of what had happened on the Hill Behind she did not speak, either at home or to those of the older *mophato* who cared for her and taught her and sometimes for her own good hurt her a little in the lessons of becoming a woman, one of the generations of women of the people.

Then came uncles of young men asking for her in marriage, and her father sent for her. 'I will make no answer that you would not wish,' he said, 'for you are the lintel of the door of my house and there is yet much which you must know and which, later, even when you are old, you will use to help our people. Yet it may be that your eyes have seen that there is a young man or an older man with whom a branch might be bent or a cooking-pot brought to boil. And although an order comes to the eyes to shut themselves, yet a small bird takes a message to the heart.'

So, after a while, Naledi said in a low voice. 'There is such a one. Indeed, his younger uncle has a well-known and beautifully-spotted ox which my father has seen.' She looked away and then she spoke again. 'But I do not know if I can be given. Kgwanyape also is my uncle and the elder brother of my father's fathers.'

So the King called together those of his people who were skilled in such matters, and they came to his house halfway between midnight and noon and consulted the *ditaola* and spoke long, both with the ancestors and among themselves. One of them had been chosen to snuff smoke and to drink the *tshitlho* which had been prepared, and so he was able to see and speak with Kgwanyape, although in a body of shadows and not as he had been on the magic hill. After this they told Kgosi that the rain-snake would not come between the Princess and her need. But also they could see something else, which troubled them, which appeared always in the *ditaola*, some question of which the answer was not plain, and they did not know what it could be, only that it was on its way. But the King was glad that the rain-snake would give Naledi to be a wife and he hoped she would have as many children as there are stars in the sky. So there was betrothal and a great brewing and cooking and singing, and the many beads which Naledi wore were like a garment of flowers on a rained-upon field before the ploughing.

But the night after the betrothal when by custom certain things are allowed, late, late, when all others were sleeping, Naledi lay on her mat at the side of her mother's house where one that was welcome could creep in along the wall, stooping, and find her. From far off there was still a singing of the people which became part of her and her body became full of hope. Then there was a rustling and a shape in the doorway. But it was not the shape of the one she waited for and it seemed to have a long neck and long legs and it was not a person at all and she, who had not been afraid on the magic climb, now screamed for fear. It went away. But all in the house had wakened and the one who had been waiting and who had been waited for, did not come.

Now this thing went on, and not only for Naledi. The comrades of the one to whom she had been betrothed spoke in jests and riddles and he answered angrily, for truly he had come, but instead of what he hoped for, a spirit with a long neck had stood in the doorway. And at last his uncle came to the younger brother of the King and asked how it was that the full gourd was taken from the lips and the honey was locked in the tree-trunk and the night-ostrich stood in the door of the house? Now this was reported to the King, for indeed the thing was most strange, and he sent for Naledi to ask what she had done, and she came in tears and distress, saying that it was so indeed

189

and no fault of hers, and what could be done?

Now it was thought at first that this could be a sorcery which had been put there by some jealous or angry person, and all that could be done was done, so that this sorcery should turn back on the head of the one who had put it there. But still the night-ostrich came and it seemed to grow larger and plainer. Now even in the daytime Naledi would look fearfully over her shoulder and catch a glimpse of it. Sometimes too her comrades of the *mophato* saw it fleetingly, so that they were doubled up with sickness. And the one to whom she was betrothed became more angry in himself and felt that it was her doing or her father's doing, and perhaps there would be the same or another curse on her wedding, which should be soon with the first new rains. Fear mixed with the anger, for this was nothing he could fight. So Naledi sent for the wise men to say that something, anything, must be done, and they in turn spoke to the King. The thing they wanted to do did not please him. But it was so, that all was becoming worse and hard words said, and Kgosi felt the anger of the family of the betrothed as something which might hurt all his people. So at last he said Yes, they had his leave to do it.

In this way certain men from the Valley went out carrying leather cords and in the evening they came back with what they had caught. It was a young boy of the outer people, the small ones, the yellow-faced whose speech is not ours. It was Tsaxau. He had run from them, but they had made a trap as though he was a beast, and now like a beast they would treat him. In the great kraal there was a sharpening of knives and with it laughter that had a cruel edge like a knife.

The Princess Naledi had been with other girls pounding grain and singing, hoping not to see the ostrich. She looked round and there it was, nearer than ever and more like a real ostrich and less like something in her mind. It flapped its wings, it hissed through its beak and it drove her, and now she ran from it trying to escape, but always it was there. By now the ostrich had become entirely solid, a day-ostrich, and many people saw it and some tried to come between it and the Princess, but it was no use. She ran and screamed, dodging between the houses, in and out of walls and yards, round grain stores and firepits, hoping to escape; but without mercy the ostrich drove her to the great kraal where Tsaxau lay bound ready for the knives. The ostrich stood over Tsaxau, and now the King, who had been called, came running and said quickly to his men, 'Loose the ox there!' For he had not cared for the thing they wanted to do.

At that they cut the thongs from Tsaxau unwillingly, for they had made themselves want to cut his throat and his stomach and cut off his hands and feet and cut out his tongue. Tsaxau stood up and he put his arms round the she-ostrich and said in his own language, 'Mother. My mother.' But in some way Naledi understood, for it came to her that she had heard this word on the Hill Behind and knew its meaning. So now she watched deeply. The eyes of an ostrich are like a person's eyes and have long and beautiful eye-lashes. The ostrich gazed at Tsaxau and tears came into her eyes and dripped down her neck into the feathers of her wings.

Then Naledi said to her father urgently, 'He will take the ostrich away, it is his mother, but let him not tell her that we have hurt him. Let the men run, get food, get drink, everything!' And so it was done by the King's word. Naledi's mother even gave Tsaxau a small iron cooking-pot and meal. He took it in his hands, wondering. But above all they brought water. And he drank and drank, and as the water went down into his stomach he seemed to grow and the tightness of his skin left him, and the great bird bent her neck tenderly over him.

Then Naledi took off the best of her necklaces and offered it to the ostrich, which lowered her head so that she could hang it over the feathered wing-shoulders of the great creature, whom now all could see. And the King gave Tsaxau a hunting-knife with a sharp iron blade. And so it was that Tsaxau left the Valley with the she-ostrich which was also his mother come back out of the magic pool, since life always returns, but not always in the same form.

All of the people had gathered and were watching, and among them was the betrothed of Naledi. She gave him a small look from under her brows. In that moment he was the swallow catching the darting fly, the leopard leaping on the buck. Out of him anger and fear flew, circled, fled away. There would be no curse on the wedding. All would be well, the honey loosed from the comb, the gourd drained to the last drop, the people at peace.

THE COMING OF THE NEW GOD

THE young man, Tebogo, came cautiously into the Chief's place through the narrow entrance in the low wall, beautifully finished, patterned with the careful fingerwork of women. It was most certainly theirs. Their houses faced warmly into it, the thatch well-trimmed, the water jars in the shade, the tall corn mortars in place, the wooden bowls and porridge spoons scrubbed and drying. Across one threshold were the poles; he looked aside—another son to the Chief.

The Mohumagadi, Morekwe, Mmaletlotse, moved out of the shadow of her house and stopped him, not with a finger laid on him but with a hard look. She was the wife of the first house, the lioness. 'What is the news from the *pitso*?' she asked, as he knew she would. He was afraid of her. She had carried the Chief's seed.

'No news yet, Mmaletlotse,' said the young man. 'Only much speaking.'

'By our lord?' she said, and motioned with her hand for the other wives to come out and join her, all but the young one, Boitumelo, behind the crossed poles. They had been watching. She was the lioness, their protector. It was she who had given them all the medicines which the *Dingaka* had made out of many rare and potent leaves and bulbs and which, taken by all together, rooted out jealousies and argument. They had been happy together. But now?

Tebogo began to speak, stammering a little, his eyes cast down amongst all these beautiful milk cows and heifers of the royal kraal. 'He said—the Bull of our people said—that we were in great danger. These men with the guns were coming again to take our land for themselves and our young boys as their slaves.'

'The *Maburro*—the Boers,' she said, and spat out the Afrikaans word like a rotten fruit. She knew Afrikaans well enough but she did not care to sully her mouth with it.

He went on. 'We have to have some kind of a something between us and them. Someone who will speak to them in the speech that they use. Or with writing. This man in the black clothes who came in the long wagon and who speaks with a loud voice—'

'The missionary,' she said and again her voice was a hard spit.

The young man went on desperately. 'He has said that he will be a shield for us if we obey him and his God in certain matters.' His

192

voice tailed off and he looked away.

'What matters?' she said sharply.

'You will know, Mohumagadi,' he said, 'as has happened to others of our peoples. Kgosi Sechele of the Bakwena—'

'I know,' she said and half turned towards the other wives. 'Kgosi Sechele was told by just such a missionary that he would get no help unless he drove out all of his wives but one. He did that. He was a coward. His headmen also were made to do this wicked thing. They were cowards. We are the Bamatsieng. We are not cowards. Besides, it did Kgosi Sechele little good. The Boers came. They burnt the houses. They took the cattle.'

The young man said nothing. It was true. It was well known. One of the young wives began to cry. Her sister had been married to a cousin of Kgosi Sechele. He had been rough. Sechele himself had sent his wives away honourably; they were sad but their families had the cattle returned to them. The wives could marry again. But this sister, not the favourite but at least a true wife and no concubine, had stumbled back unattended to her father's house, dumb with not understanding. Some cattle had been returned later but meanwhile her father and uncles had beaten her until she almost died. She had not been able to explain that it was no fault of hers. Her sister had seen her still limping from the beating. Could that happen here? Among the women there were low noises of pain. Then the Mohumagadi, Mmaletlotse, looked round, motioning them for quiet. The children clung to their mothers, silenced.

She asked, 'Was he there—this man?'

'Standing beside Kgosi at the *pitso*. With his powerful book. The book with anger. He said that no man must have more than one wife. It is against the law of his God. And if he is to be our shield the price is to worship his God. Also we must use no more medicines for war or for rain. Instead his God will help us. The ancestors, he said, are only dead men. Also we must give him land for a house for himself and also a great house for his God where we must all worship and sing.'

'I know this God,' said the Mohumagadi. 'This God of the missionaries is a law to himself. He is an enemy to the ancestors. He is also an enemy to women.'

The young man gaped and was afraid. Women were powerful in ways he could not understand but feared. When they were hot they were as full of power as a gun pointed at one's heart. He muttered, 'He has this book. When he opens it there is a pit of fire and snakes. But also good things—milk and honey, he says, and cool springs. We shall fly with wings. If we worship his God we shall never be altogether dead. He will teach us to open this book of his.'

'And what will he teach to the wives, the widows, the deserted ones?'

There was no answer from Tebogo. A thought had come into his head. It might be that there could be more wives for the younger men. That the old bulls would no longer take the choicest of the young heifers. Perhaps that was meant by the opening of the book and if it was he would be glad. He would truly worship this God.

'Have I leave to go back to the *pitso*?' he asked.

'Go,' she said, and the word was like a tree falling.

He slipped out through the narrow gap, the one that was easy to block. Had she seen him thinking?

The other wives came to her now, noisily, shouting or sobbing. 'Sisters,' she said, 'sisters—we have to face this together.'

'You are safe!' one of them screamed.

'It is I who will care for your children,' she answered, 'if this thing comes about.' And gradually they became silent and the sun beat down and the tears dried and spurted again. They had been married to Kgosi for reasons of family or alliance with other tribes. There had been fears and teasings and sighing, but he had found ways to please all of them and had left none complaining that her house was not visited, the corn in her mortar not stamped. How could that end!

'We do not know what our lord will say,' said one of the senior wives, a Mokwena.

'This that we have heard, it could be a story. To frighten us. In case we were disobedient,' another said.

'Sisters,' said the Mohumagadi, 'we must wait.'

But indeed and in truth it was many days of waiting and Kgosi himself anxious, not telling much, only seeking for forgetting-time and then the sweet sleep-time following it, to give him cover in the thorny and terrible thicket of argument and fear he was in. And word came that the Boers were gathering, they and their guns, far off still but their eyes were pointed his way. Yet each of his wives hoped that by this bodily gift of peace and sweetness to their lord they might avert doom from themselves and their children. But the

194

man with the magic book and the new God stayed as an illness stays in the body.

Then one day without warning it came. Their fathers and uncles had been summoned. They were told. The young wife, Boitumelo, came out from behind the crossed poles, fat and beautiful and shining and her sucking babe the same, but Kgosi did not look; he could not bear to, being himself in the trap. There was a lowing of cattle, the rage of a driven bull, a bleating of goats, weeping of women. They took the babes that were still at the breast, slinging them on to their backs. But the older children were taken to the Mohumagadi and told, 'There is your mother,' and the children were very quiet and held on to one another. And in a little while and yet it seemed long to many as hurting things do, they had gathered everything into their baskets, all the things that give pride and strength to women, necklaces, finely worked skins, pots, cups, spoons, knives, all kinds of adornments in gold or copper, and sweet ointments, sacks of corn and meal, the hoes and flails, the tall corn mortars where they had worked together singing, the makings of their lives. And the Mohumagadi stood silent, not allowing herself one tear, saying go well, go safe, as they flung their arms round her before they went down through the town of Ditlabeng, breaking their fellowship. It was only the hate within her that dried her tears.

Kgosi came to her but he did not speak and she did not speak. There was emptiness round them. And then who should come but the man with the book of the fire pit and the flying people. He told Kgosi that God had approved what he had done and now that he had one wife he should honour her by taking her to his God and they would both together become God's children and God would protect and love them. He spoke at length and he seemed to know this God. The Mohumagadi stood with her head bent pretending that she did not understand, but in truth she understood everything and her anger fought silently with the cruelty of his God.

Kgosi said little, seemed not to hear. He was all the time anxious; he was hoping that the man would do good for his people, the Bamatsieng, in many ways. They were, he had heard, clever at healing, *Dingaka* beyond their own *Dingaka*. They could stop pains. It was said that they would make schools; his own tribe would learn to read the powerful book. And more especially there were guns. Better guns than the white *Maburro* had. Or so he had heard. But it was hard for him to speak of all this since the man spoke only of his God and also of the land which he would need for his Mission and for the church he would build where his God would look down and judge the Bamatsieng and their Chief.

Kgosi did not care for this; he was the only judge of the Bamatsieng, he and his elders and headmen in council together. If they misjudged, the ancestors might also show displeasure. But if the coming of this new God was the price—the missionary had promised to write strong letters. When the *Maburro* and above all this Kruger of theirs, demanded this or that in writing, it was always hard to know what was real and what was a threat which was not meant to happen. When one of those letters came, Kgosi became a little sick in the stomach. And his young men wanting to fight! They were his children; he could not see them shot down before even they had the chance to blood their spears. In a while the missionary was talking about this washing with some kind of water which would take away every sin. 'You will bring Morekwe,' he said, 'and she should wear a white gown, oh so white, from neck to ankles. My wife will see to that. And afterwards she shall lead the women coming to our church in Christian clothing, to show that she has been washed and is clean in the sight of God.'

But the Mohumagadi said nothing until he was gone. Then she turned to Kgosi and he could feel the anger at the back of her throat, since by now and in his deep affection for her, he knew her moods. She said, 'My lord, I shall have many mouths to feed now. The children who are now mine. The girls will pound but I need grain. Above all there is need of meat.'

He said, 'How many cattle I gave back to the families with your beautiful sisters! So many. So many. Cows in calf. Heifers.'

She answered, 'Most certainly my lord would do all that was honourable.' Then she added in an altogether different voice, 'There is no need for my lord to buy me white cloth. If I must go with him into this water, if it is his bidding, that I will do. But I do not wish to wear this dress of the new God.'

'It will be better', he said nervously, 'and indeed, my wife must learn the ways of this God. Who, they say, is more powerful than the ancestors. Who has his hand on the rain. Or so it is said. Perhaps yes, perhaps no. It is also said that this God or his Son will take away any wrong things we may have done.'

196

'I have kept myself clean for you, my lord,' she said, 'and it was the same for my sisters in their houses.'

'Jesus—' he said, 'Jesus—I cannot remember. The wife of this man will tell you what you must know. It is something that will help us all in Ditlabeng. Truly. And you must wear this dress. It is my command.'

She bowed her head, the proud one, but her heart was not bowed. The wife of the missionary came, walking across Ditlabeng, nervously, glancing from side to side, aware that she was watched. Mmaletlotse received her; the woman was young and perhaps tender underneath her long dress. She had pale eyes. There was a man with her who tried to interpret, a Mongwato, but the Mohumagadi brushed him aside, saying she understood. 'You understand!' said the wife happily, 'You know Jesus! That is so good. Come with me!' So it seemed better to Mmaletlotse to go, lest by not going, she might be forced.

There were tents and two small houses, built hastily. 'And there,' said the wife of the missionary, pointing, 'there will be the church, God's house, where you will lead the women to worship!' She spoke with great joy, expecting the Mohumagadi to show equal joy. But how could that be? And then, inside the house, she unfolded the white garment and held it out with smiles. For a moment Mmaletlotse was afraid; it could be a trap and besides she did not at all know how to put it on. And still she did not speak, not fouling her mouth with Afrikaans. The wife gestured to her to take off her necklaces and her skirt, which was made of beautiful skins, silk-supple and carefully sewn with patterns of other skins set in. The wife caressed the fur with her hand, saying how nice it was, not looking at the dark nakedness of the other woman. And suddenly a thought came to the Mohumagadi and she spoke stiffly, 'I will give you such a one.'

'Oh,' said the wife, 'I thank you!' She was surprised at the African woman speaking and also she was embarrassed, wondering if she would be expected to wear this savage thing. But it could well cover a chair. She helped the Mohumagadi to put her head through the opening and her arms into the sleeves of the white garment and she drew and tied the neck string. She had not been in the mission field as long as her husband and she shrank a little from African flesh. Yet she knew this was wrong and that soon this black Queen would be washed in the waters of baptism and the footsteps of light would move forward. All was as it should be.

It was a great day for the missionary, one about which to write back to his headquarters, when the Chief of the Bamatsieng, his wife and many of his elders and councillors came to be dipped into the baptismal waters. All the men had put away any wives they had beyond the scriptural allowance. Two of the Chief's young sons came, but another not. It had seemed wiser to Kgosi to leave one in the old world, in case, after all, there might be a need for certain ceremonies, above all the essential rain-making. Supposing the new God failed. He did not put it this way to the missionary and indeed shook his head over the unwillingness of this son, Letlotse, who was, in fact the son of the first house, the child of Morekwe, who was, because of him, called Mmaletlotse. But that was not clear to the missionary, although it was clear enough to the headmen and elders of the Bamatsieng.

Yet some of them were sad that their Chief had been less than whole-hearted over this matter. They were mostly those who had suffered from fears and attacks of a certain kind and now, it seemed to them, that Jesus and his yet more powerful Father had made things so that they need fear no longer. The night-movers, the *baloi*, had no strength left; the terrors were over. Parents need no longer weep when their children died; the little ones had been given wings. All would meet in heaven, wearing new bodies without pain or stiffness; eyes and teeth would come back. All this had been promised after their baptism, after the touch of the waters of life. They looked back with great joy on that day, and when they began to feel fear or sadness coming at them again, they could start at once to sing the new songs they had been taught, calling on Jesus, who would most certainly hear.

But there was sadness in Ditlabeng among the cast-off wives, sadness when women met at the wells and talked: why had this happened? How was it now with the ancestors? Surely they must make some sign! Some women who had been sent sadly away from their husbands had been baptised, but even so they could not go back. There were angry brothers and uncles. Yet at least the boy Letlotse had stayed away from this Jesus. And the Mohumagadi had been above all glad about her son.

Kgosi came to her most evenings. But there were these times when it would have been wrong for her to receive him; she could have done him an injury through her blood. And if she conceived again, she asked herself, what would happen and how would the Leopard bear it if he had no comfort for his loins? She was already past her best strength, although she had never lacked for honour. But work was harder now, all the singing and playing together had gone, and at night there was no pleasant, laughing rivalry. Nor could she do otherwise than wish sometimes that there was some other sleeping mat where her Bull could slake his great thirst.

But a story came to her of how, after hunting, he had gone back to the house of a certain friend of his own *mophato*, and had been offered the services of the wife—and that wife had been one who, after her sad leaving of the royal kraal, had been taken in marriage. How happy she had been to find her true lord again, whom she had feared would never more lie with her. Other such stories drifted through Ditlabeng; the Mohumagadi was glad that her lord had found young antelopes in what had seemed a desert; one of them even, was of her own *mophato*, true sister as well as fellow wife.

Meanwhile she cared for the children, saw that they were clean and fed and that they swept out the houses of their mothers. She told them stories and played games with them in the evening when work was over and she could have wept for the other wives, her sisters whom she had not been able to save. Sometimes she would visit them, but one had gone back to her own tribe and another was in a far-out village. The young one, Boitumelo, whose *mophato* had been raised ten years after her own, was still suckling her babe and had not been sent into marriage.

These stories came back to the missionary. He rebuked Kgosi after the hymn singing in front of his headmen; others would follow the lead of their Chief, here as elsewhere. It must not be. The missionary threatened to leave them all if they did not serve his God faithfully. But that would never do, since he had written strong letters to the *Maburro* warning them not to come and to the heads of his own church, demanding protection. Also he had started to teach letters to some of the children. So Kgosi and such of the others as had sinned were shamed and made many promises.

For the Mohumagadi it was not to be borne that her lord was shamed by this man, so she remembered what had been in her mind ever since the wife of the missionary had admired her skirt of fine game skins. She went by night to visit a certain woman who was a *moloi*, taking with her two beautiful skirts, one of which was for the woman herself. Well she knew that this was now forbidden, most of all to those like herself who had been in the waters. But she had gone through them unwillingly, only because of her love and obedience given for ever to Kgosi, her lord, the Bull of the people, who was now, it seemed, to be tamed and ridden by this new God. No, she could not bear it.

She did not like to be with this woman, who treated her with all too much familiarity. She did not wish to be touched or to make certain gestures or say certain words which were demanded. When the woman put out a hand and pawed at her necklace, she took it off quickly and gave it. She had half thought this would happen and had worn the one she cared for least. Yet she was not pleased to know that now this woman owned something with her own sweat on it.

Yet in the end she had her weapon. She went to visit the wife of the minister, carefully wearing the Christian dress which she had been given for the special day of the new God, the long cloth skirt and apron and the cloth covering her breasts—yes, even her breasts where Kgosi had laid his tired head, where his babes had fed full and smiled up, milky-lipped. The new God, it seemed, hated the breasts of women. For a while she watched the men who were building the church and the new large house for the missionary. And for his wife? That was to be seen.

The Mohumagadi was welcomed at the mission. It was surely a sign that all was going well. A wife must be glad, naturally, if her husband is rebuked for sinning against the marriage bond. The missionary's wife was planting two little orange trees; she had grown them in pots. From this day they were to grow and flourish in the ground itself, the land which had now been blessed. She had been singing to herself, gently, as she pressed down the yellow earth round them, carefully making a small trench for the water they would need. Then came the Mohumagadi with her gift. They spread it out. She would perhaps not wear it as a skirt, said the Mohumagadi, but as a cloak in the cold weather which was coming. 'I will put it on my bed!' said the young wife.

'The very thing,' said the Mohumagadi. Yes, that way would be best.

So the days went by and the wife of the missionary became ill. There were medicines in the large box which they had brought with them, but these did not help. 'What will happen, my lord, if the woman dies?' asked the Mohumagadi on a beautiful evening of warm dust and golden light, of distant singing, of her best brewing of beer. She went on, 'Will the man go? Will he surely go? And will all be as before?' Kgosi said nothing at first; his fingers were on her breasts, warming her. She ached with the thought of the empty houses, the women waiting, their bull pawing and snuffing, at last entering and satisfying. How much she wished for a new young virgin, to be washed and teased and ornamented, to be looked over and touched, to be rubbed with sweet ointments here or here, to be offered and accepted. Surely, surely, this must happen again!

At last Kgosi spoke, 'I do not think so. He will stay. Whatever comes to him. And perhaps he will become more angry about certain matters.'

'This woman, his wife, does she make him happy? This one woman?'

'It is the command of Jesus and his Father. We are told that.'

'We are not told about happiness. I wish this woman would die.'

'They do not know why she is ill.' He said nothing for a long time and the glow of light drifted up from the tree tops and the stars showed. There was a small chill in the air, the beginning of winter, the time of war. But the new God was against wars. There must be other things worked out for the young men. He lifted the gourd full of beer and drank a little, but not enough to stop his thinking. Then he said, very quietly, 'You. Do you know why the woman is ill?'

She did not answer for a moment, but her breath caught and he listened for it. He held her wrist tightly. 'There is something you have done,' he said, and then, 'I brought the man in, I allowed him, because we, the Bamatsieng, were in danger. It seems that the man has stopped the *Maburro* in their tracks. I also wish, for all the Bamatseing, that there should be more knowledge. I wish that we ourselves should write these strong letters to the leaders of the *Maburro*. There is this also. The men who build the new church are getting knowledge. I do not care for the church but I care for the tools, the quick way to measure. We have bought guns, giving many good cattle for them, but we can never know if they are good guns. But the man will show us which will kill the lion that has broken into the kraal, which will bring down the fat eland. He will show us how, ourselves, we can make the powder and balls. We shall learn more about plants, about cattle and horses. Ways of digging deeper wells.' He was talking almost to himself; she listened very quietly; it was men's talk. He went on, 'Even if this man goes, another will come. We cannot escape, even if there was no good in it.' Then he turned and spoke into her face, 'Undo whatever you have done. I shall know.'

And so? And so? Had it been useless? If all was as her lord had said, if it was for the good of the tribe, the thing was in her hands. She slept on her decision; in her dream something was following her. She woke early. She ground down certain leaves and roots and perhaps other things which she had, and made them into a paste with a little milk. She did not want to go to the woman *moloi*, did not trust her to undo harm. Rather, she trusted in her own knowledge, gathered over the years.

On the ledge, at the top of the wall, where the thatch poles came down over it, leaving a space for air but not for thieves, there were bundles, carefully tied. She moved the corn mortar against the wall, climbed onto it, reached up and jumped down, sad that now she fell more heavily, just as now a night of dancing tired her feet. Yet there had been no dancing, not since the man had come. Had come with his wife. Yet should her anger have burned her fellow woman? The wife of the missionary would surely do only her husband's bidding. As she herself was doing now.

She took out of the bundle the most beautiful of all the furs, not a skirt but a winter bed covering. She had treasured it. She put on the Christian clothes, slowly, shivering at the stiff, cold touch of the cloth. She went across Ditlabeng to the house of the missionary and, although she hated him, she knew she must not hate what was good for the Bamatsieng. The servant opened the door. The servant opened the door. In the room the young wife lay half awake, breathing shallow, sweat standing on her face. And, yes, the fur of the skirt which had been doctored was pulled half over her, where she lay, as these people did, between white cloths as though dead. Oh clearly, clearly, the medicines had worked. The medicines of the *moloi* which now the Mohumagadi, for the sake of the tribe, must take on herself. That was the dream's meaning.

Gently she pulled off the fur covering and gently she laid in its

202

place the new and yet more beautiful one which, sometimes, had covered her and Kgosi in a sweet warmth. The woman who was in the room watched and saw that the Mohumagadi was feeding the wife of the missionary, and that both were smiling. She saw the Mohumagadi putting her arm behind the sick woman and helping her to sit up. Something good was happening. She saw also how the Mohumagadi tied the skin skirt from the bed over her Christian clothes before she left the house.

In another ward of Ditlabeng the young Boitumelo, she who had lain behind the crossed poles the day the bad news came, bent over her baby and feared many things, most of all that her uncles would decide to marry her to a man of their choice. She knew who it was likely to be and she did not at all care for what might happen. At least it would not be until her little son was weaned. The babe of the true lord.

She looked up. There was the Mohumagadi. How glad she was! She brought meat and porridge and milk. They spoke together. After a while the Mohumagadi asked Boitumelo, 'They have not yet made a new marriage for you? No? Child, you must keep that at a distance.' She spoke again, 'Do you remember the time of *bojale*—when we of the older *mophato* made you obey us?'

'Indeed yes!' Boitumelo went into giggles and covered her mouth. 'Yes, with canes across my hind-parts! Oh how we laughed! I have never laughed so much! You beat me, my mother, my sister, oh you looked so fierce when I wriggled round to peep, but your cane came down lightly.'

'It was only a branch,' said Mmaletlotse, smiling, 'but it meant obedience. Now I have this to say. It may be that I shall die. I would not have my lord, who is also your lord, going wifeless.'

Boitumelo was troubled. 'But Mmaletlotse, you are not ill! You must not die.'

'It could happen,' said the older woman, 'and this is why I have come to you. My child, you are young still. It is hard to be the one wife. One must be strong, stronger than I shall be soon. And there are many children. They must be cared for, fed. They must not weep for their mothers who are gone. Do you understand?'

'I understand, Mmaletlotse. But I do not wish to understand too well!'

'I will go now,' said the Mohumagadi, 'leaving you with this thing

203

which has been spoken about between us. Which is for our lord. Which is for the Bamatsieng. Which if need be, you will speak of to your uncles.' And for a moment she stood alone and listened inwardly, as though to something which might have changed its track, which might be following her. She saw also, inwardly, the face of that woman *moloi*, and fought it. But, having done one thing, others must come after. This has to happen. Lightly she touched the young woman on her shoulder, 'Stay well, my child, my sister.'

'Go well,' said Boitumelo, 'ah, go well! But if— if— I will do all that you want of me.'

REMEMBER ME

MY name is Jessie MacKinnon. I was on the District Council for ten years and since then on the Community Council; I was Vice-Chairman, and indeed I am acting Chairman now. There was this and that committee and group in our small community a few miles out from Oban. My husband had a small mixed farm, which did well enough and gave him plenty of time in the winter for reading and wood-work. He was a great reader. After he died I carried on working the farm with one old man, for I liked doing it, but Rob and Sandy used to come out with their families and help me in holiday times. Sometimes in summer I used to let to a few boarders, nice folk. They came back mostly, I remember; they were all terribly taken with my garden, all of them, and the view. I had children. I had friends. It is all past.

My little granddaughter Fiona was staying with me, Rob and Mary's youngest. It is because of her that it is at all worth my while to be alive, and sometimes looking at her I wonder. For I ask myself has she truly escaped? She is beginning to grow up, to have the thoughts that come naturally to a young girl. But then? At least she looks better than most of the other children. Better indeed than some of them, poor wee mites.

This is the way it was with me. It was a light west wind and I was out in my garden, looking into the wind, so that I never saw the flash east over Glasgow. I only—somehow knew that something had happened. I turned and I saw the cloud go up. Then another. I thought about Rob and Mary; well, I will not speak of that now, nor of much else. My other son was in the Midlands of England: himself and—all of them. No word has come through. Nor will it now.

Queer things went through my head. The old man who helps on the farm, Colin Mor, came over from the sheds. He said 'They have done it' and then he stared round and began muttering about would the pensions go on. I looked at him and it changed to some kind of prayer. And then it was one of my neighbours, Miss Paterson, who had the rockery with the fancy heaths and the gentians. She watched the cloud with me and I felt her hand on my arm. She said, in a shaky voice 'No more Strathclyde now, Jessie.' You see, we had all been speaking together about the new local government set-up and how badly it was turning out for us on the fringes, and then we both

205

looked at one another and I knew she had said that in the hope of taking my mind off what she knew it must be on. And with that I remembered how she had a sister and brother-in-law in Helensburgh. So some way we managed a small laugh, and then I said, 'We'd best get down to Connel.' That was the Civil Defence Centre by the loch, and we had both said we would go over and help if there was ever any need, though some way we thought there never would be. We could not have brought ourselves to think otherwise. They had a stock of medicines and blankets and all that down there. She said hesitating 'Have you tried the phone?' I said no, for I knew, I knew. But yet now she had said it I lifted the receiver and dialled the number I knew so well. But there was nothing, nothing at all.

I gave Fiona a book and some sweeties and a great petting, saying I'd be gone for a while. She had not noticed a thing, indoors. I told her I would lock the door in case bad people were to come, but it was mostly to stop her going out—and touching anything. The flowers were still blooming, but if the wind changed—

We drove down to Connel and even then I began to wonder about petrol. We waited with others. Some of us tried to reason out why it had happened. The laird's wife said they had been small bombs or rockets, if it had been one of the big ones we would all be dead. 'Theatre weapons' she said and somehow naming it made it less terrible. One could hold it in the mind then. But the thing was, we had thought we were out of the world danger, that a small country such as we are today need not be drawn in. We did not know then what was being done over our heads. I am not even clear today, for the news that gets through is not to be trusted. No more than one can trust the grass or the sky. Not any more.

It was on into evening before the first of the buses got through, and then the rest, and I looking, looking for my own ones. Just in case. It was not until a week or two after when they began to die that I could bring myself to be glad that Rob and Mary and Andy and Jean had not been among them; that it was all over for them, almost before I had seen the cloud. The only train that got through had been standing at Garelochhead; the driver was burned, but he carried on, the decent man; I remember he did not die for quite a while. He lifted a load all up from there to Arrochar; the woods were all on fire round him; it was the ones who had been working their gardens or that who had the burns. No train from further down

Loch Long had a chance. The ones who came on the buses were from Alexandria and Balloch, the western edge of Dumbarton even. There were a few from Helensburgh who got across to the Lomond side-road, but they had been badly caught by the Holy Loch bomb. They had the most terrible things to tell us; some of them seemed to be going to live, but they had these burns that did not heal. The blankets were mostly used to bury them in. That is, until we began to see that there would be no more blankets and we could not afford to let the dead have any of them. The laird's wife brought down stuff from the Big House. Their son and his family were in Australia; they had not heard yet when I saw them last, and if the son were ever to get here, what would he find?

Miss Paterson had given up hope for her sister and brother-in-law. She was working hard, wearing herself out. I could see how Dr. Bowles was counting on her; he was an elderly man who had come out to the highlands mainly for the fishing and golf and the pleasure of it here, as it was in those days. He had read the leaflets but had barely taken them in. The young doctor from Oban, Dr. MacAndrew, knew more. But I could see how even he flinched from the burns. It was later that Miss Paterson told me about how hard it was to forget that her sister had a baby coming, her first. There were wee coats and socks that Elsie Paterson had been knitting, put away in tissue paper. For weeks after she kept dreaming she was putting another one away in the press. And then she woke. Those were the kind of dreams I had too.

That first night the wind blew itself out and there was a calm. But even while it seemed to be blowing there must have been a current away above us that was bringing some of the evil stuff west and over. I have some sense and I kept Fiona in the house, but myself I was working for the refugees. The District Nurse was on leave. She never came back. I started by bringing all my milk over to the centre; I thought it was the best way I could help. Dr. Bowles had been pleased at first, but young Dr. MacAndrew—he is dead now but he was a fine young man—said to me that it was as good as poisoned. 'Throw it away!' he said, and he told me quick while he was dressing a burn, for we still had dressings in those days, that the milk would be full of radioactive iodine and must on no account be given to anyone, above all not a child. It could damage the child's thyroid gland and give it a cancer or turn it into an idiot.

We all know that now. Too well do we know it. But then it was news and not everyone believed. Dr. MacAndrew said to me 'Go round to your neighbours, Mrs. MacKinnon, and warn them every one, and above all those with bairns. And mind, not a drop to Fiona.' So I did just that, but half of them laughed at me; it seemed against nature that good milk with nothing at all wrong in the look of it could hurt a child. So it came about that before a year had passed I saw my nearest neighbour's three turning from lively bright children into listless miseries. One of them has just died; we all know that is best.

Yet at the time it seemed just crazy; Fiona had been with me just because she'd had the measles and was needing good food. I did not think to do this extra washing of the vegetables which I do, not until later. Even so it had me puzzled, for we get our water from the high loch and it would be bound to get as much fall-out as the grass. I had not thought it out; when I did I began drawing water out of the old well, that is fed by a spring from far underground. I look and look at Fiona and wonder, did I keep enough of the stuff away from her? Or will she have something secretly eating at her? It is, I suppose, probable that she escaped. But I cannot help thinking sometimes that I did not do enough.

I have even tried to pray for Fiona, but I just cannot get myself to believe that it is any use now. I don't know even how she has taken it all. She clings onto me, but not too badly. She never or hardly ever speaks of what has been. Only at birthday or Christmas time. Mostly she tries to take the burden off me, more perhaps than a child her age should do.

I had of course to tell her, but not until we were totally certain, beyond the reach of any hope. I think she knew by then. She asked about her uncle Sandy and the cousins, down south. Betty was her own age. I said we should not hope too much. By that time we had come to the conclusion that a string of these rocket bombs had been targetted across all the industrial parts of Scotland and England. Strategic destruction that is called. Not murder.

The police came over with their geiger counters, walking about the fields and houses. After a time they said it was safe or just about. 'Not like nearer in' I mind they said. One or two had been as far as Inveraray and they say the things ticked away there. Over the Rest they did not go. Nobody did. Arrochar—it is just a name now. But, for all they said, I found it hard to believe that our own land was unhurt.

Gradually we got a drift in of survivors, not like the first lot, though some had small burns or radiation sickness which did not kill at once; some of these have survived. But most were people who came where they thought there would be food. Some had their living knocked away. Some had been staying in hotels, though the full tourist season had not been on when the thing happened. The hotels shut and the guests had no way of going back to wherever they had come from; they were cut off except from the west. They drove as far as their petrol would take them and offered money, but what was the use of that? Still and all, those of us like myself who had rooms, took them in if they seemed decent. I had first an old lady and got mortally tired of her; she did nothing but complain. Then I took in an Edinburgh couple with two small children; I thought Fiona might like them. Mr. Drummond did not look strong; he had been in some kind of an office with good pay; he seemed to think that some day he'd be back and find it going on. Indeed he tried to bluster at first and sell me his car for a great price, but his wife had more sense and we got together.

She would help with the housework and cooking, but she turned out to be a poor cook, having only done it in a town. He would dig, help on the farm and so on. I thought, well, he could dig up the back part of my garden behind the dyke which I had not bothered about for long enough, and we would put in more vegetable seeds. He agreed. We went to Oban together and got plenty of seeds. The shops still took money, in hope, one supposes, that some day it would be worth something. He did not know much about gardening but came back with a heavy spade and fork, and he certainly worked and did not complain about his blisters or the nettle stings. But we did not see much of each other.

They were in what had been Rob and Mary's room. I would wake in the night and hear them moving and for seconds, until my mind cleared, I would have the warm feeling that they were mine, not these strangers. I was not the only one to have that feeling about the incomers.

Yet in a way it was worse for them, since they had lost everything, while we still had our homes. I knew that and yet I could not be welcoming. So they were apt to get together and let out to one

209

another how they felt about us. One can get the feel of this kind of thing in a small community and we could not blame them. But more had gone on to Oban and even to the islands and Ardnamurchan. And one or two had skills we needed; there is a brisk wee dressmaker from up Stirling way who never seems short of eggs or potatoes or even flowers.

Looking back on last year I find it hard some way to remember just when things happened. The electricity still goes on sometimes and was good enough for a while, since most of the hydro-electric stations were far enough from the towns. The others, the coal-fired ones, were put out of action at once. They say the great building at Longannet is still standing and the turbines inside it. Some day perhaps it will be possible for people to go back into it, start it all up again. Not in my time, nor yet Fiona's. But the Falkirk bomb destroyed most of the works and until we can build up some kind of industry in Scotland there's power to spare. But things go wrong at our own sub-station level and there is no way of getting repairs. Some of the men have gone into the outskirts for short times and tried to get what supplies and spares they could carry away in barrows. But it is terribly risky, even with rubber boots and gloves. We would never urge anyone to do it.

It stands to reason that there was no petrol after the first month, even with the hard rationing. There was fighting over the last of it in Oban, and two of the police badly hurt. Perhaps this was to be expected. Here we just accepted it decently. But I'm wondering how long my poor old pony will last; he had to eat the grass and it must have been thick with fall-out. For that matter, even if the wind had not changed, the stuff would have got back to us right round the world. As it must have come to everyone everywhere, even those who sent out the planes: but not strongly—I could wish it had been. We all worry about our beasts; I gave the first milk to the calves and they are not looking too grand for yearling queys and stots. The milk should be safe now with the radioactive iodine worn off and I could wish I had more of it, but the cows are just not in calf. We are hoping it will wear off as the ones with the geiger counters say, and it is great news when we hear of a new calf, even if it may be a bitty misshapen. But some of us small farmers depended on the A.I. centre with the stuff driven out to us, and that had to close down at once; it is queer how much we took for granted in the old days, now we are back to something much older. Maybe this summer when the flush of grass is on I shall be able to make a bit butter; it is something one misses, and Mrs. Drummond seemed to think there'd be bound to be margarine at least, in the shops. Some of the folk with big deep-freezes and the Oban hotels themselves bought it up, but some of this was lost when the electricity went off, and the rest of us were not sorry for them.

It was the same going back to old ways with the fishing and all the boats depending on diesel, not just the engines but the winches and every new bit of machinery. The nets they had were far and away too heavy to haul by hand. But the fishermen got going, I'll say that for them; the big boats are laid up, but the small ones are out with lines and lobster pots and their trawl nets cut up into something lighter. It's the queerest thing, but already there seem to be more fish coming back; I have dried and salted a few. Yet I am doubtful about some of them. I remember Dr. MacAndrew saying to a meeting of housewives 'It is this stuff the herring feed on, the plankton, that gets hold of the radioactive material that has fallen into the water, and it stands to reason the herring will be full of it, and so will the mackerel.' Yes, I remember that day well, for soon after that he got ill himself and knew there was nothing to be done. He had gone as far as Crianlarich to try to help the doctor there and both of them had gone down with the radiation sickness. I used to go over and sit with him once in a while. He would not go into hospital. It was crowded out and he said to me 'We mustn't waste resources. Remember that, Mrs. MacKinnon.' His voice had gone thin by then, and he was vomiting now and again; I wiped his face for him and he was saying he was sorry and trying to smile.

Yes, I have remembered. We have to make do with our own food. The tins in the shops are all done, even the kinds one never used to buy. I am lucky that my hens are still laying. Nearer Glasgow most of the poultry as well as the cattle died. They say there is hardly a cattle beast left in Dalmally and Tyndrum, as well as Strachur way. South of Tarbert there is nothing alive. One of the things had been targetted on Macrihanish. It was hard somehow the way we in western Scotland had been loaded up with these things which have brought destruction down on us and we were never even consulted. Defence, they said! When the haze came creeping over everything and the whole eastern sky glared like hellmouth—some way I had expected this—I kept in all the beasts from the inbye land and the hens, just as I kept in Fiona. I mind now I slapped her for running out. My heart bleeds for it but I know I was right. But the way I was placed I could not get the sheep from the high ground—indeed we had nowhere to put them under cover, none of us—and things have gone badly there. We would find a dead sheep here or there and when it came to lambing time, there were dead lambs and sick ewes. It is the same for all of us.

Maybe all this worrying about what we shall have to eat and to wear and how to mend our houses is some help against the deep grief which we almost all have and the feeling night and day that we are cut off. The telly went blank, though for a time some people kept trying it; they just couldn't believe it was over for ever. My radio never got much beyond Radio Scotland and Clyde. But I kept on trying. Once or twice I have heard foreign voices; I thought I could even make out a bit of French once, but it was faint and I could not get anything from it. Yet there are other people, maybe in the same fix as ourselves. If once we could get to them! But how? Fiona found an old newspaper at the bottom of a press and read the big headings, the football and all that. Finished. Finished. Then she found the strip cartoons and she was at me to know what happened next, so we made up stories. But I was glad to burn that newspaper and all the cheery lies it had in it. I can remember that it used to be said by the Americans and the Russians and the Chinese that they could stand an atomic war because it would only kill one in three or maybe one in four of their populations. I do not care one bit if there are no Americans left or no Russians or no Chinese. I would not lift one finger to help any of them if I saw one in trouble. Yet once I was a good church member with a great belief in human brotherhood. It is as though love has been killed in me.

Some of the folk round here have been going to the church and seem to be all the better for an hour of hymn-singing. But not me. I went once and the Minister kept on about sin and how we were being punished. But it seemed to me that all he had in mind was the wee kind of sins, gambling and fornication and drink. And the sins that brought all this on us were of a different kind altogether and nothing to do with God looking on to see if the boys were playing cards for money at the back of a haystack. We brought it on ourselves. It was not God. Without our intending it surely, but that made no difference.

At first we tried to go on with local government as it was. But it was too difficult. We had too much to do, all of us, and the Strathclyde administration was finished as though it had never been and the District Council could not go on. For a while we telephoned to Lochgilphead, but then the lines went down in a storm that November and could not be repaired. Even in Lochgilphead there were some people burned and a terrible lot of sickness later. The hospital there was to receive casualties from Glasgow; some got through, but most were scared of heading south again; it was too near the Holy Loch. I don't know how they got on later. Nobody has been that far for months, though we might manage it maybe next year. The District Engineer that we used to see at the Oban meetings tried to get through to Dunoon. He was a brave men, but it is just not enough to be brave. He is dead.

But when it comes to the bit, local government, whatever you call it, depends on grants from the central government. And there is no government. There is no centre. Schools only go on because we, the parents and grandparents, pay the teachers in eggs or potatoes, peats or meal. I gave one of them a box my husband had made; it had a lock and key. That matters these days. Public health is gradually breaking down for want of equipment. One of the married District Nurses who had retired came on again when it was clear that our own nurse would never come back from her leave. She had us all out gathering sphagnum moss and drying it for dressings and for use when there were no more sanitary towels to be had. We need to think of everything.

There is no postal service with no petrol for the vans. And I will never get the letters I used to look for. Never. Never. But our old Postie got hold of a pony and starting running a service on his own, in and out of Oban, with the odd passenger and letter or parcel. He says that it's happening in north and mid-Argyll, and indeed we are beginning to get in touch, though everything is gone beyond Ballachulish. It must have been Inverness and Fort William that they picked out. Postie sends in the bill himself, using up the old forms and saying what he will take instead of pounds. There are still a few people who use the old money. But it is little used compared with things, most of all food, and that is how we pay Postie.

Well then, it seemed to Miss Paterson and me that we should at

213

least get the Community Council started up again, so we called a meeting, just going round. The Chairman himself had been away at the time and, well, he never came back. So it was myself that needed to take the decision. So far we have had three meetings. It is not much more than six or seven miles for anyone to come in and up to now we have managed to give the executive committee a cup of tea, but they must bring their own sugar. There had been some thefts already, so we asked the policeman to come. Things were awkward for him because he had carried out the emergency orders, but then they had stopped. Oban Headquarters was not much better off, and there had already been some crimes there, the real thing I mean, not just young people showing off. Our own policeman came in and told me they were going out armed now in Oban, but for himself he could not see himself doing anything of the kind, for after all we were all decent folk.

I was taking the meeting and maybe I saw a bitty further ahead. Anyway I proposed from the Chair that our Police Force representative should be asked in the name of the community to go out armed. It has turned out to be just as well, though there was only the one time he has had to shoot—so far. He was upset about it himself, although he missed; but the gang were scared and ran, and it has kept certain ones away. The laird's wife brought in the gun, with her husband's compliments, and he would have come himself if he had felt able. Postie went over later and asked if he could have the pair to it. I believe he has had to use it, though he will not say.

Old Dr. Bowles came to the meeting, and I kept thinking if only it could have been Dr. MacAndrew , for the old man was flustered and seemed some way unable to think ahead. He kept saying we ought to get in supplies, vaccines and antibiotics and that, though he knew as well as the rest of us that this was nothing but speaking into the wind. I had bought bottles of aspirin and cough mixture and disinfectant before the Oban chemist I mostly went to was out of them. The shop is shut now, and so are most of the others in Oban. I wish now I had got more sugar, but I did not wish to appear grasping; most of it has gone already, though it is nice to see the jam and jelly I have. The laird has diabetes and there is no more insulin; it is weeks now since I have seen either of them. I had not wanted to ask the Minister to the meeting, but he came and started in about sin. I told him he was out of order, and a fair few laughed.

214

The incomers came to the meeting and mostly sat by themselves in the two back rows, except for the dressmaker body who sat with friends near the front. They wanted a piece of land ploughed up for themselves and one of the farmers who has a pair of good horses, offered to plough and harrow around an acre for them, free. But they must get their own seeds. It seemed fair enough to the rest of us, though clearly some of them thought they could do with more. They are managing with seeds this year and so are we all, but next year? Oats and barley will go on, and potatoes, but our turnips and field carrots will scarcely ripen seed so far north and I cannot see most of the greens doing it, still less the beans and peas.

The talk at the meeting, which used in the old days to be about the footpath to the school and danger from cars, or else about the bus time tables, was now about food and security from raiders and what was happening elsewhere. Postie was good and offered to find out where the rest of the Community Councils were getting together. Indeed he has done just that and maybe it will be possible to build something up. It could be the only way. We have even had a representative coming from north Argyll across the loch and we hope to send someone over to mid-Argyll. We hear from the fishermen that there have been troubles in Mull and the folk in the big hotel waving money about and trying to get hold of a plane, but we will face that when it comes. Meanwhile we will strengthen ourselves. Several of our young folk have got out their old saddles and are keen enough to ride to a meeting. They have been making bows and arrows, even. But most of the time we needed to talk about getting together for this and that which had to be done urgently. I suppose it will be like this all over wherever people have escaped and maybe we are luckier than some.

The old Oban Town Council, that was there before Strathclyde, had got together, such as were left of them, and they sent over, trying to rope us in, with talk of rating the district and that. But they had little to offer us, except for office space and acres of paper and clips and rubber bands, and it was clear that what they wanted from us would be oatmeal and mutton. So we decided to write back a polite and formal letter, but to let it be known we would not be playing their game.

It was clear to all of us that we'd need to go back to the old ways for the harvesting. A few of us had a bit of diesel oil laid by for the tractors, and some used it for harvesting, making out that something would happen one day, some help was bound to come. But it seemed to me that I would keep the little I had for the winter ploughing. My pony is not up to it. I slept with the key of the padlock under my pillow and I let it get about that I had a gun; who would know that I only have five cartridges? Though there was a time not so long ago when one could leave one's house door unlocked and no thought of harm.

Colin Mor has been terrible at first, asking for this or that, even if he knew I had none of it, but now he has settled in and is working hard. The queer thing was he wanted to keep getting his wages in cash. I told him that money was not worth having, but if that was what he wanted it suited me. I drew out all I had in my account, and borrowed quickly against my shares, though nobody, least of all the bank manager, knows if they will ever be worth anything again. But Colin Mor was happy, putting it away wherever it is he does put it, under his mattress maybe, and he was with us for harvest. He snares an odd rabbit and I make a stew with my onions and give him his share. The Drummonds did not like it at first, but they soon got over that. All of us got together when it came to a fine spell in September, and cut the oats with scythes and bound by hand; I tried to wear gloves at first, but they hinder one and we had to be quick; now I am worried about the skin on my right forefinger.

What we could not harvest at the back-end was fed to the beasts, though we were careful to keep plenty of seed. There may be enough fertiliser in the stores for next year's grain and grass, but it will need to be shared and not let the big farmers, least of all the ones in Mull, get too much of a share of it. By now we had almost forgotten which field was whose; we were needing to think all together. Again we needed to thresh by hand, since there was no fuel for the big thresher. But it is easy enough to make a flail, though hard and slow work using one. We had to grind the grain as best we could. I had a hand coffee mill and Fiona does half an hour at it after school. We were speaking at the last Community Council meeting about the possibility of getting one of the old water mills somewhere in Argyll working again. We were well aware by now that there would be no flour coming in and we must depend on our own oatmeal and barley meal. It is queer to think how little one used to value a loaf of bread.

We dug the potatoes with graips as we could not use the tractor

216

spinners, all getting together as in the old days. Not one wee potato did we miss! We had a good feeling that they at least would be safe, though how can we be sure, for the evil stuff works down into the soil. We would find dead worms here and there. But we notice that there are far too many grubs and caterpillars and such and not the birds that used to clear them off for us. For the poor birds that were flying about in the air while it was at its worst dropped and died; it was sad to see that. One is glad of a sparrow now even. I wonder will the swallows ever come back.

I do not know how long we can go on. For the first year we still had some stores; I even made a Christmas cake for Fiona and a few other of the young ones. I used the last bit of margarine that I had been saving up and Mrs. Drummond managed to find some sugar; there was a brooch she used to wear and I think that is how it went. But it started Fiona onto speaking about her last Christmas and all the fun and happiness they'd had together. And I had to leave the room quickly; it was more than I could bear. We have kept hoping that a ship might come in from somewhere. But it never does. And our health is going down. I have sore places on my insteps and my face, and my hair has fallen out in patches. There was a time I would have minded about that. Now I only mind anything because of Fiona. Yes, and the Community Council. But it is too soon to know what will happen either to the Community Council or to the children. Perhaps when we do know it will seem that we were still happy when we did not know.